Pm

DARK WATERS

A Selection of Recent Titles by Susan Rogers Cooper

The Milt Kovak Series

THE MAN IN THE GREEN CHEVY
HOUSTON IN THE REARVIEW MIRROR
OTHER PEOPLE'S HOUSES
CHASING AWAY THE DEVIL
DEAD MOON ON THE RISE
DOCTORS AND LAWYERS AND SUCH
LYING WONDERS
VEGAS NERVE
SHOTGUN WEDDING *
RUDE AWAKENING *
HUSBAND AND WIVES *
DARK WATERS *

The E J Pugh Mysteries

ONE, TWO, WHAT DID DADDY DO?
HICKORY DICKORY STALK
HOME AGAIN, HOME AGAIN
THERE WAS A LITTLE GIRL
A CROOKED LITTLE HOUSE
NOT IN MY BACK YARD
DON'T DRINK THE WATER
ROMANCED TO DEATH *
FULL CIRCLE *
DEAD WEIGHT *

*available from Severn House

DARK WATERS

Susan Rogers Cooper

This first world edition published 2013
in Great Britain and in the USA by
SEVERN HOUSE PUBLISHERS LTD of
19 Cedar Road, Sutton, Surrey, England, SM2 5DA.

British Library Cataloguing in Publication Data

Cooper, Susan Rogers.
  Dark waters. – (A Milt Kovak mystery)
  1. Kovak, Milton (Fictitious character)–Fiction.
  2. Sheriffs–Oklahoma–Fiction. 3. Offshore sailing–
  Puerto Rico–Fiction. 4. Murder–Investigation–Fiction.
  5. Detective and mystery stories.
  I. Title II. Series
  813.6-dc23

ISBN-13: 978-0-7278-8273-8 (cased)

All Severn House titles are printed on acid-free paper.

Severn House Publishers support The Forest Stewardship Council [FSC],
the leading international forest certification organisation. All our titles that
are printed on Greenpeace-approved FSC-certified paper carry the FSC logo.

Typeset by Palimpsest Book Production Ltd.,
Falkirk, Stirlingshire, Scotland.
Printed and bound in Great Britain by
MPG Books Ltd., Bodmin, Cornwall.

For the newest little love of my life, Josey Tucker Law

ACKNOWLEDGEMENTS

I'd like to thank Joan Hess for the many mutual plot sessions over a semi-friendly game of backgammon; my long-time reader and even longer-time daughter, Evin Cooper; my stalwart agent, Vicky Bijur, for her input and support; my editor, Sara Porter, for her advice and counsel, and a special thank you to Jan Grape, long-time reader and friend, who invited me to swim with the dolphins.

PROLOGUE

One Year Ago, Aboard Swedish Cruise Line Ship Cavalcade

The old man was way too drunk – he knew that. He could barely walk. Oops! Actually, he couldn't walk at all. He fell to his knees. There was someone there, helping him. Little someones, with their little hands all over him. Leprechauns, he figured. His grammy's little people. He always believed – at least when he had a few whiskies in him. And he knew he had more than a few in him now. Little hands pushed him down, so he was lying on the floor. OK, this wasn't bad, he thought. At least I can't fall! he told himself and laughed out loud. Hands in his pockets. No, the old man said, maybe out loud. That was the money he'd won! No, no! Don't take my money! he thought, or maybe said out loud, he wasn't sure. He needed that money. It was for his grandson! To get him out of the trouble he was in. The old man tried to sit up, and felt the stabbing pain in his chest, the ache in his left arm, the tightness in his throat, and then he didn't feel anything. Ever again.

ONE

Imagine my surprise when, while at the Rural Sheriffs of Oklahoma (or RSO for short) annual meeting in Oklahoma City, I won the big door prize: a seven-day cruise for four to Puerto Rico on the brand-new Gypsy Cruise Lines' Star Line ship. It was supposedly a smaller ship meant for more intimate travel: it only cruised five hundred, as opposed to the thousands on other cruise ships. Coming from a small town, I feel that five hundred is still a crowd. There were seventy-six people in my high school graduating class; a hundred and ten registered members at the Longbranch First Baptist Church, and eight members of my department. Yep, five hundred souls seemed like a bunch to me.

Now things would have been just fine if I hadn't mentioned my great prize to my wife. She was born and raised in Chicago, went to school at Northwestern University, and got her MD at Johns Hopkins. To her, five hundred people are what you invite for a casual lunch. And then Johnny Mac, my ten-year-old son, overheard us, and the mention that I had won four (and us being only three) tickets, and decided then and there that we could do this at spring break and take his best friend Early Rollins with us.

I harped on the fact that the air fare to Galveston, Texas, from where the cruise ship set sail, wasn't included, but Jean countered that by suggesting a quick day-and-a-half car trip which would be, and I quote, 'fun and educational.' She's a shrink. You would think she'd know better.

'Honey,' I said, 'I'm thinking that's not a good idea.'

'Why not?' she demanded.

'We're talking a ten-hour trip with two ten-year-old boys cooped up the entire time—'

'That's why I suggested a day and a half. We cut the ten hours in half – or better yet, say seven hours the first day, if we get up early. And speaking of Early, he'll spend the night with us the day before we leave so we can get out of here at the crack of dawn, drive until lunchtime – so seven hours – stop at a motel with a swimming pool, let the boys swim off their pent-up energy, then finish the trip the next day with plenty of time to board the ship in Galveston!'

And she smiled. Now my wife is a good-looking woman: almost as tall as me, she's got short reddish-brown hair turning gray a little bit, green eyes, bodacious ta-tas, a killer ass and well-shaped legs, even if they didn't work too well due to childhood polio. She's got a real pretty face, but her smile – I can't do much against one of my wife's smiles. They not only light up her face, or the room – it's like the whole universe smiles back. And they not only make me weak-kneed, but weak-willed to boot. So that's what we did. And it wasn't pretty.

Our crack-of-dawn departure on the Saturday morning of the first day of spring break did not occur. Early, Johnny Mac's best friend since first grade, had wispy blond hair and watery blue eyes and, although he made the same Little League team as Johnny Mac, couldn't throw or hit a ball worth a damn. His one really good point, as far as I could see, was that he seemed to idolize my son. Jean disagreed, saying he was bright, inquisitive and very funny. Hadn't seen that yet. Anyway, he forgot one of his bags, so we had to go into town to his house and pick it up, which Early, Johnny Mac and I did while Jean stayed home and fixed treats for the trip (and we all knew they'd be organic, non-sugar, non-fat and non-fun), then we had to drive back to the house to pick up Jean and her treats, and then we had to go back into town because I forgot to gas up Jean's minivan, which is hard for me to drive because it has multiple hand breaks and stuff on account of Jean's polio when she was a kid. We didn't leave until after ten and I had the pleasure of teaching the boys military time, 'cause adding seven hours to ten o'clock made seventeen hours, and you can't do that on regular time. Meanwhile, Jean sat fuming in the shotgun seat, blaming the whole getting out late thing on me because of the gas. I'm just saying, it wasn't all my fault. She also might have been a little miffed when nobody ate her homemade granola – oatmeal, dried fruit and raw nuts, with nothing to stick it together. It wasn't pleasant. Even the boys wouldn't eat it.

We made it about thirty miles south of Dallas before we decided to find a motel with a pool. We found one around seven that evening that had a coffee shop as well as a pool. It was right outside a town the size of a postage stamp, but right off the freeway. Unfortunately the pool hadn't opened yet for the summer, and the coffee shop had a sewer leakage problem and was closed for the foreseeable future. We got a double room, then got in the car to find someplace to eat.

'Why don't we find another motel?' Johnny Mac whined. 'You promised us a pool.'

'Well, he didn't exactly promise—' Early started, but Johnny Mac cut him off.

'Shut up!' my son said.

'You shut up!' Early said.

I'm pretty sure my son instigated the first blow.

'OK, you two!' Jean said, turning around in her seat to glare at the boys. 'Knock it off and I mean now!'

There was one more bout of slapping, then they retired to their respective corners. Turning around, Jean said, 'If you say a word I'll slap you!'

'Wouldn't that be lowering yourself to their level?' I said, keeping my eye on the road and the smile off my face.

She hit me anyway, in the thigh, and it wasn't a love pat. 'Ow!' I said.

Then we spied a Denny's. I pulled in and we had supper. In lieu of swim time, Jean let the boys have whatever they wanted for dessert. It was a God-awful mess and we had two bloated and moaning young'uns on our hands as we headed back to the motel.

At three o'clock in the morning I made Jean get up when Early started puking. He puked so loud that it woke up Johnny Mac, who decided sympathetic puking was in order. At that point I thought it would be just cruel if I didn't get up to help. But feeding them hot fudge sundaes and molten lava cakes hadn't been my idea. I rolled over and stuck Jean's pillow over my exposed ear. I figured she wouldn't be back for a while.

The next morning was no crack-of-dawn experience either. Jean decided both boys needed to sleep it off, which she explained to me in a no-nonsense, I-don't-like-you-much tone with no eye contact, and then demanded I go out and find coffee and fruit. The only thing I could find open in this East Texas burg of maybe twenty-three citizens was the Denny's (and how they deserved a Denny's and Longbranch didn't, I'll never know – OK, they had a freeway and we didn't, but still). I got two large coffees to go, a fruit plate, an extra-large orange juice, two small cereal boxes and a medium milk. I carted all this back to the motel.

The boys were up by then.

'I was sicker than you,' Early was saying as I walked in the door.

'No, you were just sick first. I was sicker than you!' Johnny Mac insisted.

'I was so sick I puked up dinner!' Early proclaimed.

'I was so sick I puked up green slimy stuff!' Johnny Mac countered.

'I was so sick—'

I interrupted whatever it was Early was going to say. 'Got the fixin's for your ills, boys! Come sit down at the table.'

I handed my wife a coffee and the fruit plate, and grabbed two of the plastic glasses from the bathroom sink. I poured some of the OJ in each glass, opened the cereal boxes so that they would be their own bowls, and poured in some milk. I'd been brazen enough to demand plastic spoons and forks from Denny's. The boys were settled and I headed with my coffee and its accompanying sweeteners back to the bed I'd shared the night before with my wife. Or part of the night before, whatever.

'You want some sweetener?' I asked, handing her the bag.

'Thank you,' she said, not looking up but taking the bag.

'There's some forks in there, too, for the fruit plate,' I said.

'How very nice,' she said, and it hardly sounded sarcastic at all, but still she wouldn't look up. She put the bag on the other side of her as I sat down next to her.

'Can I have one of the forks?' I asked.

'Certainly,' she said, handing me the bag.

I grabbed two real sugars out of the bag and the one fork left over. 'Is this the silent treatment?' I asked her.

'I hardly think you could call this the silent treatment,' she said, studiously spearing a pineapple chunk.

'Well, you're saying words, but they don't seem real, if you know what I mean,' I said.

'I have no idea what you mean,' she said.

'You want me to explain?' I asked.

'Hardly,' she said, then got up and, using her crutches that were by her side of the bed, went into the bathroom.

I sighed and ate the rest of the fruit, and the donut I'd stashed in my jacket pocket.

Milt – Day One

The line to get on the boat – ship, whatever – was really long. And again, my warnings came true (Jean insists it was a self-fulfilling prophesy) – the boys were hell-bent on making life miserable.

Just coming over the causeway onto Galveston Island had been a real treat for our two landlocked boys. Each grabbed a window and exclaimed the virtues of their side, then switched, then switched again. We were a couple of hours early for boarding, so we drove to the sea wall, found a parking spot and took the kids down to the Gulf of Mexico. The water was still pretty cold, but we let them play with the small waves and pick up seashells and throw them at each other. Had they been girls, I suppose they may have kept the seashells to make necklaces or something; thank God we had boys, or I'd have to wear a seashell necklace for the entire cruise. Even though it was mid-March and the day was pretty overcast, the beach was crowded with people and there were quite a few surfers riding the paltry waves of the Gulf. They weren't very good waves, but they were all they had.

The hell that is traveling with children started when we needed to leave the beach to go find the ship.

'No! I wanna stay!' Johnny Mac whined.

'Yeah, please?' Early, not biologically ours so therefore polite, said.

'No, guys, we got the boat to catch,' I said.

'Ship,' Jean corrected.

'I don't want to go on any stinking ship!' my son said.

My wife turned and gave him a look. It was the same look my mama had given me when I'd been a whiny pest. It worked on Johnny Mac the same as it had me.

He turned, his face a mask of sulking, and headed back to the car, Early following him. When they were far enough away that we could hear only the sound of words but not the words themselves, the two began talking, and what they were saying was pretty damning to someone – or maybe two someones.

The two sulked all the way to the boat. Having never been to Galveston, I was gaping big time at the old houses surrounding the sea wall. Due to last year's hurricane a lot of them were under reconstruction, but a bunch had been finished, and the fresh paint on these old-painted-lady Victorians was pretty neat, with combinations of colors I wouldn't have chosen, but somehow worked on these: cerrillium blue with orange shutters, and purple with green, and all sorts of crazy combos.

'Aren't these glorious?' Jean said, and I was grateful for the beginning of the thaw.

'Yeah, I like 'em,' I said.

'We had some like these in our neighborhood in Chicago when I was little – before we moved to the 'burbs. I always wanted one,' she said. 'But to have one this close to the water would be awesome!'

'Yeah, we could go surfing every day,' I said in a playful voice.

My wife laughed, but my son – with the big ears – said, 'Daddy, are we gonna move here? Can we? Please?'

'No, buddy. Your mama and I were just kidding,' I said.

There was silence from the back seat, then, 'Well, it's not funny,' he said in a very-much-not-amused tone of voice.

Jean and I looked at each other and grinned. We were back.

But then we had to park. The parking lot was extremely crowded and Jean's handicap sticker did us no good as all the handicap spaces were full. So I drove up to the back of the line waiting to get aboard and deposited Jean, the boys and the luggage before heading for a parking spot.

I ended up in the back row of the lot, about four city blocks from the boat. I got out, locked up and headed seaward. By the time I got there, Jean, the boys and the luggage were gone.

Meanwhile, Back In Prophesy County

Emmett Hopkins, chief deputy and temporary acting sheriff for Prophesy County, Oklahoma, looked out over the bullpen at his charges. Dalton Pettigrew was staring moon-eyed at Holly Humphries, the new civilian aid (only called new because the last aid, Gladys, was at the job for twenty-something years). Holly stared moon-eyed right back at him, which meant a lot of work wasn't getting done. Emmett was thinking he might have to separate those two. Maybe put Dalton back in his office while he was occupying the sheriff's office. Milt hadn't said it was OK for him to use his office, but Emmett figured if he had the job, however temporary, he should look the part. And how could he look the part when he was stuck in his cubbyhole of an office? The sheriff's was big with two walls of windows, whereas Emmett's just had the one wall with a window. Hell, Milt used to bitch about it all the time when it was his office. So of course he'd understand Emmett moving into his – however temporarily.

That settled in his mind, he glanced once more at the bullpen. Jasmine Bodine, now Jasmine Hopkins, his wife, sat at her desk on the phone. He was going to pretend it was work related and not her talking to the babysitter about their daughter, Petal. She was in the second grade now and one of Emmett's worst fears had come true: his beautiful daughter had come home crying from school, telling her mama that the boys at school were calling her Petal Pusher. He'd been assured by his wife that they didn't call those short pants for women that aren't pants and aren't shorts petal pushers anymore – they were called capris; no one used petal pushers at all. Well, all he could say to his wife was, 'Oh, yeah?'

But Jasmine had been adamant. She was one of four sisters and a brother and all the girls were named after a flower: Iris, Rose, Jasmine and Daffodil, the baby. Her brother's name was Paul. Emmett always thought they shoulda named him Stem, but he never said that to Jasmine.

At the desk next to his wife's sat Nita Skitteridge, their newest deputy, an African-American woman, who, despite Emmett's misgivings, had turned out to be a pretty good deputy. The only deputy not in the bullpen was Nita's cousin, Anthony Dobbins, the department's first African American ever, who would come on duty at noon and stay until eight when they locked the doors and the phone was switched over to the deputy on call. Tonight it was Jasmine, which meant Emmett might have to do some babysitting, although he'd never say that out loud. Jasmine hated it when he said he was babysitting, because as far as she was concerned it wasn't babysitting when the kid was your own. Emmett stipulated that might be true.

Emmett wandered down to his office just as Holly transferred a call to him. He picked up the phone and said, 'Acting Sheriff Hopkins.'

'Hey there, Acting Sheriff Hopkins,' said a familiar voice. 'This is Bill Williams, and I'm not acting like a sheriff, I really am one.' And then, of course, he laughed like it was funny.

'Hey, Bill,' said Emmett. Bill Williams was the sheriff of the next county over, Tejas, which was a might smaller and had a much smaller budget than Prophesy County. Of course, Prophesy County housed the township of Bishop, one of the higher property-taxed communities in the state.

'Just called to let you know I got a call from McAlester that they released Darby Hunt yesterday.'

'Darby Hunt?' Emmett said, knowing the name was familiar but not being able to place it. McAlester was the town that housed the Oklahoma State Prison.

'Yeah, you were probably at the police department when this went down, back in 'eighty-seven,' Bill said. 'He lived in your county and beat his wife something awful. She ran away – came over here to her mama's house. He found her and gutted her like a chicken in front of her entire family, most of whom live in your county. Everybody testified and he said he'd kill 'em all when he got out. Well, like I said, he got out yesterday – no prior warning – so I thought I'd give you a heads up.'

'Why'd the parole board call you instead of me?' Emmett asked.

''Cause the killing was here in Tejas. Trial was here and everything. But like I said, he lived in your county and most of his wife's folks that testified against him live in your county. Of course, maybe he got over them sending him to prison, but he never did have what you might call a good disposition, and I doubt if twenty-five years in prison made him all warm and fuzzy.'

Emmett was nodding his head. 'Did Hunt and his wife have any kids?' he asked.

'Yeah, a daughter, Elizabeth, but she was too young to testify against her father. According to the warden – I checked – she never went to see him.'

'How old was she when this happened?'

'About four, I think. She went to live with her aunt until her eighteenth birthday – the aunt in Prophesy. You might ask the aunt where she is – if the aunt ain't dead by now.'

'Hush that kinda talk. OK, can you fax me or email me or whatever the names of the family members in Prophesy?'

'Already done. Check your fax machine.'

'Will do, and Bill, thanks for letting me know.'

'Hell, Emmett, I know you'd do the same for me,' Bill said and hung up.

Looking up, Emmett saw Holly Humphries standing at his door. In her usual fashion, Holly was wearing bright yellow leggings with pink hi-tops, a black lace skirt that almost reached her crotch, a patchwork T-shirt, too many bracelets and a huge pendant of a skull hanging at about chest level. The bleached streaks in her jet-black hair were tinted green today. Her smile made the hardware on her face sparkle.

'Acting Sheriff,' she said.

'Stop. It's still Emmett, Holly.'

'OK, Emmett, here's a fax for you from Tejas County,' she said.

He took the sheet, said thanks to his civilian aid and began to peruse it. There was a list of six names, with three at the same address. The other three were two at another address and one living alone.

The sheet also told him that the deceased wife's name had been Cheryl McDaniel Hunt, and of the six names, the three at one address were Cheryl's brother David McDaniel, his wife Brittany and their daughter Emma, age twelve. The two at another address were Cheryl's sister, Lisa McDaniel Atkins, her husband Roger, and the one living alone was their twenty-year-old son, Malcolm. Lisa would have been the aunt who took in Elizabeth, Hunt's daughter. Emmett knew Dave McDaniel, the uncle, from back when he was chief of police of Longbranch. Dave had a paint and body shop and used to do the repairs on the city patrol cars. Nice enough guy, Emmett remembered.

There was a second page to the fax, with a short biography of Darby Hunt and the addresses of his family members. The biography detailed where he went to school, what jobs he'd had, and his arrest sheet. He'd been locked up twice for domestic abuse, charges dropped, and twice for drunk and disorderly, which was the dropped-down charge in both cases from assault. Seemed like nobody wanted to get on the bad side of Darby Hunt. He counted a list of seventeen family members, many of them cousins – a couple of whom had been arrested with Darby – and all of whom lived in Prophesy County.

This wasn't going to be good. Emmett did something he'd promised himself he wouldn't do. He picked up the phone and called Milt.

Milt – Day One

The entryway to the ship was in the bowels of the beast, and there was a man standing guard there in a phony-looking naval officer's uniform. I walked up to him.

'My wife and kids already boarded,' I said.

'Did they leave you a boarding pass?' he asked.

'No, were they supposed to?'

'You can't enter the ship without a boarding pass, sir,' he said.

'So where do I get a boarding pass?' I asked.

'Inside,' he said.

'Huh?' I said.

'Inside, sir,' he said.

'Inside what?' I said, my temper beginning to flare.

'The ship, sir,' he said.

'Are you frigging kidding me?' I said at the top of my lungs.

Then I saw the guy's mouth begin to twitch, and Jean and the boys came out from behind him all laughing.

'We saw you coming, Dad!' Johnny Mac shouted. 'And Mom said we could play a trick on you!'

'And they talked you into this?' I said, looking at the guard.

'It was my pleasure, sir,' he said, sticking out his hand to shake. 'You can go in now. Your wife has your passes.'

I shook my head and slipped in behind my wife and the boys. I was wrong. We weren't in the bowels of the ship. It was some sort of holding place with roped-off lines, but the big room was empty so the guard moved the ropes so that Jean wouldn't have to circumnavigate them.

'You sure you don't want me to get you a wheelchair, ma'am? To just get up to the ship. It's a pretty steep rise,' the guard said.

'No, Max, we're fine,' Jean said. She does that. She gets at least the first name of everybody anywhere. I know the first names of my dry cleaner, my barber, my banker, etc., mostly because I went to school with them or their mama or daddy, or sister or brother, or in some cases, arrested some relative, or in others, them. But Jean knew the names of the bellhops, maids, bartenders and waitresses at the hotel we stayed at in Las Vegas, knew the names of the toll takers on the toll road to Oklahoma City, knew the names of both our garbage men and their back-up guys, knew the names of – OK, I think you get the drift.

We started up the ramp to the ship. Our luggage, thankfully, had been taken by ship's personnel to our room – excuse me, cabin. So all we had to do was just get ourselves on the ship. That didn't work so well. Jean should have taken Max's advice. A quarter of the way up she almost fell, and I called down to Max for the wheelchair. He brought it up and between me and the boys we got Jean and the chair to the check-in level – against her continued protests. My wife never wants to appear needy, and she isn't. It's just that sometimes she could use a little help from her friends.

Finally we got on the ship, checked in with another phony naval officer, then went through a doorway to Vegas.

I swear to God it was everything I hated about Las Vegas. Lots and lots of noise, the sound of slot machine bells and whistles, people bustling about, thick phony-smelling, perfumy air – just very Vegas-like. And not one peek of the Gulf anywhere. A woman in a fake naval uniform holding a clipboard came up to us.

'Name?' she said with a big smile.

Well, that was nice, I thought. 'Kovak, Milton, party of four.'

She ran her finger down the clipboard. The smile brightened her face once again. 'Here you are. We have you in a small suite, Mr Kovak. Is this Mrs Kovak?' she said, extending her hand to Jean.

Jean said, 'Yes, I am. And you are?'

'Oh! I'm so sorry! The first thing I'm supposed to do is introduce myself.' She leaned down closer to Jean in her wheelchair. 'This is my first tour.' Straightening, she said, 'I'm Louisa and I'll be your steward all day today.'

'Nice to meet you, Louisa,' Jean said. 'And these two young men are John Kovak, our son, and his friend, Early Rollins.'

Louisa shook hands with both boys and said, 'I'm so glad you could join us. Seems like it's spring break in a lot of places right now! We've got a lot of children on-board. You two should have a great time.' Turning to Jean and myself, she said, 'And we've a lot of supervised activities for the kids also, leaving the parents a little alone time,' she said, and actually winked at me.

Then she led us to an elevator, went down two floors, and we followed her down one hallway after another, me pushing Jean's wheelchair, her crutches lying across the armrests of the chair, until we got to a door that looked exactly like every other door we'd seen since leaving the main deck.

Louisa used a keycard to open the door, then handed that card to me and pulled out a second card from her pocket for Jean. 'Here you go, folks! Let me show you around!' The smile she flashed us seemed to indicate we were going into the bowels of the Taj Mahal. That's not where we went. The room was about as big as our guest bathroom back home. Walking in, there was a bathroom to the left and a closet/drawer thingy to the right. The bathroom was the size of – hell, we didn't have anything in our house that was quite that small. Evinrude's litter box, maybe, but that was about it. I knew from looking at it that Jean was going to have a hell of a time. First off, there was a high step into it, then the toilet sorta sat under the sink, and the shower – well, I think I'd probably touch all sides of it. But OK, it was a ship. There wasn't a lot of room. Getting past the bathroom and closet thingy was the rest of the room: two twin beds with a night stand between and on the other side of the far bed a sliding glass door led onto a balcony with a view of – joy of joys, the Gulf! OK, I liked that. Across from the beds was an archway that opened into the suite part of our accommodations. Smaller than one of my jail cells back home, there were two bunk beds and a small table, and that was it. No extra bathroom or closet thingy. The alcove didn't have a balcony, but did have a window with a deep window sill that worked as a shelf the boys could use to store some of their junk. What with Louisa in the space and the four of us, plus Jean's crutches, we had some work cut out to get Louisa out of our 'suite.' But finally she was gone and we all sat down for a minute on our beds.

'Seven days in this?' Jean whispered to me, her face drawn.

'We'll get used to it,' I said, trying to put on a brave face.

Turning her face away from the boys, she whispered, 'There's no escape from them.'

'You mean . . .' I started.

Jean interrupted, saying, 'You're not getting any this trip, mister man.'

'Remember what Louisa said,' I reminded her. 'Supervised time for the kids.'

She grinned. 'Halli-fucking-luia.' That was the first time in almost eleven years I'd ever heard her drop the F-bomb. I sat there with my mouth open. She stood up. 'I'm going to attempt to go pee. If I must, I'll use the shower.'

'Rinse,' I suggested as she struggled through the small space with her crutches and tried to get up the steep step to the bathroom. Some people might have tried to help her. Me? I didn't feel like getting a crutch in my gut.

TWO

Milt – Day One

Luckily they didn't take the wheelchair away. It was parked outside the cabin when we decided to check out the ship. I talked Jean into using it 'just this once.'

Using the map we'd been given, we headed upstairs to the promenade deck and found an opening to the outside that looked out to the dock. We stood with five hundred of our closest friends and waved goodbye to total strangers. More navy guys came up and offered us fancy cocktails for only $6.50 each. I bought two of those – two kinds of rum, pineapple juice, grenadine, and a shot of apricot bandy – and two Shirley Temples for the boys.

'You realize that's a gateway drink, don't you?' my wife the shrink said.

'Huh?' I said. I'm clever that way.

'Shirley Temples. It's a mixed drink for children to get them ready for alcohol,' she said.

'Huh?' I said again.

'Are you paying attention to me?' she asked.

'Hey, look down there! See that guy next to the woman in the red dress? He looks just like Al Pacino!' I said.

'No,' she said, looking down. 'He looks like Robert De Niro.'
'Right. The other one. I always get them mixed up.'
'You're such a bigot,' she said, but there was a smile in her voice.
'What?' I said in all innocence. 'I'm a middle-aged southern white guy. What do I know about east coast eye-talians?' I said, stressing the 'eye' to make her laugh. I got the desired result.

The boys had put down their Shirley Temples and were using the extra-long straws as swords to assault each other. I put my arm around Jean and stared at Galveston. We wouldn't be seeing that bitch for seven whole days.

Let me just say this: I'm not a big gambler, I don't play golf (there was a putting green aboard ship), and I'm not much for Vegas-style shows. But give me a free meal in a semi-star restaurant and you've got me for life. The restaurant spread from one side of the ship to the other, with windows looking out to the ocean on both sides. The tables had tablecloths and fancy china and silverware and crystal glasses. I wanted to mention to the boys not to touch the crystal, then figured the ship's people had to allow for a little breakage or they wouldn't let kids aboard, right? Then we sat down to a menu of stuff I loved and stuff I'd always wanted to try. Like an appetizer of escargot in garlic lemon butter with toast points, a main course of Chateaubriand with truffles, roasted new potatoes and white asparagus, and for dessert a chocolate soufflé with raspberry sauce. I wanted to lick each plate but figured that might embarrass my wife. The boys weren't that crazy about the restaurant, wanting to know where on the menu were the chicken nuggets, so after a little fine dining we took them across the ship to the buffet line/food court-type place where they were able to find all sorts of kid-friendly foods: chicken nuggets, corn dogs, tacos, spaghetti and meatballs – you name it, it was there, along with some more adult treats like Chinese food, Mexican food, Greek food – and of course, hamburgers, hotdogs and fried chicken. There were vegetable dishes, too, and a salad bar with lots of fruit, but the only things the boys even looked at were the corn on the cobs. I figured no way was I going hungry on this trip, and say what you might about organized fun, as long as I wasn't hurting for food, I really didn't care.

That first night we took the kids to see a magic show, got them to bed around eight-thirty, all tucked in, gave Johnny Mac his mama's cell phone and told him to call me for anything, and then locked the door and left.

Jean kept saying, 'This isn't a good idea.'

'They'll be fine,' I kept saying back.

Johnny Mac – Day One

The only thing more adventurous, more spontaneous and more inquisitive than a ten-year-old boy is two ten-year-old boys. Where one boy alone might be a little reticent and a little nervous, add another and the word 'dare' and you have a situation. So it was on the first night of the voyage of the Star Line, Gypsy Cruise's newest and proudest ship.

After the parents left the two boys, Johnny Mac in the top bunk, Early in the bottom one, talked about things. Like ninjas and zombies and who would win in a fight; about vampires and aliens and what it must be like to live on Jupiter. About inventions like a ray gun that could shoot candy into your mouth from a thousand miles away. After about thirty minutes Johnny Mac climbed down from the top bunk, got the flashlight off the night stand and, with Early behind him, crept into Johnny Mac's parents' room to check out their stuff. On the night stand between the two single beds, Early found a book. Since it was a hardcover and fairly big, Johnny Mac claimed it was his mother's. 'Dad only reads paperbacks,' he told his friend. Early nodded his head. He totally understood that.

The volume of his mother's was entitled *Early Childhood Development*, and the boys eagerly took it into their part of the 'suite' where they sat on the bottom bunk with the flashlight on and quickly turned pages looking for boobs. It was with great regret that they returned the book to his mother's side of the bedside table, pictures of the developing boobs never found.

It was then that they heard a sound. Knocking on doors – not theirs, but other doors on the corridor – first one, then another, coming closer. Then, their own door! The boys looked at each other then ran to it. The knocking had moved on so they opened the door and leaned out. Three kids – two girls and a boy – were running down the corridor, the boy on the left, the two girls sharing the right, knocking on doors and laughing.

'Hey!' Johnny Mac called out. 'What are y'all doing?'

All three turned around in shock. Seeing that it was just two other kids, the boy said, 'We're knocking on doors randomly, dumbshit.'

'Why?' Johnny Mac asked.

'Why not?' the boy shot back.

'You guys want to join us?' one of the girls asked.

Johnny Mac and Early looked at each other, then at their pajamas. 'Let us get dressed.'

'Meet you on C deck,' the boy said and they were off, knocking on doors again and laughing.

Meanwhile, Back In Prophesy County

Dalton couldn't keep his eyes off Holly. He loved the way she dressed, all crazy-like. And her hair – he liked running his fingers through the funky colors when they kissed. Most of all, he loved kissing her. And that time when she stuck her tongue in his mouth, he loved the feel of that little ball in the center of her tongue where it was pierced. He never thought he'd like that kind of thing – he always thought he'd go more for the Trisha Nixon type. He'd had a mad crush on Trisha when he was a boy. He'd fallen for that type the weekend he'd met Holly, but it turned out this Trisha lookalike was a guy. Very disappointing.

But there was a problem. Holly wanted to meet his mother. His mama didn't know he was dating. Whenever he went out with Holly, he told his mama he had to work overtime, and he wasn't wearing his uniform because it was undercover work. The problem was, his mama wouldn't approve of Holly, not one little bit. She kept trying to fix him up with women from his church, and they were nothing like Holly. They dressed more like his mama, and they talked about recipes and quilting and other women. Fact is, most of them were pretty old. Older than him, anyway. Maybe in their late thirties, early forties.

Dalton was thirty-five, and he knew Holly was only twenty-seven, but she fit him in almost every other way. Like sitting on her couch in her living room, watching TV, he'd put his arm around her and she'd snuggle up and she fit just perfect. Or walking hand in hand; he was pretty tall, but so was she for a girl, so their hands fit. And in the important places, like in his heart, she fit just perfect.

He'd seen a little house, near downtown, for sale the other day. And he thought that would be a perfect place for him and Holly, after they got married, to live and raise a family in. But he wasn't sure how to ask her. Surely, before they started having kids, she'd have to meet his mother.

Milt – Day One

We were headed down the promenade when my phone rang. I'd just got an iPhone and didn't know exactly how it worked, so Jean had to turn it on for me. My old phone had been just fine – a fliptop I'd had for about fifteen years – but peer pressure had forced me into it. I took the phone from Jean and said, 'Hello?'

'Hey, Milt, it's Emmett,' came a faraway voice.

'Hey, miss me already?'

'Well, you took a hell of a time to leave,' he said.

I stopped walking and motioned to Jean, then moved to as quiet a spot as I could find on the promenade. 'What's up?' I asked, falling easily back into sheriff-mode.

'You remember a fella by the name of Darby Hunt?' he asked.

'Oh, shit, yeah. He's not getting out!'

'Already did – yesterday,' Emmett said. 'Bill Williams just called, mentioned how Darby threatened everybody in his wife's family, and we've got like six of 'em here in the county, and all of his relatives.'

'Man-o-man,' I said. He was right – I took a hell of a time for a vacation.

'Just wanted to give you a heads up. I know you can't do anything about it from where you are, but just wanted to see if you had any insights for me.'

'Let me call you back later tonight, 'k? I'm in the middle of this damn boat's playground and can't hear a damn thing. I'll call you from the cabin.'

'Are you having a good time?' he asked.

'The food's damn good,' I said.

We hung up and I made it back to my wife. First we tried a cabaret-type show, but the singer couldn't sing, and one of the dancers fell on her ass, so Jean and I decided to leave. We found a quiet little bar not far from the theater, parked the wheelchair outside, and Jean used her crutches to go in. We took a table at the back. The place was not crowded – two guys at the bar, a couple at a table near the front, and us. Jean ordered a cocktail and I got a beer. And we sat there and talked like we never had the time to do at home. So this was vacation, I thought. Not bad. We needed this. We didn't talk about who did what to who in my job, or who thought what about what in her job. We talked about us, our son, and our past and our future. And a little bit about our now.

That's when she said, 'You think the boys are still up?'

I looked at my watch. It was almost midnight. 'I wouldn't be surprised.'

'Should we call them?'

I pulled out my phone. 'You want to do the honors?'

Jean took my phone and dialed her own cell phone number. After about three rings, Johnny Mac picked up. Jean put it on speaker. 'Hey, big guy,' she said. 'Did I wake you up?'

'Mom?' he said in an exaggerated sleepy voice. 'Yeah. I was asleep.'

'Just wanted to let you know we're headed back. Didn't want to scare you when the door suddenly opened.'

'No problem,' our son said. ''Night, Mom.'

Jean hung up the phone and I said, 'They're still awake.'

'Oh, definitely,' Jean said.

We smiled that secret smile parents share when they know their kids are trying to pull a fast one. Boy, did we have his number.

Johnny Mac – Day One

'Oh, crap,' Johnny Mac said. 'That was my mom. They're on their way back to the room.'

'Cabin,' said the other boy, now known as Ryan, who was eleven.

'Whatever,' Johnny Mac said in an attempt to impress the girls – now known as Janna – nine, with curly blonde hair and big blue eyes – and Lyssa, ten, with long, straight black hair and big brown eyes. Mature for his age (or possibly just his father's son), the attractiveness of the two girls had not gone unnoticed.

'I guess we should get back then, huh?' Early said.

'Have I mentioned that's a dumb name?' said Ryan.

'What's a dumb name?' asked Johnny Mac, with just a touch of heat.

'Early. Who names a kid Early, for gawd's sake?' Ryan said and sneered.

'My name is Earnest Eugene Rollins the fourth, if you must know!' Early shot back. 'But I was a month and a half early, and my mom didn't want me being a fourth of anything, so she called me Early and it stuck.'

'Sweet story,' Lyssa said, smiling at Early.

'Oh, yeah, real sweet!' Ryan said, still sneering.

'Jeez, Ryan, leave him alone!' said Janna and swatted Ryan on the arm. 'Y'all go on. You don't want to get in trouble.'

The two boys waved goodbye, mostly to the girls, and headed back to their suite. They got turned around and couldn't find their way back, but luckily, as they found out later, Johnny Mac's mom had lost her wheelchair and had to use her crutches to get back to the suite. The boys got back in plenty of time.

Unfortunately they never thought about the fact that the door to the suite might have locked behind them. Panicked, Johnny Mac and Early looked all around, trying to find something with which to break down the door. Nothing. Then they saw Louisa, their steward, walking toward them down the long, long corridor.

Johnny Mac jumped up and down, waving his arms. Louisa hurried to their sides. 'Are you OK?' she asked, slightly breathless.

'Miss Louisa, please don't tell my parents!' Johnny Mac knew that a lady as young as Louisa would really like the 'miss' he added. The southern gentleman stuff worked like a charm. His dad had taught him that. 'We went out for just a minute to get a milkshake at the soda fountain, but we locked ourselves out!' he said, letting a little water fill his eyes.

'Oh, honey, don't worry! I won't say a word.' She pulled out a card key and opened the door.

'Wow!' Early said. 'You had the right key card for our room?'

Louisa looked down at the card. 'Oh, no. This is like a skeleton key, but a card. It opens all the rooms.' She smiled and shooed them inside. 'Better get changed and in bed quick, you guys!' She giggled and shut the door behind them.

Milt – Day One
When we left the bar the wheelchair was not where I'd parked it. 'What the hell?' I said, looking around.

'That's OK,' Jean said. 'I don't need it.'

Like I said, she does this kind of shit. Wants to be totally independent. I guess that comes from having been single for so long.
She was in her early forties when we married. But it had been
eleven years now. Time for her to realize she didn't have to be so
goddam strong all the time. She had me. I could do that part every
once in a while.

We took our time getting back to the cabin. I found a bench in
the foyer by the elevators and asked Jean if we could sit for a
minute. 'I need to call Emmett back. It won't take a minute,' I
told her. I'm a good liar.

It was pretty late, but Emmett picked up on the first ring. ''Bout
damn time,' he said.

'What a way to greet your boss,' I said.

'Boss? Didn't you hear? I'm the new sheriff-in-charge.'

'That's *acting* sheriff, in charge of not much!' I said. Sobering,
I said, 'Now, about that asshole Darby Hunt. And I *do* mean
asshole. When they lived together in Prophesy he used to beat
Cheryl something awful. And I hate to say it, but I'm the one who
encouraged her to finally leave him.' I shook my head, remembering. 'Didn't think he'd do that. Bad as he was, I didn't think
he'd do *that*.'

'Man, we never know, Milt. Don't beat yourself up over it.'

'Yeah, I stopped doing that at least ten years ago, but now? I
can't believe they let him out. Can't be for good behavior.'

'He did twenty-five. What was his sentence?'

'Huh. Twenty-five. Didn't realize it had been that long. No
parole for that asshole, happy to note. But they coulda kept him
longer, just for the hell of it.'

Jean was getting fidgety. 'Go on to the cabin, honey,' I said,
my hand over the phone. 'I won't be much longer.'

'OK, but, Milton, we're on *vacation*! Do you know the defini-
tion of that word?'

'Yes, ma'am,' I said.

She gave me a look and headed for the cabin.

'She gone?' Emmett asked. 'Now we can talk.'

'I *am* on vacation,' I reminded him.

'Yeah, but you're not dead. So tell me about this asshole Hunt.'

'Bad to the bone,' I said. 'Him and two of his cousins, same

age as him, used to terrorize Longbranch High, so much so that
we got called in a couple of times, mostly when they were doing
athletics outside of town.'

'Yeah, I was about to say. The high school's in city police
jurisdiction and I don't remember getting any calls on them.'
Emmett used to be police chief of Longbranch until politics got
him booted out and I was lucky enough to talk him into joining
the sheriff's department.

'Yeah, they turned over a car at a game against Bishop.'

He snorted. 'A Volkswagen?'

'No,' I said. 'A Chevy Impala. All three were big boys. Anyway,
at the school rodeo at the arena out by Jasper, they got in a fight
and put a kid in the hospital. Then one of 'em, never found out
which, punched out a bull.'

This time he downright laughed. 'You're shitting me!'

'No, and it might have been funny if it hadn't been for the kid
in hospital with a punctured eardrum and a caved-in sinus cavity.
Doctors said he'd never ride a bull again.'

'Shit. Sorry I laughed.'

'Well, punching out a bull is kinda funny,' I admitted.

'Did the bull go down?'

'Like two tons of brisket,' I said.

'I got a list here of his cousins. Which ones were his wingmen?'

'Billy and Shorty Hunt.'

'I thought you said they were big?' Emmett said.

'Yeah, Shorty was the runt of the litter. Only six-two, two
hundred and ten pounds of pure mean.'

'Ouch.'

'Yeah, no shit, ouch. He went after Dalton once, and big as
Dalton is, it took two deputies to pull Shorty off him.'

'Yeah, well, Dalton may be big but he's not mean.'

'That's the truth,' I said. 'There were more cousins – boys –
both older and younger than those three.'

'Yeah, I got a shitpot of names here, mostly male.'

'One girl in the bunch – Vivica. She was as big as the boys and
a little bit meaner.'

'I'm not looking forward to this,' Emmett said.

'Look, keep me posted, but if I don't get back to my cabin
pronto I'm in for a world of hurt.'

'I hear ya,' Emmett said. 'But you know I'm gonna be calling?'

'Without a doubt.' I hung up and headed toward the cabin.

When I opened the door, the one small light between the beds was still burning but the rest of the suite was dark. Jean was in the bathroom, and when she heard me come in she opened the door. Her face was clean of makeup – the way I liked it best – and by the taste of her kiss, her teeth were brushed.

She whispered, 'I thought I'd wait for you to check on them.'

We tiptoed into the boys' part of the suite. Early was snoring like he meant it. Johnny Mac was totally still, almost rigid. Oh, they were both awake all right!

We went ahead with our nightly rituals, careful not to discuss anything we didn't want the kids to hear. But then I decided to get creative.

'So what did you think of that show tonight?' I asked my wife.

'The show?'

'Yeah. Did you believe that was a real vampire?'

'Well,' she said, picking it up quickly, 'I wasn't quite sure about the vampire, but that thing with two heads was definitely real!'

'I want to go back tomorrow night after the kids are down and see the mummy,' I said.

'Do you believe it really walks?' she asked.

'More than I believe there are real-life zombies,' I said.

I caught movement out of the corner of my eye in the boys' area.

'I'm not so sure,' Jean said. 'There is some medical evidence regarding the existence of zombie-like creatures, at least in nature. And if it's true in nature, why not with humans, too?'

'Gosh, I didn't know that!' I said. 'Tell me all, but keep it quiet. We don't want to wake up the boys.'

'OK,' Jean whispered, and it wasn't two seconds before both boys were in the room with us.

'Mom, really? What part of nature? What do they look like? Have you seen one? Are we talking reptiles, insects, or mammals?'

'We're talking you should go to bed when we tell you to, instead of staying up all night talking!' I said.

'There are no zombies. Or vampires,' Jean said.

'Or mummies, or two-headed things—' I started, but Jean cut me off.

'Well, there are two-headed calves, occasionally.'

I laughed. 'Honey, you've been to too many carnival sideshows.'

'No, they're real!' she insisted.

I laughed indulgently. That pissed her off. She grabbed her laptop, pulled up Google and downloaded a video of a two-headed calf somewhere where the one-headed people didn't speak English. So we had to watch the video and discuss the phenomenon. That took us to almost two a.m.

We finally got the boys down and ourselves in bed. No reading for either of us tonight. Tomorrow would be our first full day aboard ship.

Milt – Day Two

Having seen the menu for breakfast posted in the main dining room the night before, I knew where I was going, but the boys were having none of that. So I took them down to the buffet line where they got all the crap they wanted to eat, got them seated at a table, gave Johnny Mac his mother's cell phone and told him to call me when they were ready to leave the buffet area.

I got lost on my way back to the cabin and ended up on the first deck, where they rented jet skis, water skis and other watercraft fun. They also rented scooter chairs – those things they advertise on TV for old people. I went in, rented one and drove it up the elevator to the right deck and to our room. I honked at our door. Jean opened it, looking lovely in pink and turquoise plaid Bermuda shorts and a pink golf-type shirt.

'What the hell?' she said, staring at the scooter.

'They rent these downstairs,' I said.

'You really feel you need that?' she asked.

I shot her a look. 'Better this than me pushing you in a wheelchair. Those are your options.'

'I prefer my crutches,' she said, turning her back on me.

I got off the scooter, took out the key and pocketed it, and headed in the cabin after her. 'I can say there were at least two hundred people on the promenade deck last night who would prefer you took the scooter.'

She turned and gave me a withering look. 'Oh, I'm sorry,' she said, the sarcasm dripping off her tongue. 'Did my pesky old handicap get in your way?'

'For Christ's sake, Jean! There is absolutely nothing wrong with finding a way to fit into your environment! These corridors are not the streets of Longbranch where there's plenty of room for people to get around us if they're in a hurry. This is a smallish ship with five hundred people on it, half of 'em going the way we're going. Besides, girl, you've got the biceps of a weightlifter,' I said, reaching for one of them. 'Which I find incredibly sexy.' I shrugged my shoulders. 'Who knew?'

Jean laughed and sat down on her bed. 'So I need to worry if Arnold Schwarzenegger comes to Longbranch?'

'Oh, baby!' I said and sat down next to her, kissing her neck. 'God, I'm hungry,' I murmured. 'I wish we could live on love alone.' Then I took an innocent nibble.

'Uh uh,' Jean said, standing up. 'If you want to bite something let's go eat.'

'You'll try the scooter?' I asked.

'Only if I can take my crutches along so I can park the scooter at the restaurant, or outside a shop, or whatever. You understand?'

'Completely,' I said, already working my head around the breakfast menu I'd seen last night.

Johnny Mac, Day Two

Johnny Mac went for seconds on pancakes and Early was behind him waiting for seconds on waffles. While they stood in line they grabbed some extra bacon, a couple of sausages, some fruit and three donuts each. Neither of them even ventured a thought toward the night before last, when they'd hugged a toilet for over-indulgence.

They'd barely started on their second helpings when Janna, one of the girls from the night before (the blonde with the big blue eyes), came by with her parents.

'Hey!' she said, smiling mostly at Johnny Mac. 'Those pancakes are delish, right?'

'Yeah, real good,' Johnny Mac said, around a mouthful of said pancakes.

'Janna, introduce us to your new friends,' her mother said.

'Oh, yeah, sure. Johnny Mac, Early, this is my mom, Lucy Tulia, and my dad, Mike Tulia. This,' she said, putting her hand on Johnny Mac's shoulder, 'is Johnny Mac and this,' she said, using only her head to point in Early's direction, 'is Early.'

Lucy Tulia smiled at the boys. She was a short, thin woman with pointy features – chin, nose and cheekbones. Her hair was highlighted and mostly blonde. 'I think you might have last names, is that right?' she said and laughed slightly.

'Yes, ma'am,' Johnny Mac said, trying to stand up in the presence of a lady, like his dad had taught him. He made it up, brushed his hands off on his shorts, and held out his right hand to Mrs Tulia. 'Johnny Mac Kovak, ma'am. And this is my friend, Early Rollins.' Early rushed to stand up and shake hands with both parents. Johnny Mac thought the whole thing went quite smoothly and was very grown-up.

'And how did you meet?' Mr Tulia asked. He towered above his shorter wife. Well over six feet, he had dark hair and eyes and pleasant features.

Janna answered quickly, 'They're friends of Ryan's.'

'Oh,' Mr Tulia said and smiled. 'He's a nice boy.'

Johnny Mac nodded, although he figured it was a pretty big stretch of the imagination to call the Ryan he'd met the night before 'nice.'

'My dad and Ryan's dad are partners,' Janna explained.

Johnny Mac nodded again, this time echoed by Early.

'Mom, can I go with Johnny Mac and Early to the kids' pavilion?' Janna asked, the big blue eyes turned up to her mother's face.

'Sure. Are you kids finished eating?' Mrs Tulia asked.

'Mom! Look! Their plates are still full!' Janna said, sliding in the seat next to Johnny Mac.

'We're almos—' Johnny Mac started, but felt Janna kick him in the leg. 'We won't be long,' he said.

'Well.' Mrs Tulia looked at Mr Tulia, then at the children's pavilion at the far end of the food court. Then they both turned to look at the three fresh-faced children. 'OK, but go straight there and stay there until we come get you.'

Janna smiled at her mother. 'I've got my cell, Mom. Just call when you're on your way, OK?'

Mrs Tulia kissed her daughter, as did Mr Tulia, and then they were away.

'Gawd, I thought I'd never get rid of them!' Janna said. 'I'm so glad I ran into you two!'

'It's nice seeing you, Janna,' Johnny Mac said.

'Whatever,' she said. 'Let's dump that food and get out of here.'

'How far is the children's pavilion?' Early asked.

Janna laughed. 'The children's pavilion? Are you out of your mind? It's right there!' she said, pointing at the far end of the food court. 'But Lyssa's waiting for us – well, me anyway – on the top deck. We're going to spit in the ocean!'

Johnny Mac and Early looked at each other and shrugged. Johnny Mac said, 'Cool,' and they were off.

Meanwhile, Back In Prophesy County

The next morning Emmett decided it would be a good idea to go check out Darby Hunt. The address listed in the release papers faxed over by Bill Williams showed him living at his mama's house, just outside of Longbranch. It was the other side of the town from where the sheriff's office was located, but the town wasn't that big, so going through it to the other side took only about fifteen minutes, even accounting for both stoplights. Mrs Hunt lived in a defunct subdivision started back in the seventies. The builders had mowed down a lot of trees and only managed to put up six houses. Hers was on the one street, Camino Real, in the middle on the right. Like the rest of them, it was rundown, the brown brick looking tired and the mustard-yellow trim needing a paint job – preferably, Emmett thought, in a different color. There wasn't much grass, just bare spots interspersed with still-brown weeds that would blossom in about a week or two. The driveway led to an attached garage and was filled with vehicles: a Ford F150 pickup, probably an eighties model; a rusted-out Chevy Camaro with a faded racing stripe, a ten-year-old Cadillac, and on the walkway to the front door a spanking new Harley, bright red, with saddle bags.

Emmett brought Dalton with him, just as a visual aid, and the two walked up to the front door and rang the bell. It was obviously still working because Emmett could hear it in the house. At first no one answered, so he tried a knock. Before he could draw his hand back, the door was wrenched open and an elderly woman with a walker barked, 'What the hell do you want?'

She was hefty, close to three hundred pounds, Emmett figured, wearing a short-sleeved house dress, her upper arms big and floppy, and slip-on slippers. Her dyed brown hair was sparse and the look on her face was not what you'd call pleasant.

'Good morning, Mrs Hunt,' Emmett said. 'I'm with the county sheriff's department. I was wondering if I might speak with Darby.'

'You got no call coming here and harassing my son!' the old woman fairly spat out. 'He's not on parole so you got no reason to come checking on him; 'sides, he never did it in the first place! And even if he did, that little bitch deserved it, the way she treated my boy!'

Emmett tried to shake off the disgust he felt and asked again, 'May I see Darby, please?'

'No!' she shouted and slammed the door.

Dalton turned and started back to the squad car, but Emmett grabbed his arm. 'No way,' he said. He looked at the motorcycle sitting on the walk. No plates. Well, unless he found Darby with it on the street, nothing he could do about that. He was contemplating other ways to get at an ex-con when the door to the house opened.

In the file Bill Williams had faxed to Emmett the day before had been a fax-faded picture of Darby Hunt. Even just looking at a headshot, you could see he was a big old boy, and the type some women would find handsome. Blond hair in a mullet which, truth be known, was actually popular in the eighties, a big smile with straight teeth and dimples, dark eyes with long lashes – all that crap women think looks good on a man. Unfortunately the man standing at the door didn't look a lot like the Darby Hunt of the picture.

'And you are?' Emmett asked.

'Who you're looking for. I'm Darby Hunt,' he said.

The Darby Hunt of yesteryear was not present – this man was skinny to the point of being frail, the blond hair turned gray, what was left of it. The face was taut and wan, his pallor almost matching his hair for grayness.

'Y'all wanna come in?' he asked, holding the door wide.

Emmett hesitated.

'Mama's in her room,' Darby Hunt said, a smile showing missing teeth but still a hint of the dimples.

'Good. I'd hate to have to shoot her,' Emmett said, crossing the threshold of the Hunt home with Dalton right behind him.

'She'd probably outdraw you,' Darby said, still smiling. The front door opened immediately into the living room, which smelled of dust and sickness. There was a beat-up recliner and a sagging couch, but against one wall was a new and big flat-screen TV. Darby pointed them to the couch and took the recliner.

'What can I do for y'all?' the ex-con asked.

'I heard yesterday that you got out. You'd made some threats against your late wife's family at your trial. Just wanted to come by and encourage you not to act on those threats,' Emmett said.

'Do I look like I have enough strength to hurt a fly?' Darby asked.

'Doesn't take much strength to pull a trigger,' Emmett said.

Darby nodded his head. 'True enough.'

'Besides, as I understand it, you've got a lot of cousins who could do your dirty work for you.'

Darby laughed. 'Not so you'd notice anymore,' he said. 'You might be thinking of my old running buddies, Billy and Shorty, right?'

'It crossed my mind,' Emmett said.

'Well, Billy died in a car wreck back in 'ninety-three, and they wouldn't let me out for the service, damn their eyes,' he said, the glassy-eyed stare making Emmett think he was seeing the past now, not the present. Darby shook himself and looked up at Emmett. 'And Shorty moved to California where he currently resides in one of their fine institutions for the criminally stupid.'

'Pardon?' Emmett said.

Again, Darby grinned. 'The boy never was much without me and Billy. He held up a diner where his girlfriend's mother worked. He pulled some pantyhose over his face, but he couldn't breathe, so he picked a hole in them. You know how a hole in pantyhose just grows and grows?'

Emmett couldn't help himself. He smiled. 'Showed most of his face before he was through, huh?'

'Oh, yeah. Enough so that the girlfriend's mama goes, 'Shorty Hunt! You can't date my daughter no more!' All he could do was plead guilty.'

The smile faded and Darby Hunt rubbed his face with his hands and leaned forward, his elbows on his knees. 'Look. I got nothing against Cheryl's kin. They did the right thing. I killed my baby right in front of 'em.' He shook his head. 'I deserved what I got, if not more. I'da died with her, if I could, but I know my baby doll went to heaven, and I doubt I'll be visiting there ever.' He shook his head. 'What I did—' He shook his head again. 'That never can be forgiven, by God or anybody else.'

'Have you seen your daughter?' Emmett asked, more out of curiosity than anything else.

Darby shook his head. 'No, sir. Haven't seen her in twenty-five years. Not since the day I killed her mama – right in front of her.' Tears sprang to Darby's eyes. 'I'll never forgive myself for that. Ever.'

Emmett stood up. He wasn't going to shake Darby Hunt's hand, but he felt satisfied that the McDaniel family was safe for now.

'Thanks for the time, Hunt. We'll let ourselves out.'

Darby stood and grinned. 'Y'all hurry now. 'Fore I let Mama out.'

Emmett refused to hurry inside the house; once outside, however, it was a completely different story.

THREE

Milt – Day Two

The breakfast was everything I thought it would be and more. I loved cruising. I was going to go on a cruise every other week if the food would always be this good. Strawberry crêpes, eggs Benedict, champagne, beignets, croissants, Irish oatmeal, Greek yogurt and Cajun coffee. Oh my God! I didn't want to leave, but Jean made me.

Once we got Jean on the scooter she used my phone to call Johnny Mac. She put it on speaker.

'Hey, sweetie. We're on our way to the buffet.'

'Oh, Mom, listen! We met some kids who told us about this children's pavilion and we came with them here! This girl's parents went with us and dropped us off. I hope that's OK?'

'You should have called first, buddy,' I said.

'I know, Dad, but I'm not used to having Mom's cell phone and I just forgot,' he said.

'Are you having fun?' Jean asked.

'Yeah, it's a blast!' Johnny Mac said.

'OK. Well.' Jean looked at her watch. 'Did you wear your watch this morning?'

'Yes, ma'am.'

'OK, mine says fifteen after ten. We'll meet you at the pavilion at fifteen after eleven. That gives you an hour more, OK?'

'You sure we can't stay longer?' he begged.

'No. Eleven-fifteen. We're going to have some family fun. 'Bye, sweetie,' Jean said and hung up.

And I stood there and she sat there and we stared at each other, then Jean turned the scooter around and we headed back to our cabin.

Twenty minutes later we were back on the promenade deck checking out the stuff. Shops everywhere, most of them full of crap you'd never need in your lifetime. But some stuff you might have forgotten to pack – like sunscreen and sunglasses and big floppy sun hats for women and golf hats for men and purses that jangled with geegaws and T-shirts that said everything from 'My parents went on a cruise and all I got was this lousy T-shirt' to 'Fuck a bunch of 'em, I'm going to Puerto Rico.' We didn't buy anything, although Jean did linger a bit over the jangly purses. We peeked into the casino and I managed to lose twenty-five cents in the nickel slots, then got caught by a country song coming out of one of the smaller auditoriums. We went in and sat at the back, listening to two songs before we continued our slow progress toward the bow of the ship. We stopped for a moment to check out today's shows and programs, then made our way toward the pool area.

This was open to the actual sky, but still the only way you could see the actual ocean was to look out the saltwater-stained windows. This area was a little less maneuverable for Jean and the scooter. The pool was surrounded by deck chairs sitting in mostly sun, while the shaded areas were filled with tables and chairs. Although I'm sure first thing in the morning all the chairs – deck and normal – were appropriately placed, by this time they'd been moved by passengers to the point that it was almost impassable.

But, like Indiana Jones moving through the jungle with his machete, I led the way for my wife, moving a chair this way, another that way, until we'd reached the other side, which led to the food court and, beyond that, the children's pavilion. Part of the pavilion was an attachment to the food court, glassed in and air-conditioned, while the other part was open, half-covered by a roof, half-open to the sun, but surrounded by a high picket fence. To the extreme starboard – or port? I couldn't keep that straight – was an exit from the food court onto an open deck around the ship.

We headed into the air-conditioned part of the children's pavilion. And it was packed. Everyone from two-year-olds to early teens. I spied Johnny Mac and Early out in the fenced-in area and told Jean to wait while I went and got them.

Working my way out there – after having signed my boys out with the lady in charge – I saw them talking to two little girls and a bigger boy.

'Hey, guys,' I said.

'Oh, hey, Dad,' Johnny Mac said.

'Hi, Sher— I mean, Mr Kovak,' Early said.

I gave Early a look for his slip – I didn't want anyone to know my profession as you get all sorts of demands on your time when you let people know what you do for a living when you're in law enforcement – and said, 'Who are your friends?'

Johnny Mac pointed at the boy. 'This is Ryan.' Then the dark haired girl. 'This is Lyssa, and –' at this point he looked longingly at the blonde and said with a sigh, 'this is Janna.'

'Hi, kids, nice to meet you,' I said, and Ryan shook my hand. I was turning around, ready to grab the boys and head out, when three more adults entered the patio area, or whatever it was called. They turned out to be the little blonde's parents, Mike and Lucy Tulia, and Ryan's dad, Vern Weaver, who was Mike Tulia's partner in a tool and die company out of Houston.

We all worked our way back into the air-conditioned area and I introduced Jean to everybody.

'We're going to play miniature golf,' Lucy Tulia said. 'Why don't y'all join us?'

So we did. My phone rang just as we got to the top deck where
the miniature golf course was – out in the open, with sun and the
ocean and all. I let Jean and the boys get ahead of me and answered
the new phone like my wife had taught me (I have no illusions of
manly self-esteem any longer – that's all gone), and said, 'Hello?'

'Hey, Milt,' Emmett said.

'Hey your ownself. I'm still on vacation, you know.'

'Just wanted to let you know I spoke with Darby Hunt this
morning. Boy's a shadow of his former self. I say he's probably
dying of something nasty. Aids, cancer – something that eats the
body up.'

'Can't see it happening to a more deserving guy,' I said.

'Now, Milt, he seemed real remorseful about killing his wife,'
Emmett said.

'Yeah,' I agreed, 'every time he beat the crap out of her, he'd
feel all remorseful in an hour or two. Didn't stop him killing
her.'

'Well, there's that.' Emmett cleared his throat. 'By the way he
looks, and the fact that his running buddies, Billy and Shorty –
Billy being dead and Shorty locked up in California—'

'Did you check both of those stories?' I asked.

'You just insulted me, Milt. I want you to know that. Of course
I checked out those stories. Both true. Anyway, I think the
McDaniel family should be OK.'

'That's good, real good. Just keep your eye out—'

'Milt—'

'I know, I know,' I said. 'I worry.'

'OK, Mom, get back to your shuffleboard,' Emmett said and,
as I was telling him that they didn't have shuffleboard on this boat,
he hung up.

By the time I made it to the first hole, Jean was already putting
for our team. Even with her crutches she did more than OK, basically beating the crap out of the rest of the adults. After that we
split with the Tulias and headed to a puppet show in one of the
smaller halls. I think it may have been a little immature for the
boys because they talked all the way through it, mostly in whispers
and giggles. I know, I'll never say 'giggles' out loud about my
son, but that's exactly what they were doing.

Meanwhile, Back In Prophesy County
Emmett hit the intercom and asked Holly Humphries to send in Anthony Dobbins.

'Yeah, Emmett?' Anthony said, sticking his head around the corner of his door frame.

'Do a background check on Billy Hunt and Shorty Hunt. Billy's supposed to be dead, and Shorty's supposed to be in prison in California. You might check the files to find Shorty's real first name.'

'Relations of Darby Hunt?' Anthony asked.

'Cousins,' Emmett replied.

He'd lied to Milt. It should have been the first thing he did, and he would have if it hadn't been for the whole 'petal pusher' bullshit. The call Jasmine made the day before had been to Petal's afternoon sitter, Carol Anne Haynes, who said Petal told her that one boy had called her that early in the morning and then everybody else picked up on it. Jasmine had insisted Petal go to this special Christian school, rather than the public school, but Emmett was beginning to think public school might have been a better idea.

At least Milt and he would have their kids on break at the same time. This Christian school was weeks behind the public school. Their spring break coincided with Easter, giving the kids almost as much time off on that holiday as at Christmas.

'So who was it?' he'd asked his wife the night before.

'Riley Sturgis!' she said, hands on hips, like Emmett was supposed to know who that was.

'OK,' he said. 'That's some kind of Yankee fish, right?'

She didn't even laugh. 'That's sturgeon, you moron,' she said. And she wasn't kidding.

'It was a joke, honey,' Emmett said.

'Well, this isn't funny! It's not bad enough she did this to me all through high school – now she's doing it to my child!' And she burst into tears.

It took a whole hour before Emmett finally heard it all. The gist of it was that Riley Sturgis was the son of Jasmine's rival for everything in high school, one Mary Ann Cummings, who used to make fun of Jasmine and her sisters and their flower names, calling them 'the weeds.' And yesterday, after talking to an old friend from high school, Jasmine found out that Mary Ann had been making fun of Petal's name to one of her old crowd, saying that Jasmine just couldn't stop it with the stupid names, ending with, 'If she were in my class, I'd call her petal pusher.' Her son had not been too far away.

So Emmett had been up real late dealing with that, thinking he might have some ammunition to get his daughter out of that damned Christian school and into the public school (he swore to himself it had nothing to do with money, although the school was scarily expensive). He wasn't able to sleep after that, worrying about his little girl. She was so tiny, so sweet-natured. This was a hell of a thing to be happening to her.

He went and got himself another cup of coffee. The new civilian aid made a dynamite cup of coffee. Made you kind of not miss Gladys at all. Ill-tempered, uncooperative and the maker of really bad coffee, it was a joy not to see her sour puss every morning.

Anthony motioned to him from the bullpen.

Emmett ambled over, sipping his coffee.

'What ya got?' he asked.

Anthony put down the phone and said, reading from his notes, 'William Jason Hunt, aka Billy Hunt, died in a one-car accident on the early morning of June 14, 1993. Autopsy showed an extremely high alcohol content. John Wesley Hunt, aka Shorty Hunt, is currently incarcerated at the Elwood Moody Correctional Facility in Moody, California. He'll be eligible for parole in 2014.'

Emmett nodded and took another sip. 'OK, then,' he said and walked back to his office, at which point an inconsistency finally dawned on him. A guy fresh out of prison, living with his mama in a rundown house without much more than a pot to piss in – where in the hell did he get the money for that fancy new Harley and that big old flat-screen TV?

Emmett decided another trip out to see Darby Hunt was in order. He took Anthony Dobbins with him this time. Unlike poor Dalton, Anthony might have something to contribute to the interview.

The street, the house and the driveway all looked the same as they parked the squad car at the curb. Darby Hunt must have seen them coming because he opened the door before their knock.

'Sheriff,' Darby said. 'What can I do you for now?'

'It's just Acting Sheriff, but you can call me Emmett. Can we come in for a minute?'

Darby looked hard at Anthony standing behind Emmett, but opened the door for them to enter. When he did, Emmett noticed on the flap of skin between thumb and index finger on Darby's left hand, which was holding the door open, was a tattoo of a swastika. Made sense. The Oklahoma Penitentiary, like so many others, had two main gangs – the white supremacists and the black Muslims. If you wanted protection, you joined the gang of your color.

The swastika wasn't missed by Anthony Dobbins. He gave Darby Hunt the stink-eye right back as he and Emmett went to the sagging sofa and sat down.

'What do you want now?' Darby asked.

'Something I forgot to ask you earlier,' Emmett said.

'What's that?'

'Where did the new motorcycle and TV set come from?'

Darby Hunt raised an eyebrow. 'Why in the hell do you need to know that?'

Emmett shrugged. 'Just wondering how a con straight out of prison comes to live with his obviously poor mama and has the wherewithal to purchase a motorcycle and a big ol' TV. Makes me think he's been up to no good.'

'When have I had time to be up to no good?' Darby asked. ''Sides,' he said, taking a long breath, 'where would I find the strength to rob a bank or whatever?'

'So you saying the pen has upped their release stipend to like $10,000 or so?' Emmett asked.

'Woo doggies, you haven't been pricing motorcycles or TVs lately, have you, Acting Sheriff Emmett?' Darby asked, that snaggle-toothed and dimpled grin very much in evidence.

'Where did you get 'em?' Emmett asked, not smiling back.

'They were gifts,' Darby said, grin still in place.

'From a grateful nation?' Emmett asked with a sneer.

'From a grateful lady,' Darby answered, his grin getting bigger.

'Hum,' Emmett said, 'you got out yesterday and already you got a girlfriend?'

'No, this lady's been my, um, friend, I'd guess you'd say, for about eighteen months. Started out as pen pals, then she started bringing my mama to see me. Real nice lady.'

'And she bought you the motorcycle and TV because . . .'

'Because I'm so fucking handsome,' Darby said and laughed.

'And how can she afford to buy you such expensive gifts?'

'She's got a real good job. She's the principal at that Christian school in town.'

No more discussion. Petal was moving to public school.

On the way home the night before, Dalton had called the realtor who had the listing for the little house near downtown and made an appointment to see it on the way in to work that morning. He pulled up outside the house about ten minutes early. Dalton never, ever got any place late, or even on time. He was always early. He never wanted to keep anyone waiting. But Holly wasn't that crazy about that habit. He'd show up at her apartment and she'd never be ready, and although that didn't bother him a bit, as he didn't mind waiting for her – either inside her apartment, sitting on the couch, or even outside standing on the porch – it seemed to bother her.

But while he was waiting for the realtor, he got an itch. He wanted her to hurry up because he wanted to see this house. The outside had him all atwitter. It was what the realtor had called a pre-war bungalow. He wasn't sure which war, but he didn't really care. It was a wood-frame house, painted yellow with white trim, and had a big front porch. In his mind he could see a white porch swing and maybe some push toys and a tricycle or two. There were evergreen shrubs on either side of the porch and mulched flower beds just waiting for planting. The driveway was paved and led to an old-fashioned garage with one of those doors that went from right to left, rather than up and down. He thought he'd probably want to replace at least the door – get one of those electric garage door openers and make it easier for Holly, especially when she'd be carrying groceries and a child or two. Or three.

A fancy Lexus pulled up in the driveway and Dalton got out to meet the realtor. She was an older lady, probably in her fifties, wearing glasses with great big fancy frames, and slacks, a top, a jacket, a bunch of scarves and jewelry.

'Mr Pettigrew?' she called as he approached. 'Or should I say Officer Pettigrew?'

'That would be Deputy, ma'am,' Dalton said, taking her outstretched hand. 'But please call me Dalton.'

'Well, fine, Dalton, I'm June O'Hara, and you can just call me June! Isn't this a lovely home? Like I told you on the phone, it's a two bedroom, one bath with an extra room, a one-car garage, or,' and here she patted his arm, 'a workroom! You look like a man who likes to work with his hands.'

'Yes'm, sometimes,' Dalton said.

'Is your wife joining us?' June asked.

Dalton blushed. 'No, ma'am. Not today.'

'Well,' she said, and looked at the gun in Dalton's holster.

'Oh,' Dalton said. 'Would you be more comfortable if I left my service revolver in the car?'

June smiled. 'That would be lovely,' she said.

Dalton headed back to his squad car and put the gun in the glove box, locked the box then relocked the car. He joined June on the porch and they headed inside. The front door opened into the living room, which was a good size, a fireplace on the right with bookcases on either side, with a small window at the top of each bookcase, and on the left what the lady had called 'an extra room.' It had glass French doors separating it from the living room, and big windows on two sides. It wasn't a big room, but it would be perfect as an office, Dalton thought. Although he had no idea what he would do with an office.

Beyond the living room was a large dining room, and Dalton couldn't help thinking about the Thanksgiving dinners he and Holly could host in that room with his mama, his best friend Milt and his family, and anybody else they wanted to invite. He smiled big just imagining it.

'And here's the kitchen,' June the realtor said, opening a swinging door.

It was just like his mama's kitchen. Real big with lots of cabinets and drawers. Some of these cabinets, however, had glass doors and he thought that would be a good place to put their wedding china and stuff like that. There was a closet by the back door that, when opened, revealed a space for a washer and dryer.

'Where are the bedrooms?' Dalton asked.

June the realtor led him back to the dining room where there was a doorway into a hall. There was a small bedroom straight across, with one window – perfect for a nursery, he thought – a bathroom in the middle, then the master bedroom at the back. Huge windows on two walls looked out on the backyard.

'This house sits on a half-acre, most of which you're looking at,' she said, indicating the backyard, which seemed to go on forever. The houses on either side were fairly close, but the back yard was at least half a football field long. 'It backs up to Mason Creek,' June said. 'But they fixed it up two summers ago so there's not supposed to be any more flooding.'

Flooding? Dalton's face fell.

Again, June put her manicured hand on his arm. 'Now, honey, they fixed it!' she said. 'It's not going to flood anymore. Stop with that hangdog expression!' And she laughed and squeezed his arm.

'This place is a real steal,' she said, and named a figure that made Dalton's head swim.

He nodded his head for a while, then said, 'I'm gonna have to think on it.'

'Well, of course, but don't take too long! At this price, this little beauty's gonna be snapped up in a New York minute!'

They heard the sound of breaking glass, and Dalton ran for the front door. Having been in the back bedroom, it took him more than a minute to get to the front porch. He couldn't see anyone, but he did see what was broken: the side window on his patrol car. Inside, the glove box had been prized open and his service revolver was gone.

'Oh no,' he said.

'What was it?' June the realtor asked as she came out of the house and down the porch steps.

'Somebody broke my window and stole my service revolver,' he said.

'Oh my God!' June the realtor said, looking around her in fear of being shot.

Dalton looked around with her. 'Wonder who did it?' he said to the world in general.

'Well, I had nothing to do with this, Deputy!' June the realtor said in huff. 'If you're accusing me—'

Dalton's face showed his complete and utter bewilderment and surprise. 'Oh, no, ma'am, I'm not doing that! I just wonder who did it, that's all.'

'Well, I didn't!' she said, emphasizing the point.

'Yes, ma'am, I know,' he said and moved around the car to the driver's side, as June the realtor headed quickly to her Lexus.

Dalton swept the broken glass off the driver's-side seat, got in his squad car and sighed heavily. He didn't dwell on it, but things like this seemed to happen a lot to Dalton Pettigrew. But he did worry about how he'd tell Milt. Well, not Milt. He was on vacation. Emmett, then. He'd have to tell Emmett. Dalton sighed again. He and Emmett weren't real good friends like him and Milt. Or even him and Anthony. Maybe it was because of Jasmine, Dalton thought. Jasmine never had liked him, since her first day on the job. Dalton didn't know why, but he knew it was true.

But still and all, he was going to have to tell Emmett. Dalton sighed yet again and started the car.

Milt – Day Two

That night was the dress-up event in the dining room. Dressing up is not my idea of a vacation, but Jean was very happy about it. She'd bought a new dress just for this occasion and had insisted that the boys and I bring suits. The boys were adamant about not going to the dining room.

'Mom! I don't like the food there! And besides, I don't want to dress up! And I forgot my jacket anyway!' Johnny Mac whined.

'I packed your jacket for you. Along with your dress pants, your belt, black socks and your good shoes. And Early's mother did the same. You have no excuse.'

'How about I don't want to?' he yelled.

Well, now, you just don't yell at Jean. That got him sent to the top bunk for the half hour before dinner. And, although Early had not participated in the yelling, he was punished nonetheless by having to stay out in the main part of the suite with me and Jean. He brought a book.

We had the early feeding that night – they have two, one at six and one at eight – so we got the boys dressed, against their wills, got ourselves dressed, and headed out. I decided dressing up was worth it when I saw Jean all dolled up. She had on a red one-shoulder dress that hit above the knee at the front and went down a little more in the back. My wife has truly beautiful shoulders and I was gonna have to try like crazy to keep my lips off that exposed one. Even Johnny Mac managed to say, 'Mama, you look really nice.'

And Early, looking up at Jean, managed a 'yeah,' before the blood infused his face and he turned around and headed out the door. Poor guy; I hoped he'd outgrow that before high school.

Everybody was dolled up when we got to the dining room. Women in full-length gowns and what they call cocktail dresses, men in suits, and one guy who wasn't a waiter in a tux. And the boys saw their friends only a couple of tables over, having to endure the same torture as them. The little blonde waved at Johnny Mac and he waved back, and I was pretty damn sure the little guy had his first serious crush. He beat me: I was in the sixth grade and her name was Bobbie Jean Murdock. She was beautiful. Her family moved to Dallas after that year and I never saw her again. Truth be known, I do believe that that night, watching my son crush on the little blonde, was the first time I'd thought about Bobbie Jean Murdock since she moved away. I couldn't help wondering what she was up to now. Being my age, probably a grandmother.

Jean and I greeted Mike and Lucy Tulia and the bigger boy's dad Vern Weaver. He was sitting next to a much younger and very sexy-looking redhead in a strapless gown showing a lot of cleavage, and across from her was the boy Ryan and next to him an older boy we hadn't met. He looked like a youngish teenager.

'Milt!' Vern Weaver called. 'Come on over and meet my wife!' He was all smiles, as well he might be, as ugly as he was sitting next to someone like her. Vern was a big ol' guy, most of it running to fat, with a bad comb-over, wiry eyebrows and fat earlobes. Not a pretty guy.

'Hey, Vern,' I said and ambled over, Jean keeping up with me on her crutches. The boys headed straight for the little girl, kneeling down and talking in whispers with her. I shook hands with Vern and Mike, nodded at Lucy and the kids, and was introduced to Crystal.

'We're on our honeymoon, and Crystal wouldn't have us leaving my boys behind! So they came along with us! Ain't that the damnedest thing?' Vern said in his booming voice. I could see by the almost-empty bottle of wine by his plate that he'd had a little bit to drink.

'Vern, honey,' said the lovely Mrs Crystal Weaver in a sultry Jessica Rabbit voice, 'you're embarrassing me, and the boys! Right, boys?' she said, looking at mostly the teenaged one. And he was a sight. Dusty-looking brown hair that needed cutting, a forehead covered in zits, and so skinny you could actually see his bones. He looked down at his plate. The other plates were near empty, like at the end of a meal. The boy's plate hadn't been touched.

'I don't believe we've met your older son,' I said to Vern.

'Yeah, and you may not now. He's acting like a shithead and I'm about to send him to his cabin for the rest of the fuckin' cruise. Excuse my French, ladies.'

'This is Joshua,' Crystal said. 'Joshua, say hello to Mr and Mrs Kovak.'

The boy looked up and said, 'Hey,' in a voice that was halfway through the change.

'Please eat, Joshua, honey,' Crystal said. 'I would hate for your dad to send you to your cabin.'

The boy played with his food.

'It was nice meeting you, Crystal,' Jean said, 'and you too, Joshua. But we need to get seated before they give our table away!' She laughed. It was that tight little laugh she gives off whenever she's secretly pissed at me but doesn't want anyone else knowing. It works. The only one who knows is me, and what I did this time I'll never know.

We said our goodbyes and headed to our table. 'Can we sit with Janna and Ryan?' Johnny Mac asked.

'No, dear,' Jean said. 'There isn't room at their table, and besides, they're almost through eating.'

'Josh isn't,' my son said.

'John,' Jean said and gave him that look.

The boy sighed and picked up the menu.

After we interpreted the menu for them, the boys, being good Oklahoma cattle country young'uns, both ordered steaks and baked potatoes and salads with ranch dressing. When they grow up, they're both gonna regret giving up this opportunity to partake in some righteous chow they're not likely to get at home.

I had an appetizer of marinated beef steak tomatoes with bleu cheese crumbles, a main course of lobster gratin with risotto and baby artichokes, and a dessert of flan with flaming strawberries. And Jean and I shared a bottle of Chardonnay. Not that I know that much about wines, but it tasted OK to me.

When we finished and left, we found the Tulias with their daughter and the Weaver boys talking with an older couple and two younger women. One of the women was holding the hand of the other little girl we'd met – Lyssa, I think her name was.

'Oh, Milt, Jean, we want you to meet some people,' Mike said, grabbing my arm.

If we'd been in Prophesy County and somebody I didn't know that well grabbed my arm like that, I'd have a gun under his chin and be reading him his rights in a New York minute. Unfortunately my gun was in the cabin, and this was, I suppose, a social exchange. I tried a smile.

'These two ladies,' he said, indicating the younger ones, 'are Esther Monte – you've met her daughter Lyssa, right?' I nodded. 'And Rose Connelly and her sons Trip and Jacob. And these two,' he said, indicating the older couple, 'are Baker and Linda Connelly, the boys' grandparents.'

I shook hands, as did Jean, as Johnny Mac and Early moved over to where Janna and the Weaver boys stood.

'You're all traveling together?' Jean said, a sweep of her arm indicating the whole bunch of 'em.

The dark-haired Esther Monte laughed. 'Oops, no, not us,' she said, her arm around her daughter's shoulder. 'We just met Rose and her boys at the pool earlier today. And they asked us to tag along this evening.'

'Where are y'all off to?' Mike asked. 'Vern and Crystal went to their cabin,' he said, winking at me, 'so we've got the boys—'

'Hey, Uncle Mike,' the older Weaver boy said, 'I can take all the kids to the children's pavilion, if that's OK with everyone?'

Everyone looked at everyone else and then Lucy Tulia said, 'There's a comedian I saw on Letterman one time in the comedy club tonight. It's supposed to be racy, so this way we can actually see it.' She spoke softly and nodded slightly at the kids. The implication was simple: get rid of the kids and we can go get drunk and talk dirty. Worked for me.

Everybody gave instructions to the older Weaver boy on how

to handle their children, and the kids took off. The older couple
– the Connellys, I think it was, decided to skip the comedy club.
'Linda's not big on smut,' Mr Connelly said, 'so we'll bow out
of this.' Looking at his daughter-in-law, he said, 'Rose, don't stay
out late and keep an eye on the boys.'

'Of course, Dad,' she said and, if I wasn't mistaken, I think she
choked a little on the 'dad.' Rose Connelly was a pretty woman
– one of those ethereal-looking ladies, with just a bit of blue vein
showing through parchment skin, blonde hair with very little
pigment and blue eyes so light in color that on an overcast day
the irises might appear to be missing. She was wearing a flowing,
hippy kind of dress. It suited her.

So, we were all dressed up with someplace to go.

Johnny Mac – Day Two

Joshua Weaver led his little band of misfits from the dining room,
around the casino, past the shops, by the bars and auditoriums, to
the open deck where the pool was located. There he sat them down
at a large table.

'Is this the children's pavilion?' the younger of the two Connelly
boys asked. 'I didn't bring my swimsuit.' Like his mother, he was
exceedingly fair and had the same blue eyes, with hair so light
that in Oklahoma they would have called him 'Cotton.'

'Who are you?' Joshua asked.

For a moment the child looked scared, until his older brother
took over. 'What's it to you? You're supposed to be taking us to
the children's pavilion, right? This ain't it. Lead on, asshole!'
Unlike his mother and younger brother, Trip Connelly bore more
of a resemblance to his grandfather – tall, brown-haired, with a
ruddy complexion and brown eyes.

Joshua laughed. 'Got quite a mouth on you, huh, kid? Here's
the deal. I think we can have more fun out here, playing some
games – and I'm not talking Monopoly, 'k?'

'Whatever,' the older Connelly boy said.

'So what's your name, hotshot?' Joshua asked.

'Baker Barnet Connelly the third,' he said. 'But you can call
me Trip.'

'OK, Trip. And the kid, he got a name?'

The younger one said, 'I'm Jacob.'

'How old are you, Jacob?' Joshua asked.

'Seven, but I'm pretty strong and I know how to play Monopoly.'

His older brother sighed. 'We're not playing Monopoly, numb-nuts! Jeez!'

'Hey, he just misunderstood!' Janna said.

'Yeah,' Johnny Mac agreed.

'You freaks want to play a game or not?' Joshua said.

'Sure,' Trip said, leaning back in the chair and crossing his arms over his chest.

The others nodded their agreement.

'OK, here's what we do,' Joshua said. 'I'll count to three, then y'all scatter. Everybody look for something someone left behind on a table or a chair. Grab it and bring it back. Best thing wins.'

'But isn't that stealing?' Johnny Mac asked.

Joshua sighed. 'Not if we give it back, silly!'

'Oh,' Johnny Mac said, trying out this concept in his mind.

'Now, one, two, three, go!'

Milt – Day Two

The comedian was just stupid, and not that funny. Jean and I left and headed to the bar next to the auditorium. We were followed out by Lyssa's mom, Esther Monte, who joined us at the bar, with a tall, dark and OK-looking guy in tow.

'I swear if he said the C word one more time I was going to throw something at him,' she said. 'You guys, this is Lance. He was sitting next to me and had the good taste to hate that guy as much as I did.'

Lance took off his suit jacket as he sat down and I saw Armani on the label. I decided to keep my Sears best on. Didn't need any label comparisons going on. Though the comparisons of the ladies' dresses were quite obvious: Jean's red, one-shoulder dress looked fairly classy up against Esther Monte's black minidress with what they call a sweetheart neckline (Jean told me later) that showed way too much cleavage (she also told me this later – personally, I thought it was just enough), had a plunging back, and (again according to Jean) was entirely too tight. She looked fine to me. I'm just saying.

The new guy held out his hand to me and I shook it. 'Milt Kovak,' I said.

'Lance Turner,' he said.

'My wife, Jean,' I said.

'Ma'am,' he said, shaking hands with Jean.

Rose Connelly came out of the auditorium alone. She was wearing a gauzy dress of pale pastels, kinda like a kaftan. I thought she looked like a nun, but Jean told me later that it was a lovely gown. Women – totally different mindset, I'm telling you.

Esther called out, 'Rose!' raising her arm to wave. Rose saw us and came over. We'd been at the bar, but with three new people we'd moved to a table.

'I think "funny" is a generational thing,' Rose said as she sat down and introductions had been made.

'Definitely,' Jean said. 'My parents thought Bob Hope was funny; my generation had George Carlin.'

'Personally, I'm an Andy Kaufman kinda guy,' Lance said.

'Should I call John?' Jean asked, holding her hand out for my phone.

'You never gave it back to me,' I said.

'Oh, right!' She dug in her bag and came up with it.

'Your son has a cell phone?' Esther asked.

'No, not one of his own,' Jean said. 'We lent him mine to use when we're separated aboard ship. It seems to be working,' Jean said. She held up a finger. 'Hi, honey,' she said into the phone. 'Are you two having a good time?' She listened for a moment, then looked at her watch. 'Well, it's almost midnight—' She stopped. Then, 'Well, OK, one o'clock. But you and Early take care of each other, OK?'

Esther waved her hand at Jean. 'Let me talk to Lyssa!'

Jean said, 'John, put Lyssa on the phone for her mom.'

It took a minute, but Lyssa obviously came on the line and Esther spoke for a moment.

Rose Connelly asked Jean, 'Do you think I could speak to my boys? How late does the pavilion stay open?'

'John said it's open until one a.m., and of course you can talk to your boys,' Jean said.

'Children's pavilion?' Lance asked me, an eyebrow raised.

'Yeah, the ship provides daycare of sorts for the kids. Babysitters and a nice-sized play area. Our son and his friend who's traveling with us both enjoy it a lot.'

Lance was a little too pretty for me to want to engage him in small talk, other than 'what do you do?' which would lead to him asking me what I do, which would blow my anonymity. So I was actually glad to see Mike and Lucy come out of the auditorium.

'Funny guy!' Mike said, pointing with his thumb behind him.

'If you like misogynistic assholes!' Lucy said.

'Which you certainly do!' her husband said, kissing her on the neck.

Lucy laughed. 'I guess you've got my number.' Jean's comments on Lucy's attire were nicer than those on Esther's but not as nice as those on Rose's. Lucy was wearing one of those cocktail dresses (difference being, I think, the length – this one hit her at the knees), black like Esther's, but with sparkly things on the top and the bottom made of some silky material. I thought she looked fine, but Jean said the dress wasn't that expensive. Well, she said it looked cheap, but I hate to report it when my wife sounds like a snob. Which she does, occasionally.

Since the women were all huddled around the phone, I introduced Lance to the Tulias.

The phone got passed to Rose, who spoke to one of her boys.

'What's going on?' Lucy asked.

'Everybody's talking to their kids,' I said. 'Johnny Mac said the pavilion stays open until one o'clock and we told him we'd come get him then. Rose and Esther are telling their kids the same.'

'Lord, I'm a rotten mother!' Lucy said, digging in her purse for her phone. 'I didn't even think about calling Janna!' She dialed her phone and got her daughter on the first ring.

I ignored her conversation as Mike and I pulled up two extra chairs for our table. Finally, after all the mothers had secure knowledge of their children's whereabouts, we could relax and order more drinks. Except my phone rang in Jean's hand. She answered it, said, 'Emmett, he's on vacation!' Then she sighed and handed me the phone.

I excused myself and went to the bar's bathroom where it was pretty quiet. 'What now?' I asked.

'Sorry to call so late, but I'm at a murder scene,' he said.

'No shit?' I said. 'Who got killed?'

'Darby Hunt,' he said.

I sat down in a stall. 'Is this a joke?' I asked.

'I'm serious as a heart attack.'

'What happened? I asked.

'Somebody fired through his mama's front window, got him right between the eyes,' Emmett said.

'Damn good shot,' I said.

'Yeah, well in this state, that doesn't exclude anybody.'

'I hear ya.' I sighed. 'Shit, Emmett, there's not a damn thing I can do about this—'

'I know that, Milt, for God's sake! I'm just keeping you informed.' He sighed too. 'I talked to him late this afternoon. I noticed he had a new motorcycle and a new TV in the house, and wondered where he got 'em. He said a lady friend gave 'em to him as a get out of jail gift. Guess who the lady friend is?'

'I have no idea,' I said.

'The principal at Petal's school,' Emmett said.

'Jesus H. Christ on a bicycle,' I said.

'Guess who starts public school next week?'

'Any leads on who killed old Darby?' I asked.

'It was a rifle – we're getting ballistics on that now. No footprints in the packed dirt in his mama's front yard, no cigarette butts or candy wrappers or other shit. I'm afraid I'm gonna have to talk to the McDaniel family.'

'It'd be hard not to. They're your most likely candidates. Keep me posted,' I said and hung up without a goodbye. I sat there on the toilet for a few moments, pants up, wondering why I decided I could possibly take a vacation. Then I remembered: I never decided that – Jean and Johnny Mac had decided it for me. When you're a cop for a big city, it's no big deal taking time off, but when you're the top cop in a small county, it *is* a big deal. A *very* big deal. I had to say, as much as I liked the food, I'd rather be home finding out who killed the killer.

I finally got up and made my way back to the table. More chairs had been pulled up, leaving an empty seat between my wife and Rose Connelly. I pulled it out and sat down.

'This is the first moment I've had alone since we came aboard,' Rose said.

'Ah, Rose, you're not alone now,' I said.

The women laughed. 'We know what she means,' Lucy said. 'Alone in this instance means sans child.'

'And in-laws,' Rose said.

'Yeah, Rose, how is that?' Esther asked. 'Vacationing with your in-laws? And your husband got out of it?'

Rose's face got a pinkish tinge to it. 'My husband died in a car wreck three years ago – with no insurance. I've gone back to school to get a degree so I can get a job. Meanwhile, the boys and I are living with Mr and Mrs Connelly.'

'I'm so sorry,' Esther said, putting her hand atop Rose's. 'But that really sucks – having to live with them. Mr Connelly seems like a—'

'Bit of a control freak?' Rose supplied.

'I was going to say asshole,' Esther said.

Rose laughed. 'Right on both counts. Thirty years in the air force, last ten as a colonel, makes for a tight ship. Did I mix a metaphor there?'

'No,' Lucy said. 'Only one metaphor. Just seemed like it because you mentioned the air force, then a navy metaphor.'

'Right,' Rose said, giving Lucy 'the obvious' Tulia a look.

'Hey,' Mike said, 'don't mind her. She's a teacher. And when she drinks she gets even worse! After two beers she not only corrects my grammar, she cuts my meat up for me.'

Lucy hit him on the shoulder. 'I have to!' she told the rest of us. 'His grammar is atrocious. And I'm sorry about the metaphor, Rose!'

Rose laughed. 'Don't worry about it. But,' she said, turning to Esther, 'speaking of husbands, where's yours?'

'Never had one,' she said. 'Met a gorgeous guy at a bar one night,' she said, glancing at Lance who sat beside her and slipping her arm into the crook of his. 'I figured I had the smarts, he had the looks, we'd make a great baby. I was right about that – she's smart *and* beautiful. The guy doesn't know though. Never got his last name!' She laughed and finished off the Scotch in front of her. 'God, I can't believe I just said that to you guys! I mean, you're my best friends, and all, but you're still perfect strangers!' And she got a good case of the giggles.

We all laughed with her. 'I know. I can't believe what I said about my in-laws,' Rose said.

'Your mother-in-law seems OK,' Lucy said.

'Have you ever read that book, *The Stepford Wives*?' Rose asked.

'Oh!' we almost all said in unison.

'Is this what y'all do when you get together? And by y'all, I mean you hens. Just sit around and talk bad about people?' Mike said.

'Ah, honey, if only you weren't here!' Lucy said and laughed.

'By the way, Mike, I'm gonna get an earful about your use of the word "hens" when we get back to our cabin,' I said.

He doffed an imaginary cap. 'My apologies, ladies. I'm sorry I called all you bitches hens.'

'Now, that's more like it,' my wife said.

FOUR

Johnny Mac – Day Three

'You did what?' Joshua said, grabbing Johnny Mac by the arm.

'I told her to pick us up at one o'clock,' Johnny Mac said, a little afraid of this big boy with the stranglehold on his arm.

'You stupid shit! The children's pavilion closes at ten!'

'But it's after midnight now –' Johnny Mac said, tears stinging his eyes. Don't cry, he told himself. Don't let this bully see you cry!

'And I coulda told them some story! Now we're in big trouble!' Joshua tossed Johnny Mac and his arm aside and paced the emptying pool area. 'So the rest of you, y'all told your parents the same thing?'

All the kids agreed and Jacob, the seven-year-old, teared up. 'I just wanna go back to Mom!' he said.

'Oh, man up, Jacob, for shit's sake!' his brother Trip said, punching him on the arm.

'God, you're an awful brother!' Janna said, putting her arm around Jacob. Jacob leaned his head against the part of Janna's anatomy that would one day, God willing, sprout boobs. He snuck a peak at Johnny Mac and grinned. Johnny Mac did not grin back.

'OK, here's what we do,' Joshua said. 'We go to where they are. Do we know where they are?'

'In that bar right next to the comedy club,' Johnny Mac said.

'OK. Good. That's not too far. Just keep your mouths shut and let me do the talking! Got that, Kovak?'

'All right! Jeez!' Johnny Mac said, and fell into line next to Early as they headed out in twos toward the parents.

Milt – Day Three

It's funny how people gravitate toward their own. It turned out that all of us were basically from the South – Jean, a native of Chicago, being odd woman out, but accepted as one of 'us' for having lived in Oklahoma for over a decade. Mike and Lucy, along with the Weavers, were from Houston, Esther and her daughter were from Atlanta, and Rose and her family lived in Memphis.

We were sitting at the table in the bar, discussing our Southern roots, when I looked up and saw a rag-tag group of kids heading to our table. Unfortunately one of them was my son – another his pal Early. The boys were carrying their dress-up jackets, and the girls looked a little less put together – hair-wise – than they had earlier.

'Hey, now,' I said, 'we were coming to y'all!'

'Sorry, Mr Kovak,' the big one – Vern Weaver's oldest son, I forgot his name – said. 'They decided to shut down early. They usually close at ten o'clock, and this was an experiment staying open this late – one that I guess failed. We were the only ones there. We were having a good time, but they kicked us out!' he said and laughed. The other kids made disappointed faces or laughed along with him.

Mike and Lucy got up. 'We need to be heading back anyway. Tomorrow we stop for a few hours in the Grand Caymans. We're definitely getting off,' Lucy said.

'So are we.' Jean used her crutches to stand up. 'I wonder if I can take the scooter off the ship?' she said to me.

'I'll find out in the morning. Johnny Mac, Early, let's head back,' I said, gathering my boys.

While we stuck Jean's crutches in a slot that seemed made for them on the scooter, I noticed the only people still at our table were Esther Monte, her daughter Lyssa, who had her head in her mother's lap and appeared to be asleep, and the new guy, Lance

Turner. You're on vacation, I told myself. And Esther's a big girl, she can handle herself. I sighed as Jean hopped aboard her scooter and we headed back to the cabin. The boys were asleep about the same time their heads hit their pillows, or maybe a little before.

Meanwhile, Back In Prophesy County

Emmett took the names and addresses of the members of the McDaniel family home with him, so the next morning he called in to Holly at the sheriff's department.

'Prophesy County Sheriff's Department,' Holly Humphries said upon answering the phone.

'Hey, Holly, it's me,' he said.

'Hey, Emmett, what's up?'

'Gonna ask you the same question. Anything going on there I need to know about?'

'No, sir. Nita's at the middle school doing that safety talk, Jasmine's on call here but Dalton called in early, left a message saying he'd be a little late. I heard about that guy, that Hunt, getting murdered last night! Awful!'

'Yeah. Why I'm calling – I'm going to go interview his late wife's family members, see if they know anything about Darby Hunt's unfortunate accident.'

'Yeah, I hate it when those bullets go accidentally flying through my front window,' she said.

'I got my cell. Call me if you need me,' Emmett said.

'Yes, sir. Try to be nice.'

'When have you ever known me not to be nice?' Emmett asked.

Holly said, 'I'm hanging up now,' and matched the deed to the words.

Lisa (née McDaniel) Atkins and her husband lived in a nice ranch-style house in an area inside the city limits of Longbranch. It was long and low, with a white-painted rail fence going around it, leaving the driveway open. Obviously not a privacy fence, or a fence to keep in a dog, because it accomplished little more than looking ranchy. Before he got out of his car, Emmett called Charlie Smith, police chief of Longbranch, to let him know he was in Charlie's territory and to see if he wanted in on any of the interviews he (Emmett) would be doing with members of the McDaniel family.

He got a clerk, asked for Charlie, told the clerk who he was and was put through pretty quick. Charlie always seemed slightly embarrassed to have the job Emmett had been kicked out of, but that had happened before Charlie's time. He'd been hired out of Oklahoma City and had nothing to do with the politics that had been going on three years before when Emmett had left. But Charlie's embarrassment might have been the reason he picked up on the first ring, which to Emmett's mind was not a bad thing. Let him be a little embarrassed.

'Hey, Emmett!' Charlie said. 'I hear you're acting sheriff with ol' Milt out of town. Heard anything from him?'

'He likes the food,' Emmett answered. 'And he denies they got shuffleboard.'

'Well, I'm not believing that! He's probably won a shuffleboard trophy already and he's just embarrassed to tell you.'

Emmett laughed. 'That's probably it.' Sobering, he got down to business. 'Listen, Charlie, you heard about Darby Hunt?'

'Sure did. Was gonna call you today, see if you needed any back-up on this.'

'Thing is, I'm sitting outside the dead wife's sister's house right now. Wanted your permission to interview the family or, even better, get you in on the interviews.'

Emmett was lying through his teeth. He wanted permission, all right, but he certainly didn't want Charlie looking over his shoulder. Emmett liked to do his interviews solo.

'You got my permission, but I'm afraid I'm hip-deep in alligators around here. Do you really need someone?'

'Naw,' Emmett said, breathing a sigh of relief. 'It's OK. Rather not wait out here anyway.'

'Well, good luck, and if you need anything, give me a call,' Charlie said.

'Will do,' Emmett said, and stepped out of the car.

The house was made of wood, stained to look like redwood, or maybe it was old enough to really *be* redwood, but he doubted it. There was a lion's head knocker on the front door and he used it. A woman in her mid- to late-forties opened the door. She was a pretty woman, with blonde hair turning silver in places, a bright smile, beautiful blue eyes and a slim build.

'Yes?' she said on seeing him on her doorstep.

'Mrs Atkins?'

'Yes, and you are?'

He showed his badge and said, 'I'm Chief Deputy Emmett Hopkins with the Prophesy County Sheriff's Department, ma'am, here in the role of acting sheriff. May I come in?'

The smile faded from her face. 'If you're here to tell me that Darby Hunt is back in town, I already know. Sheriff Williams from Tejas County called me yesterday.'

'No, ma'am, it's not that. May I come in?' he asked again.

She sighed. She was sort of dressed up, wearing what Jasmine called a 'pencil' skirt, black, with a royal blue, silky-looking shirt and blue heels.

'I need to get to work,' she said, her body language denying him entry.

'It's important, Mrs Atkins.'

She sighed again and dropped her hand from the door. 'All right,' she said.

The front door opened into a foyer. To the right was a dining room with Shaker-looking furniture, and to the left was a living room, well decorated but still comfortable-looking. Mrs Atkins took a seat on the sofa, her butt barely touching, indicating that he take what he could only assume was her husband's chair. It was a manly brown leather with a comfy butt spot all ready for him. He sat.

'I *do* need to get to work,' she said.

'Ma'am, could you tell me where you were last night?' Emmett asked.

Her eyes got big. 'Excuse me?'

'I need to know where you were last night around eight-thirty.'

'I watch enough TV, Deputy, to know you're asking me for an alibi. Did Darby Hunt' – the name spoken as if the words were poison in her mouth – 'accuse me of doing something?'

'Could you please answer the question, ma'am?'

She raised her hands up in exasperation. 'I was here, Deputy. With my husband, watching TV at that time of night. Then we went to bed a little after eleven. I like to watch Dave.'

'Ma'am?' Emmett asked.

She sighed. 'David Letterman,' she said, indicating his stupidity was equaled only by his desire to make her late to work.

'And your husband can vouch for that?' Emmett asked.

'Of course! Now what has that horrible man accused me of?' she demanded.

'Nothing, ma'am. Darby Hunt was killed last night. Rifle through the front window of his mama's house.'

A grin broke out on Lisa McDaniel Atkins's face and she said, 'Hot damn! About fucking time!' Then she covered her mouth and giggled. 'Excuse my French, Deputy.'

'No need, ma'am,' Emmett said. 'Can you think of anyone who might want Mr Hunt dead?' he asked, already knowing the answer.

'He doesn't deserve to be called "mister,"' she said. 'Slime bucket, I feel, works best. As for anyone who might have wanted to kill him? Let me go get the phone book.'

Since she didn't get up, Emmett figured it was her way of joking at the deceased's expense.

'Ma'am,' he said. 'Could you answer my question, please?'

'Other than my brothers and me?' She shrugged. 'Well, my daddy, but he'd have to haunt the slime bucket to death, since he's been dead ten years now.' She teared up. 'He never did get over losing Cheryl like that. Right in front of all of us. It killed my mama, too,' she said, looking Emmett in the eye. 'Just downright killed her. Wasn't six months before she just keeled over dead. So that man didn't just kill my sister, he also killed my parents.' She stood up, her look showing she thought he should do the same, which Emmett did. 'I don't even think God can forgive that man for what he's done, so I'm sure he's already in hell. I won't get out of my hell until I join my sister and parents.'

She walked to the front door, Emmett following. 'As for who killed Darby Hunt, I don't know, and actually, Deputy, I really don't care. Except I'd like to pin a medal on him.'

'Ma'am, before you throw me out, could you tell me please where I might find your sister Cheryl's daughter? Elizabeth, right? I can't find the name Elizabeth Hunt anywhere in Oklahoma.'

'That's because her name isn't Elizabeth Hunt. My husband and I legally adopted her when she was eight. And she hated the name Elizabeth because she was named after Darby Hunt's mother.

So she asked and we agreed that her first name be changed to Beth. She's a teacher at Longbranch High School.'

'And your son?'

'Jeez!' she said and heaved a huge, conspicuous sigh. 'He has a small house over on Trinity Street.'

'What's the number?' Emmett asked. He already knew – he just wanted to see what she'd say.

'Look it up,' was her reply, and she shut the door in his face.

Milt – Day Three

Shortly after deciding we were taking the tickets I won and informing the cruise line of their luck in having us, we were sent a brochure about the ship with two add-ins – one for our first stop – the Grand Caymans – and one for our second stop – San Juan, Puerto Rico. Each of these add-ons had lists of activities to be had in each port, how to go about booking said activity, and how much they cost. The activities in Georgetown, Grand Caymans, were such joys as scuba diving, horseback riding or jet skis. There were also hikes, tours on buses and walking tours, but the three of us – me, Jean and Johnny Mac – had narrowed it down to scuba diving, horseback riding or jet skis. Then we'd had Early for a sleepover, did a vote of those three, and ended up with jet skis. Personally, I was excited. I figured it would be like riding a motorcycle, except on water. What's not to like about that?

The next morning we woke up docked at Georgetown, Grand Caymans. Once off the ship we found an open-air three-wheel contraption – with a small trailer on the back – that would fit the four of us and Jean's scooter. We paid our guy a little extra and got a quick tour of the city. The island was beautiful. White beaches, green everywhere, and the perfect blue of the Caribbean. The city of Georgetown was an old city with lots of old buildings and rock walls and stuff. Real pretty. So we tooled around a bit, our driver telling us about this building and that, before we hit the jet-ski rental place. The add-on that came with the brochure said they had dressing rooms, so we'd brought along our swimsuits to change into, rather than wearing them from the boat. Not so bad for me and the boys, but for some reason women have a hard time going to pee, especially in a one-piece – at least, that's what Jean said. So we changed, then headed out to the jet skis. One of the guys took Jean's crutches and the one brace she still had on her left leg. The jet skis had hand controls, so she wouldn't need to use her legs, which I'd found out before we booked this activity. Early rode with me and Johnny Mac rode with Jean, and we were off. We stayed out for almost two hours, used up an entire bottle of sunscreen, and managed to have loads of fun. We fell off a couple of times – well, Early and I did. Jean and Johnny Mac, after flooding us with a giant wave, managed to stay on their skis. Still, by the time we turned them in we were all tired and a little sunburned. We showered – boys with me, Jean on her own – got dressed and met outside.

We'd agreed to meet up with the Tulias and the Weavers in town for lunch, and headed to a meeting place. It was a chain restaurant that we even had back in Oklahoma. Personally, I would have picked a local place. I was getting a little adventurous with grub. But we had a decent enough meal – it wasn't the ship's food, that's for damn sure, *and* we had to pay for it – and got out in plenty of time for a little sightseeing.

'Hey, y'all, would it be OK if us kids did a little sightseeing of our own?' Vern Weaver's oldest boy asked. 'I'll take care of everyone.'

Crystal Weaver beamed at her new stepson. 'Oh, Josh,' she said, 'what a wonderful big brother you are! Isn't that a great idea, Vern, honey? Then we grown-ups can just wander around at our leisure!'

Mike and Lucy looked at each other, as did Jean and I. Finally Jean said, 'Where are you thinking about going?'

He pointed at a group of shops closer to the ship. 'I thought we'd just go over there and look at stuff,' he said.

'Oh, Vern, honey, give both the boys some money!' Crystal said.

Jean sighed and punched me in the ribs with her elbow. 'Well, be sure you stay in that area, OK? Milt, give them some cash. Boys, you listen to Josh, OK? And look at several things before you buy. Be smart.'

'Yes, ma'am,' the two boys said in unison.

'Mom?' Janna said, looking up at her mother and tugging on her hand. 'Please?'

Mike said, 'Ah, honey, let her go!'

Lucy's whole body seemed to capitulate. 'All right.' She dug in her purse and took out some cash. 'Were you listening to Mrs Kovak? Be smart! And listen to Josh!'

'OK!' Janna said, almost jumping up and down. She ran over to where the boys all stood. ''Bye!' she said, waving. Everybody waved and they were off. And I didn't like it not one little bit, but I couldn't tell you why.

Johnny Mac – Day Three

'So here's what I want you to do,' Josh said, gathering the kids around him outside the first shop. 'This is the first test to see if you can make it in the pirate brigade.'

'What's that?' Early asked.

'It's the new club. If you don't pass you don't get to play with us anymore,' Josh said.

'So what's the test?' Janna asked.

'There are four of y'all and five stores. I want you each to pick a store – no two kids in one store, got it?'

They all nodded their heads. Josh went on: 'And the one who brings out the most expensive thing without paying for it gets to be second in command in the pirate brigade.'

'That's stealing,' Johnny Mac said.

'I'll take everything back when we're through! Jeez, Kovak! You accusing me of being a thief or something?' Josh said, a mad look on his face.

'No, I didn't mean that—' Johnny Mac started, but Josh cut him off.

'Look, Kovak, you don't have to play. Go back to your mommy, OK? Let the rest of us have some fun. I doubt you'd be very good at this anyway. Probably get caught before you get out of the store!'

'I would not!' Johnny Mac said. 'I can do this!'

'Well, then,' Josh said, 'pick your store!'

Johnny Mac picked the first one, not even seeing what kind of store it was.

Walking in, he wished he'd paid attention. He didn't know what to do in a jewelry store.

Milt – Day Three

After three stores, Mike and I ended up at the nearest bar with a wide-screen TV and ESPN while the women did their thing. I can only 'ooh' and 'ah' so long before I get a headache, know what I mean?

I knew Mike and Vern Weaver were partners in a tool and dye shop, so I hadn't really brought it up, not wanting him asking me what I did for a living. I wouldn't lie, but I didn't want that particular cat out of the bag. Like a doctor getting asked about imaginary ailments, a peace officer can get lots of people asking questions and trying to involve that peace officer in things that were basically none of his business. Like family squabbles. And if I knew anything at all about Mike Tulia, it was the fact that he'd have me refereeing a fight between him and Lucy in a New York minute. But, unfortunately, there's only so much you can do.

'So, Milt, what do you do for a living?' Mike asked about five minutes after we sat down. ESPN was playing a retrospective of the Texas/Oklahoma rivalry over the last forty-odd years. Now that's something I coulda gotten into.

I sighed. 'I'm in law enforcement,' I said, hedging my bets.

'Yeah? What do you do?' Damned if he wasn't going to make me spell it out.

'I'm the sheriff of a county in Oklahoma,' I said.

'No shit?' Mike said. 'Man, I've always wanted to do that. Have your own little fiefdom, huh? How cool is that?'

'Very,' I said. Then, changing the subject, I asked, 'So how long have you and Vern been partners?'

'About ten years. I was working in oilfield supply, used to call on Vern, then the bottom fell out of that and I needed a job. Had some 401K to transfer, bought up half of Vern's business. He needed the cash and I needed a job.' He took a long pull on his beer. 'That old boy's made me a millionaire – on paper, anyway. Only drawback is, in sales, I used to get an eyeful of some lush tush here and there, but shit, haven't seen a woman in our shop since that bowlegged postal lady got a new route.' He held up his hands in a stopping motion. 'Not that I ever did anything about it! Looking's one thing, touching is a whole nuther ball of wax.'

'Yeah, I hear ya,' I said, glad for the new subject. 'That's a headache I don't want to ever get near. 'Sides, who'd take a chance on losing everything – wife, kids, house, money, everything – for a piece of ass?'

'Huh,' Mike said, nursing a beer and staring at the wide-screen TV. 'That's a good point. Never thought about it like that. I just never did it because Lucy would put lye in my food if she caught me.'

'Seriously?'

'You should hear her daddy's deep and gravelly voice,' Mike said, looking at me and wiggling his eyebrows.

'Shit,' I said, finding a new respect for Lucy – and her mother.

Johnny Mac – Day Three
Johnny Mac could barely see into the jewelry cases, and what he could see all looked like diamonds! Millions of diamonds! He gulped in air, thinking about the prison they'd put him in if he even *tried* to take one of these million-dollar diamonds! If they didn't just shoot him! Oh, crap, he thought, what have I gotten myself into? He felt the tears at the back of his eyes. Stop! He told himself. Get a grip! That's what Daddy always said. Count to ten and get a grip. So he did. He counted to ten and he gripped his hands together behind his back. No way he could get at those diamonds if his hands were behind his back, he thought.

Even if Josh was going to return everything, Johnny Mac wasn't sure these store people, or the police, would believe that. He turned and looked out the window. Janna was already back and handing something to Josh. And then, there was Early, pulling something out of his T-shirt! Early did it! OMG, Johnny Mac thought. If Early did it, then I have to do it too!

Johnny Mac turned again and looked at the display cases. They opened from the back and that's where the store people were. The grown-ups in here were asking to see this and that and the store people would open the case and pull something out and let the person hold it. Would they do that for him? And then what? Just run out the door with it? They'd be after him in a heartbeat! No way. Then he saw a whole display case with no one behind it. The only thing on top was a ballpoint pen. Johnny Mac grabbed it and ran.

Meanwhile, Back In Prophesy County

Emmett stopped for lunch at the Longbranch Inn, a hotel/mostly restaurant where he and Jasmine had spent their first married night, and where he and Milt had been eating lunch together for over twenty years. Loretta, who may have come to Oklahoma in a covered wagon with the pioneers who settled Longbranch, was his usual waitress, but he was a little afraid to sit in her section today, for fear she'd ask about Milt's vacation. How could he tell her that Milt found the ship's food to be even better than that at the Longbranch? He couldn't. But if he sat at another waitress's table, how would he explain that?

He took a chance she wouldn't ask after Milt and sat in Loretta's section.

'Hey, Emmett,' she said, bringing him his usual glass of iced sweet tea with a water chaser, and a basket of melt-in-your-mouth yeast rolls. 'How's Milt liking his vacation?'

Well, there it was. She hadn't wasted much time on that! He wanted to say, 'just fine,' or even, 'real good.' Instead he said, 'He likes the food on the ship more'n he likes the food here.'

It came out real fast and then he just sat there, trying real hard not to make eye contact with Loretta.

'Don't I know it!' she said. 'My sister Lucile and me went on that Alaskan cruise one time, couple years ago, and the food was to die for! I hope Jean's just letting him go for it and not trying to keep him on one of her crazy diets!' Emmett finally found her face and saw her smiling. He smiled back. 'What'll it be?' she asked.

'Usual,' he said, and sat back in relief.

The thing was, Loretta, who didn't approve of diets, was a big woman, as tall as she was big, with a short temper when it came to anyone dissing the Longbranch Inn, Longbranch itself, Prophesy County, the State of Oklahoma, or the good ol' US of A.

It wasn't that he was exactly afraid of her, so much as he had a healthy respect for the parts of his body she could reach while he was sitting down.

It didn't take long for her to bring out his chicken-fried steak with cream gravy, French fries and fried okra. Manna of the gods.

He thought he'd wait until school let out at three-fifteen before tackling either the principal at the Christian school (Darby Hunt's girlfriend) or Beth Atkins at the high school (Hunt's daughter). So after wiping his face, taking a last long drag of his iced sweet tea and leaving a generous tip for Loretta, Emmett headed to David McDaniel's house, him being the older brother of Cheryl Hunt.

He'd called Dave's place of business first, a paint and body shop over off Highway 5, that had the contract for repairs on the squad cars when Emmett had been police chief, and found Dave had taken the day off. Since he owned the place, Emmett figured he had that prerogative.

Dave, his wife Brittany, and his last-at-home child Emma, age twelve, lived only a couple of blocks from his sister Lisa's house. The McDaniel house was a nice size, as befit a family of two parents and three kids. Two stories, with a one-story wing on the right that made the house look sort of crooked. That one wing, Emmett figured, had been an add-on.

Dave McDaniel opened the door before Emmett even knocked. 'Hey, Emmett. Figured you were coming to see me next,' he said, opening the door wide and ushering him in. McDaniel held out his hand and Emmett shook it. 'Long time no see,' McDaniel said.

'Been a while, Dave. How's Stevie doing?' Emmett said, asking after Dave's eldest son who had done a short stint as a patrolman for the LPD (Longbranch Police Department) before heading up to the state troopers.

'Keeps getting them promotions,' Dave said. 'Won't be long before he's in charge of Oklahoma.'

Emmett smiled, then sobered. 'Dave, the reason I'm here—'

'Yeah, Lisa called. Come on in the den.'

The front door opened into a foyer with a huge family room straight ahead, a large dining room to his left and a smallish formal living room to his right. Dave led him into the family room. To the left was a large open-plan kitchen, separated from the family room by a bar with barstools. The furnishings were plain and sturdy, as befitted a houseful of kids, mostly boys. A woman was in the kitchen with her back to them.

'Haven't seen you in a dog's age,' Dave said, indicating Emmett take an easy chair while he took the couch. 'Honey!' he called toward the kitchen, 'Emmett's here.'

Emmett had never met Dave's wife; theirs had not been that kind of relationship. And Emmett's wife back then, Shirley Beth, had been a recluse, a secret drinker, truth be told, which kept Emmett's socializing down to the bare minimum. Emmett still found it hard to think about her killing herself with his service revolver. That had been a bad time. Real bad.

The woman who came out of the kitchen took Emmett's breath away. She was medium height: not big but not little either. Her hair was dark brown with some gray showing, and when she smiled at him he couldn't help smiling back. All that was nice enough, but it was her eyes. Huge, like one of those dumb pictures of cats, and turquoise, with black lashes longer than any mascara ad could claim. They sparkled and danced with light and he thought if the lady ever went into hypnotism, she could do a hell of a lot of damage.

'Emmett, my wife, Brittany. Brit, this is Emmett Hopkins. We worked together when he was police chief, but you're with the sheriff now, right?'

Emmett nodded, dragging his eyes away from Dave's wife's turquoise ones. 'That's right. Head deputy, but the sheriff's out of town, so I'm more or less acting sheriff at the moment.'

Brittany shook his hand and beamed a bright smile his way. 'I hear you're here to give us the good news that somebody awesome killed that rotten son-of-a-bitch Hunt!'

'Well, ma'am, I don't know about awesome. He coulda hit Hunt's mama instead,' Emmett said.

The grin never leaving her face, she said, 'Well, hell, Acting Sheriff, that would have been awesome too!'

'OK, Brit,' Dave said, putting his arm around his wife's waist and encouraging her to sit down next to him. He nodded at Emmett and he too took his seat. 'Thing is, Emmett, Hunt's mama's been calling us every few years, every time the asshole was up for parole, asking us to stay home and not protest his release, and when we showed up anyway she'd then call us for weeks on end afterwards, saying awful things, and she didn't give a good goddam who answered the phone – me, Brit or one of the kids. And the woman could cuss like a sailor.'

'It didn't take a rocket scientist to figure out where Darby Hunt got his charm!' Brittany said.

'Well, Dave, I'm sorry, but I gotta ask y'all where you were last night,' Emmett said.

Dave nodded. 'No problem. I understand. Brittany and me were here watching TV until, what, honey? Ten, ten-thirty?'

'Something like that,' Brittany said. 'And Emma, our youngest, was here, too. But she's twelve and has a nine-thirty bedtime. So she was probably asleep and wouldn't know if Dave and I slipped out to go kill Darby Hunt.'

'Honey!' Dave said.

Brittany laughed. 'I'm kidding! Emmett knows I'm kidding, don't you, Emmett?'

'I assumed as much,' Emmett said. 'I know you got some older kids—'

'Two boys,' she said. 'All grown now. And you know our oldest! You were Stevie's boss when he worked here in Longbranch!'

'Yes, ma'am,' Emmett said.

'He spoke very highly of you, Acting Sheriff Hopkins,' she said.

Emmett couldn't tell if the 'acting sheriff' business was a jab or sincere. He was hoping for sincere. To get back to business and his eyes off Mrs McDaniel's dancing ones, he said, 'Your other son – he's living here in town?'

'You want to know if one of my boys killed Darby Hunt?' Brittany McDaniel asked. 'Only Stevie would even have reason to think about it. He's the only one who knew his Aunt Cheryl. And he and Beth, Cheryl's daughter, were really close. He was five when Cheryl was killed and he heard talk. I think all that might be why he went into law enforcement. And besides, he lives in Oklahoma City and it's been two weeks since he's been home. Grady was just a baby when Cheryl was killed, but of course he knew about it. But Grady's not the type to go killing anybody, even though he lives here in Longbranch. Well, outside Longbranch, actually.' She laughed. 'In your actual jurisdiction! I take it you're not in your jurisdiction now, right, Deputy?'

He noticed acutely the change from 'acting sheriff' to 'deputy.'

'No, ma'am, I'm not, but Police Chief Charlie Smith knows I'm here, ma'am, so everything is copacetic,' Emmett said.

'Well, Emmett,' Dave said, 'much as I hate to admit it, my boy Grady's a knee-jerk pinko liberal who don't even *own* a gun and never shot one since I made him try when he was ten. Didn't take to it then, and I doubt he'd take to it now. Chances are real good Grady might think, wrongly, I know, that old Darby Hunt'd been rehabilitated up there at the Oklahoma Penitentiary. 'Course, the boy's wrong at least every four years or so.'

'I'd still like to talk to him,' Emmett said.

Dave and Brittany McDaniel shared a look, then Brittany got up and went into the kitchen where she wrote something on a slip of paper and brought it to Emmett. 'Here you go, Deputy. This is Grady's address. When you throw him in jail please be gentle – he has a trick knee.'

'Brit,' said David, his tone one of exasperation.

'I'm just kidding, honey,' she said, looking at Emmett with those turquoise eyes. They didn't dance so much at that moment, more like icy heat boring a hole through his soul. She turned and sat back down next to her husband.

Emmett stood up. 'Well, thank you, folks. I appreciate your time.'

Both Dave and Brittany McDaniel stood up. 'I'll see you out,' Dave said, patting Emmett on the back.

'Nice to meet you, Acting Sheriff Hopkins,' Brittany said, still standing by the sofa.

Emmett turned and smiled. 'You, too, ma'am,' he said, more than ready to get away from those turquoise eyes.

He was in his car, heading for his next interview, when he got a call on his cell phone. Seeing that it was the shop, he said, 'Hey, Holly.'

'Sorry, Emmett,' came Dalton Pettigrew's slow-talking voice. 'It's me, Dalton.'

'OK, well, hey, Dalton. What's up?'

'Ah, you coming in anytime soon?' Dalton asked.

'I've got some more interviews about this Darby Hunt mess. You need me?'

'Yeah, I heard about Darby Hunt. Huh. Well, I gotta tell you something. You driving?'

Exasperated, as he usually was with any discussion with Dalton lasting more than two sentences, he said, 'Yes, Dalton, I'm driving! What the hell is it?'

'I think you need to pull over, Emmett, is all I'm saying.'

There was a strip mall in front of him. Emmett pulled into it and cut the engine. 'OK, Dalton, I'm all yours. I pulled off the road and cut the engine. What do you want?'

'Well, I didn't see you yesterday, so I couldn't tell you in person, and I wanted to tell you right away, in person, but you aren't here again today, so—'

'Dalton, if you don't spit it out I'm going to hang up,' Emmett said.

'Well, I was somewhere yesterday morning and I couldn't take my gun in with me, so I locked it in the glove box?'

'Why couldn't you take your gun in with you?' Emmett asked.

'Ah, I don't want to tell you that part right now, OK?'

Emmett sighed. 'OK, Dalton. Then tell me the other part.'

'Well, I heard a crash, and when I came outside . . .'

After a long pause, Emmett said, 'Yes?'

'Well, somebody had busted the passenger-side window and broken the glove box and my gun was gone.'

'Christ on a crutch, Dalton! Where in the hell were you?'

'In a residential neighborhood,' Dalton replied.

'Doing what?' Emmett demanded.

'I still don't wanna tell you that part right now,' Dalton said.

'Well, you're going to! God, Dalton, have you got any idea how bad this is? Jesus! Why does this shit happen on my watch? We go months with nothing happening around here; Milt leaves for a week and all hell breaks loose!'

'Yeah, guess so,' Dalton said.

'I'm not talking to you!' Emmett said, his jaw clinched.

'Then who you talking to, Emmett?' Dalton asked.

Emmett hung up the cell phone.

FIVE

Milt – Day Three

Vern Weaver joined us after about an hour. Good thing, too, because Mike and I were running out of things to talk about.

'Hey, fellas,' he said, slapping us both on the back. I almost chipped my tooth on the beer mug.

'Hey,' I said back without much enthusiasm.

'Where are the girls?' Mike asked.

'Ah, hell, with Crystal along they may never come back. I just gave her the credit card and came here.'

'Vern, there are a lot of diamond shops here—' Mike started.

'Yeah, she does like her a diamond, don't she?' He shook his head and ordered a draft from the bartender. 'That's OK. I gave her a card with a $10,000 limit. She can't hurt me too bad.'

'I take it Crystal's not the boys' mom,' I said.

Vern laughed. 'Jesus, God, no! Their mama's my first wife, Lois. She's back in Houston waiting on her boys to come home. She's got custody of 'em, and I didn't fight that. Children belong with their mother, unless she's unfit or something, and God knows Lois is a good mama. 'Sides, me and Crystal need some time to get to know each other.'

'I take it y'all are newlyweds,' I said.

'Married at a JP's in Galveston the day before the ship sailed! Boys were our witnesses,' Vern said.

'Wow,' I said for want of anything more meaningful to say.

'That's not the half of it!' Mike said. 'Talk about a whirlwind romance! When was it you met Crystal?'

'Well, now you're just embarrassing me,' Vern said. Then he turned to me. 'Met her on a Friday night, filed for divorce on Monday. Gave Lois any and everything she wanted, got a judge friend to rush it through for me. That was twenty-six days ago. The divorce was final last Friday. We were married Saturday morning.'

'Wow,' I said again.

'Hey, Vern,' Mike said, 'guess what old Milt here does for a living?'

'A poontang inspector?' Vern said, and laughed heartily at his own weak joke.

'Now there's a job,' Mike said, a little wistfully. 'No, he's a sheriff!'

Vern turned and looked at me. 'No shit?' he said. 'Where you the sheriff?'

'Prophesy County, Oklahoma,' I said. 'County seat is a little town called Longbranch.'

'Now ain't that the damnedest thing!' Vern said, a look of shock and, yes, respect on his face. 'I want you to know I'm a card-carrying member of the 100 Club in Houston. And I don't just pay my dues, either. I give righteously.'

'That's nice,' I said. 'What's the 100 Club?'

'It's an organization in Houston, started back in the 'fifties,' Mike said. 'It's to help the widows and orphans of police officers.'

'Ah, hell, we do a lot more'n that now,' Vern said. 'We've included fire fighters and state cops like DPS, and even prison guards. It's a fine organization, but all I'm saying, Milt, is I'm on your side, one hundred percent.'

'That's good to hear, Vern,' I said.

'Always wished I'd gone to the Academy,' Vern said wistfully. Then he barked a laugh, hit me on the back and said, 'But then I'd never be the rich fucker I am and have that beauty sucking my dick!'

Mike and I turned in the direction Vern was looking and saw our women coming our way. The ladies were using my wife's scooter to pile up all their booty. I got up and met Jean as she drove into the open-air bar. I bent down, kissed her and whispered in her ear, 'Help me! I'm being held hostage by the redneck from hell!'

Jean started coughing to cover a laugh and almost choked. She patted my hand and whispered, 'You probably had the better end of it.' Out loud, she said, 'Any word from the kids?'

'Nary a one,' Vern said, 'but Josh'll take good care of 'em. At first he was acting like a shithead about Crystal and all, but he's warmed to her and been acting like a little gentleman, huh, Crystal, honey?'

'Oh, he's a doll,' Crystal said. 'They both are! Vern's got just the sweetest boys!'

Vern beamed.

'Honey, help me with my packages,' Crystal said, going to the scooter that Jean had vacated for a chair at a large table that would accommodate us all. Vern started pulling off packages as his new bride directed and when they were done there were two small bags left.

'Whose are these?' Vern asked.

'The pink one's mine!' Lucy called out.

'The brown one is mine,' Jean said.

'What did you get?' Mike asked his wife.

She held up a small clown, one of those ones like the Christmas elf who sits on the shelf? You know, sits on the mantel or something. 'I collect clowns,' she told me, I guess me being the only one who didn't know this fact about her.

'What about you, honey?' I asked Jean.

She pulled out a cloisonné letter opener in a cloisonné sheath attached to a cloisonné base. (I only know it was cloisonné because she told me. I'm still not sure what cloisonné is, but it was sure pretty.) 'For my office,' she said, and actually blushed a little. Jean's not big on geegaws, but this was real pretty.

'That's gonna look nice,' I said, and smiled at her.

'I ain't even gonna ask what you got!' Vern said to Crystal. 'But I bet there's a diamond or two in there!'

Crystal put her arms around Vern's neck, looking up at him with googly eyes and said, 'But baby, I like sparkly things!' And then she giggled.

Johnny Mac – Day Three

'Are you fuckin' kidding me?' Josh said to Johnny Mac, staring at the ballpoint pen Johnny Mac had placed in his hand.

'All the jewelry was locked up,' Johnny Mac said, blushing a little as Early, Janna, Josh and his brother Ryan all stared at him.

'Well, you lose!' Josh said, tossing the pen on the ground and smashing it with his foot. He looked at Johnny Mac and shook his head. 'You disgust me. Go sit over there and stay out of my face.'

'No way!' Johnny Mac said. 'And you can't talk to me like that! You're not the boss of me!'

'Gosh, Mr and Mrs Kovak, I told Johnny Mac he shouldn't steal this,' he said, holding out a small sailboat one of the others had stolen, 'but he wouldn't listen to me.'

'They won't believe you!' Johnny Mac shouted.

'Early?' Josh said.

Early looked from Josh to Johnny Mac and back to Josh again. Finally, albeit grudgingly, Early said, 'Yeah, Josh, I heard you tell him not to.'

Johnny Mac looked at his best friend for the past five years and couldn't believe it. Early had betrayed him, just like Harry betrayed his BFF Peter Parker, aka Spiderman.

Broken, Johnny Mac walked over to the short wall that looked out to the blue sea and sat down. This was the worst vacation of his life.

Meanwhile, Back In Prophesy County

There was nothing Emmett could do about Dalton's gun at the moment so, as it was getting on toward three o'clock, he headed to the Christian school on the south side. A couple of churches had gotten together and bought a defunct grammar school the city had condemned, fixed it up some and made it a K-12 school. Classes were real small, which is why Jasmine wanted to put Petal in there, less than ten students per class, but the curriculum, as far as Emmett was concerned, left a lot to be desired. Emmett ascribed to the big bang theory, which he tended to keep to himself in rural Oklahoma, whereas the school, of course, taught creationism. There seemed to be religion in almost every subject. Helping Petal with her homework one night, Emmett read a math problem: 'Noah brought in animals two by two. If he brought in elephants, zebras and monkeys, how many animals did he bring in?' He was drinking a cup of coffee when he read that, and almost did a spit take.

There were quite a few cars in the parking lot of the Christian school when he pulled in, but he found a spot fairly close to the door. He'd discovered that the older he got, the more he liked to park close. He was thinking about maybe getting one of those handicap stickers, but wondered if you had to be actually handicapped to get one, rather than just old and lazy. He got out and headed into the school. Some of the older kids were still in the halls, the younger ones having all been picked up. This school didn't provide buses, so you had to get your kid there and pick them up every day. Somehow Emmett and Jasmine had been able to work that into their schedules, even though it was on a daily basis.

He had never met the principal but knew where the office was, so headed there. Reba Sinclair was at her desk, head down, writing with a ballpoint. Emmett knocked on the door jamb of the open door.

Sinclair looked up. 'Yes?' she said.

She looked to be around fifty or so, with frizzy salt-and-pepper hair, so thin she looked like maybe she had an eating disorder, a really large nose – probably looking so big because of the weight loss, Emmett thought. He hoped so. Her eyes were covered with tinted glasses. She was not an attractive woman, which may have been one of the reasons she dated through the prison system and bought her boyfriend expensive gifts.

'Ma'am, I'm Deputy Emmett Hopkins from the Prophesy County sheriff's department. I'd like to talk to you, if I may—'

She stood up at her desk, glaring at him. 'You have no right coming here and harassing me!' she fairly hissed at him. 'My personal life is none of your business, Mr Hopkins, and just because you're a deputy gives you no right to tell me who I can see in my private life!'

'Ma'am—'

'The children are in no way affected by my relationship with Mr Hunt! He will not be coming near the school, I can assure you of that! Now if you will please leave my office—'

Emmett reached behind him and shut the door to her office. 'Ms Sinclair, I'm not here about Petal. I'm here on official business. Ma'am, I need you to sit down a moment,' Emmett said.

Reba Sinclair remained standing for a long moment, then slowly sat down. 'What is it?' she asked.

'I'm sorry to inform you, ma'am, that Darby Hunt was killed last night.'

She covered her mouth with her hands, her eyes wide. 'Oh, my God!' Tears sprang to her eyes. 'What happened?'

'Drive-by shooting, ma'am,' Emmett told her.

'He was a wonderful man, Mr Hopkins,' she said. 'He was terribly sorry about Cheryl. He had a bad temper back then. He found Jesus with the help of the prison chaplin and,' she blushed, 'me, I guess. We were going to be married.'

'I'm so sorry for your loss, ma'am.'

'How is his mother?' she asked.

'Distraught, I'm sure,' Emmett said.

Reba Sinclair stood up and wiped her eyes. 'I must go to her.' She stopped in her tracks and said, 'Unless you have questions?'

'Can you tell me where you were last night?' Emmett asked.

She nodded. 'At home going over administrative paperwork.

Although I should have been with him. I was supposed to be, but . . . this problem . . . with the paperwork . . .'

Her voice trailed off and she sat back down. 'I can't believe he's really dead,' she said.

'Again, ma'am, I'm really sorry for your loss. Would you like a ride over to Mrs Hunt's house?'

'No. No, thank you, Mr Hopkins. I'll be heading over there in a minute,' she said, and turned in her swivel chair to stare out the window.

Emmett left, again leaving behind the walking wounded.

While Emmett was interviewing Reba Sinclair, something wonderful was happening at the offices of the sheriff's department.

Dalton was sitting at his desk in the bullpen, not even looking at Holly. He didn't dare look at her, knowing what a mess he'd made of things. No way would she want to be with him now. He'd heard it all his life, but he never believed it until now. Dalton, he told himself, you *are* a screw-up.

But, as usual, there was an angel watching over Dalton, the same angel that got him out of that mess in Tulsa and led him to meet Holly in the first place. And that angel opened the front door of the shop and in walked a lady named Inez Walker, dragging in two boys by their shirt collars.

'Anybody missing something around here?' the lady said at a very high volume.

Dalton jumped up from his desk and ran to the counter, praying like it was Sunday. 'Ma'am?' he said.

'My name is Inez Walker and these two terrors are my grandsons – my boy's son Michael Walker and my daughter's boy Taylor Dunham. Boys?' She let go of their shirt collars and stared down at them.

'We're sorry, Deputy,' the one called Michael said. 'Yeah,' echoed his cousin.

'And why are you sorry?' demanded their grandmother, handing Michael a bag out of her purse.

'We stole your gun,' Michael said.

His cousin echoed, 'Yeah.'

Michael handed Dalton the bag and, sure enough, his service revolver was inside, the bullets tossed in separate.

'I emptied it to be on the safe side,' Inez Walker said.

'Thank you, ma'am,' Dalton said.

'Now tell the man the rest,' she said to the boys.

'And we'll pay to have the window and the inside thing fixed.'

'It may not be cash, Deputy,' Inez Walker said, 'but these are two strong, strapping young men, and they sure can wash cars and clean toilets until it's paid off.'

'Nana!' said the younger one.

She glared at him and he shut up.

Dalton was nodding his head. 'Well, ma'am, I'll take that up with our acting sheriff when he gets back, and if you leave your number, we'll get back to you,' Dalton said. 'But, ma'am, may I ask the boys a question?'

'Certainly, Deputy. You can even lock them up for a few hours if you want.'

Both boys stared up at their grandmother with wide, wounded eyes.

'No, ma'am,' Dalton said. 'That won't be necessary.' Turning to the boys, he said, 'How come you broke the window in the first place? What made you think there'd be something to take?'

Michael, the older one, said, 'Well, sir, we saw you take your gun out of its holster and put it in your glove box. We were standing there right across the street.'

'Oh,' Dalton said. He should have been paying more attention, he thought. As usual.

Inez Walker dug in her purse and came up with a card. 'It's got my home number, cell number, email address and website address right there,' she said, pointing it out. 'I had these made up to hand out to the men at the senior center. Gotten a few dates out of it,' she said, grinning.

'Nana!' Michael said.

'Don't be embarrassed, child. Everybody needs a little lovin'.'

With that, she grabbed her grandsons by the backs of their shirts and headed out the door.

Milt – Day Three

My smart wife asked the Weavers and the Tulias which dinner they were going to; when they said the late one, we went to the early one. I was fixing to take Johnny Mac and Early down to the buffet when my son said, 'I'd rather eat with you and Mom. Early can do whatever he wants.'

Kinda quick, Early said, 'Me, too. I want to eat with y'all.'

Thinking maybe the boys had had a tiff of some sort, Jean and I welcomed them to what had become our table, up one step and down three tables to the left. That night I had mushroom caps stuffed with lobster and crab for an appetizer, an endive salad with a cucumber dressing that was weird but good, and a crispy-skinned duck served with candied sweet potato spears and a smidgen of cooked cabbage – I know, sounds homey, but it wasn't. It was goddam wonderful. And for dessert I had cherries jubilee that they set on fire at the table. The boys were impressed enough to order their own each. They still weren't in a sharing mood.

The boat pulled out of the Grand Caymans while we were eating dinner. By the time we'd finished, the ship had hit a squall and we could see lightning through the windows of the dining room. Because Jean and I both like a good storm, we made our way to the pool area where we could hear the thunder and watch the rain and lightning while safely under its half-roof. All the swimmers and sunbathers had deserted the area and we had the place to ourselves. The boys went with us, although I could tell Early wasn't a storm aficionado like the Kovak family. He flinched every time he saw the lightning and covered his ears when the thunder boomed.

'Is the ship going to sink?' Early asked me at one point.

'No, it's not. They go through storms like this all the time, son—'

'He's not your son!' Johnny Mac said, standing up and moving closer to me. 'I am!' He stared hard at Early, who moved away from us and sat down at the end of the covered area. I could see he was getting wet.

At that point I suggested we take the boys back to our suite. Letting them walk ahead of us, Jean said, 'Let's leave them alone in the cabin, OK? They need some time to work out whatever's going on with them.'

I nodded my agreement. Looking at the menu of activities earlier, we saw this country singer we'd heard the first night was going to be on around ten in one of the smaller auditoriums, and I'd talked Jean into going. She's not much into country music, but she's a good sport, I'll give her that. We got the boys ready for bed, kissed 'em both goodnight and headed to see Miss Lily Sullivan White.

Johnny Mac – Day Three

'I'm sorry,' Early said from the bottom bunk.

Johnny Mac didn't reply.

'I said I'm sorry!' Early said with a bit more bite.

'Yeah, you're a sorry asswipe!' Johnny Mac countered.

Early stood up from his bunk and looked up at his friend. 'I was scared, OK? I'll admit that! Josh scares the crap out of me!'

Johnny Mac sat up and looked down at his friend. 'And that's supposed to make what you did OK?'

Early shrugged. 'No, I guess not. It's just that –' Early shrugged again. 'OK,' he said, crawling back in the lower bunk. 'I'm an asswipe.'

Johnny Mac jumped down from the upper bunk and leaned into the lower one. 'Yeah, you are,' he said, 'and I can't believe you stole that boat!'

Early sat up and grinned. 'But I didn't,' he said. 'I bought it with the money your dad gave us! I just threw away the sack before Josh could see it!'

Johnny Mac laughed. 'Cool! And Josh thinks he's so smart! What an asswipe!'

'Yeah,' Early echoed, 'what an asswipe!'

There was a knock on the door. The two boys looked at each other, then went together to open it. Janna and Lyssa stood there. 'I saw your parents with mine,' Janna said. 'So let's go party!' She grinned big time at Johnny Mac.

'We have to get dressed,' Johnny Mac said.

'Is Josh gonna be there?' Early asked.

'God, I hope not!' Janna said.

The boys got dressed, then the girls showed them how to stick something between the door latch and the door jamb to keep it from locking. 'This way,' Janna said, 'you won't risk getting caught.'

Milt – Day Three

We ran into Mike and Lucy as we headed to the small auditorium where the country singer was going to perform.

'Hey!' Mike had shouted and we couldn't do anything but stop and say 'hey.'

'Where y'all headed?' Lucy asked.

So we told her. 'Oh, I love country music!' Lucy said.

'Me not so much,' Mike said. 'But I like to humor her.'

'As does my wife me,' I said. 'Y'all can make fun of me and Lucy while we listen, OK?'

So we headed to the music.

Johnny Mac – Day Three

That night the four, Johnny Mac, Early, Janna and Lyssa stayed away from spots they thought might contain Josh Weaver. 'He's just a big bully,' Janna told them. 'I never have liked him. Ryan's not much better.'

'It's too bad you have to spend so much time with them,' Johnny Mac said.

'Tell me about it. We go over to their house almost every Sunday for bar-be-que – well, at least we did, before Mr and Mrs Weaver got a divorce. The first Mrs Weaver, I mean. I call her Aunt Lois. She's really nice and down to earth, my mom says. Not at all like Crystal. But Dad says we have to hang out with Mr Weaver and Crystal now because Dad and Mr Weaver are partners.'

They sat on deck chairs pulled up close to the rails of the top deck of the ship. They would occasionally lean down and spit in the ocean. 'That sucks,' Johnny Mac said.

'Yeah. But, and don't tell anybody this,' Janna said, looking around, but Early and Lyssa had made their way to the bow of the ship and were leaning over, staring at something. 'My mom talks to Aunt Lois all the time – at least once a day. And she's even called her from here! Last night I heard her telling Aunt Lois all about the stuff Crystal bought when we were in Georgetown.'

'What did she buy?' Johnny Mac asked.

'Mom said she bought a solitaire diamond that was like four carrots.'

'What does that mean? Like big as a carrot?' Johnny Mac asked.

Janna shrugged. 'I dunno. But the way she talked it must have been pretty big. And she said she bought a lot of other stuff – mostly diamonds – and maxed out the credit card she had!'

Johnny Mac just shook his head. He knew ladies liked

diamonds a lot, although his mother wasn't like that. She had a small diamond in her engagement ring, and that was all. But his Aunt Jewel, his dad's sister, she had loads of them! Rings and necklaces and bracelets and earrings! His dad told his mom one time that Aunt Jewel had so many diamonds he hoped he never saw her when the sun shone directly on her – it could put out his eyes. Johnny Mac was pretty sure he was joking, but was still careful not to look directly at his aunt when they were outside.

'Did you really steal something today?' Johnny Mac asked Janna.

She shrugged. 'Sorta,' she said. Not looking into Johnny Mac's eyes, she continued, 'Some kid knocked this toy to the floor in the store I was in and it was close to the door. I just kinda kicked it out.'

Johnny Mac didn't say anything.

'I never stole anything before,' Janna said in a weak voice.

'I don't think I like these games Josh wants to play. Did he take that toy back to the store?' Johnny Mac asked.

Janna shrugged again. 'I dunno.'

Johnny Mac patted Janna on the shoulder. 'It's OK, Janna. It's not your fault. Josh is a bully.'

Janna started to cry and put her head on Johnny Mac's shoulder. He wasn't sure what to do or where to put his arm or anything; all he knew was he liked her head on his shoulder a lot. So he just said, 'There, there.'

After a minute Janna raised her head and said, 'What time is it?'

Johnny Mac checked his watch. It was almost midnight. 'Time to head back, if it's not too late already!'

He helped Janna up and they walked back. After dropping the girls off at their cabins, Johnny Mac and Early went to the suite they shared with Johnny Mac's parents. As he opened the unlatched door, Johnny Mac spied an envelope on the floor. He picked it up and saw 'J.M.' on the outside, so opened it and read:

'You breathe a word about today and you'll be sorry. Sure would be a shame if your mom had an accident! Don't tell anyone about this note or anything else, or oops, SHE FELL DOWN THE STAIRS, OFFICER.'

Meanwhile, Back In Prophesy County

The day before, after leaving Reba Sinclair's office, Emmett had found his daughter Petal waiting by his squad car.

'Daddy!' she said on seeing him, tears in her eyes. 'I was so worried!' She ran up and threw her arms around him.

He knelt down to hold her. 'Oh, baby, I'm sorry! I forgot it was my day. I was talking to your principal about some county business. You OK, Petal?'

She nodded her head against his chest and gulped. 'Yes, sir.'

He'd hustled her into the car and on home, so hadn't had the chance to interview Beth Atkins or her cousin, Dave McDaniel's pinko liberal son Grady.

He had, however, received a call at home from Dalton Pettigrew telling him, in great detail, about Inez Walker and her two grandsons.

'Well, you lucked out this time, Dalton,' Emmett said.

'Yes, sir, sure did.'

'Are you gonna tell me what you were doing that you had to leave your service revolver in the glove box in the first place?' Emmett demanded.

'Not ready to talk about that part yet, Emmett. Sorry.'

'Whatever,' he said, wondering what the hell Dalton Pettigrew was up to, thinking it couldn't be anything too elaborate or even all that interesting. 'Just get the car fixed. We use Dave McDaniel's shop?' Emmett asked.

'No, sir, they got the city contract. We use Jasper Paint and Body in Jasper,' Dalton said.

'OK, well, get it over there. Have someone from the office follow you and drive you back to my house, pick up my squad car and take it for the day, OK?' Emmett said and rang off, hoping Dalton had got all that. He'd tried to be specific. Milt said that's how you had to be with Dalton – tell him all the parts.

When Emmett got into the shop early that morning, Holly met him with two emergencies. 'Accident on FM4712, gave it to Dalton,' she said. 'And an overnight burglary at Sylvia's Gifts. Gave that to Nita.'

'Great,' he said, taking the two incident reports out of her hands and walking to his office. 'Dalton get that squad car fixed yet?' he said over his shoulder.

'No, sir, he had to take that call first. He used Anthony's. Anthony left his here last night.'

'Just make sure Dalton takes care of that, you hear me?'

'Loud and clear,' she said.

'I'm just checking in,' he told her as he sat down at his – or Milt's – desk. 'I need to head out and interview a couple more people. You know what time class starts at the high school?' he asked her.

'No, but I'll find out,' Holly said and picked up his phone. Dialing out, she said, 'What time does Mercy go to school?' She listened, thanked the person on the other end of the line and turned back to Emmett. 'That was the lady who has the other side of my duplex,' she explained. 'Her daughter's a sophomore. Nine a.m.'

Emmett looked at his watch. Ten after eight. He had plenty of time to get to the high school and interview Beth Atkins if he left right that minute. 'I'm outta here,' he said, as Holly waved goodbye.

The new high school was in a recently incorporated section of Longbranch on the west side. It looked like a college campus: three two-story buildings, one long one-story building and a gymnasium, circled around a courtyard with trees and tables with umbrellas. Emmett wasn't sure he liked the idea of his tax dollars going to buy umbrellas, but figured it was better than the brats getting skin cancer and his tax dollars paying for their care later. The one-story building housed administration, the cafeteria and the theatre, yeah, with an 're' instead of an 'er'. That's what the sign said.

Emmett went into the one-story building, to the administration office and asked to see Beth Atkins, either there or in her classroom. He showed all the right credentials. He was told to wait there and Ms Atkins would come to him.

Beth Atkins showed up less than five minutes later. He figured she must have been in the one-story building all along. She was a short, squat young woman, wearing trousers, a button-down shirt, Bass loafers, and had a very short haircut. She also had a pretty face, and Emmett felt the usual stab of jealousy whenever he saw a pretty woman obviously batting for the other team.

'Ms Atkins?' he said, holding out his hand.

She took it and gave it a firm shake. 'I expect you're the acting sheriff I've been hearing about from my relatives.'

He nodded and smiled. 'Yes, ma'am, that'd be me – Emmett Hopkins. Is there some place we can talk private?' he asked.

'Sure,' she said, then looked over at the school secretary who was obviously listening to every word. 'Wanda, can we have the counselor's office?'

Wanda nodded her head and Beth Atkins led the way down a hall laden with offices. Opening a door marked 'Counselor,' she went in and sat in one of the two chairs in front of the desk. 'The counselor only comes in twice a week, and this isn't one of her days,' she said.

'Then we shouldn't be interrupted,' Emmett said. She nodded her head, and Emmett began. 'I take it you've heard about your father's death.'

'No, sir, my father is very much alive. His name is Roger Atkins. If you're referring to Darby Hunt, yes, I did hear that he was shot. Someone did the world a favor.'

'May I ask where you were the night before last, Ms Atkins?'

'Please, call me Beth. And yes, you may ask. Actually, I was with several of my students at a showing of Laurence Olivier's *Hamlet* at the Beanery last night from six until ten.'

'Long movie,' Emmett remarked.

'There was eating involved. And a lot of talking, both before and after the showing.'

'I haven't been to the Beanery. Any good?' Emmett asked.

Beth laughed. 'If I say it's great and you go there and decide it's not great, will you assume I was lying when I said it was? Or vice versa, for that matter.'

Emmett smiled. 'No, ma'am. Just wondered. My daughter gets tired of me and my wife always dragging her to the Longbranch Inn whenever we go out to dinner.'

Beth cocked her head. 'Well, I doubt if it's going to last long around here. It's vegetarian, but the food's very good. I'm not a vegetarian myself, but I don't mind occasionally getting my protein from sources that don't have faces.'

Emmett grimaced. 'I dunno about that. No meat, huh?'

'Egg dishes, cheese, tofu. I had the Portobello mushroom burger. Better than the real thing.'

'Maybe once,' he conceded. 'Anyway, back to business. Had you seen your— Darby Hunt since he got out?'

She shook her head. 'I haven't seen that man since I was four years old and he eviscerated my mother.'

'And your gran— Darby Hunt's mother?'

'She tried to get custody of me when my mother was killed, but the judge wouldn't hear of it. She tried several times after that to get visitation, but she'd always do something stupid and get shut down. Evil and stupid – not a good combination,' Beth said.

'I'd like you to try to answer this truthfully, Beth. Have you heard any of your relatives threaten Darby Hunt since he got out of prison?'

'You mean *to* him or just in general?'

'Either.'

'Well, I don't know that anybody actually saw or spoke to him. But if you're asking if threats have been made in general and by whom, I'd have to say everybody, including myself. He was not well liked,' she said with an ironic grin.

'Have you seen your cousin Steve in town since Hunt got out?'

She shook her head. 'No, Deputy. Steve's got bigger fish to fry in the city.'

Emmett glanced at his watch. It was getting close to nine a.m. 'What course do you teach?' he asked.

'English lit, sophomore level, and American lit, junior level.'

'So you were out with the sophomores the night before last?'

Beth laughed. 'And a few juniors tagged along. You want a list of their names and numbers?'

'No, ma'am,' Emmett said, standing up. He held out his hand. 'Thanks for your time, Beth.'

She took his outstretched hand and shook it. 'It was my pleasure, Deputy. And don't mind us – the McDaniel brood. We can't help being happy that the SOB is dead.'

Emmett nodded and left, this time leaving behind a happy camper.

SIX

Milt – Day Four

When we woke up on the fourth day aboard ship, we were already docked in San Juan, Puerto Rico. Standing on our balcony, Jean and I could see everything: the sea and sky, both the same shade of turquoise blue, the green and white of the island, touches of red and yellow flowers sprouting everywhere. This beat the hell out of a March in Longbranch where the grass was still winter brown and nothing was even thinking about blooming.

Jean turned to me and her eyes were shining with excitement. 'What's on the agenda for today?'

'I let them keep the deposit I gave 'em when we took the scooter off the ship in Georgetown, so we don't have to do anything but get off.' We went back into the suite and grabbed the menu of things to do in San Juan. 'Maybe some snorkeling?' I suggested.

'That would be great for you and the boys. I think I might lie on the beach and work on a sunscreen-challenged tan,' my wife said.

'But first, like we did in Georgetown, maybe we can find a car and driver to take us to see the sights. And, oh, look, they've got canoes to rent. That could be fun. Check out the shore line?'

She smiled. 'Let's just wing it,' she said. 'I'm up for anything!'

And so we grabbed the boys and deboated. Probably not a word, but, hey, if you can deplane, why not deboat? Or would that be deshipped? None of the taxis waiting at the gate had a trailer for Jean's scooter, so we got one of the ship's people to take the scooter back and we got on two bicycle-driven cabs – Johnny Mac and Early in one (since they seemed to be friends again this morning), and me and Jean in the other, with strict instructions to the two operators not to get separated. And off we went with a running monologue from our driver with all sorts of trivia – like did you know San Juan is the oldest city under US rule? I didn't. Or that Puerto Rico has its own rainforest?

We left the more modern area around the docks and headed into old San Juan with its blue cobble-stoned streets and candy-colored houses. And Jean and I, of course, discussed retiring to San Juan and becoming beach bums who lived in a candy-colored house. This time Johnny Mac didn't hear us and get disappointed that we were only joking.

By the time we got through snorkeling, we were all slightly sunburned – Jean a little more so – and ready to get back to the ship. We would take off again during dinner and head straight back to Galveston with no more stops. We were on the downside of the trip and I was a little bummed. I was going to have to start getting used to my wife's cooking all over again.

Back at the ship we rescued Jean's scooter and got ready for dinner. I took the boys down to the buffet, with a stipulation that they were to go straight to the children's pavilion after they ate and to call me when they got there, then I headed to the dining room to meet Jean.

It may have been the back end of the trip but the food sure didn't suffer. I had fresh mozzarella with prosciutto and melon for an appetizer, a wedge salad with bacon, blue cheese crumbles and cranberries, and a Cornish game hen stuffed with dates, wild rice and feta cheese, with a spinach soufflé. For dessert Jean and I shared a chocolate soufflé. After I just leaned back and wished I smoked. It was that good.

Johnny Mac called me during the main course, saying they were heading for the children's pavilion. Jean reached for the phone and gave a few thousand instructions, and then we finished eating. After, we headed to a large room off the casino where they were calling bingo. It wasn't Jean's idea of a good time, but I'm damned good at bingo. I got my way when I mentioned there was a good chance I could win the big prize – a three-hour massage and facial package at the ship's spa.

Johnny Mac – Day Four

Janna was dropped off to sit with Johnny Mac and Early by her parents, with instructions to go straight to the children's pavilion after eating. Lyssa joined them a little after that.

'What all do they have to do in the children's pavilion anyway?' Early asked. During the short time the kids had been at the pavilion the first night Johnny Mac and Early had joined the girls and Ryan Weaver, they'd barely had time to check out the trikes and push-toys in the open-area section.

Janna shrugged. 'I don't know. I've only been there that once with y'all,' she said.

'Me, too,' Lyssa said and laughed. 'Maybe we should go check it out for real, just in case one of the parents asks us!'

The four hopped up and headed to the pavilion at the end of the large food court area.

They signed themselves in and checked the place out. There were a few kids there, little ones, like five or something. They were definitely the oldest in attendance. Checking out the shelves of toys, Johnny Mac and Early found a box of Lego and a bag of toy soldiers. The girls discovered a Barbie Dream House and a whole bag of Barbies and her clothes. And all four got very busy.

Far away, in the middle of the ship, a man named Clifford Dunne was winning big time at the blackjack table. He often noticed that he played better the drunker he got. Nancy, his wife, said he disgusted her and had stormed off to their cabin over an hour ago. Clifford thought, 'This'll teach her!' as he pulled in yet another win, bringing his total for the night up to $4,940. He was on a roll. Definitely on a roll. Unfortunately the roll was off his stool and onto the floor. Clifford began to laugh.

The dealer helped him up and then there was someone else there putting his winnings in his pocket and leading him toward the promenade. 'Sir, this is it for tonight,' the man said with a smile. 'Why don't you go back to your cabin and apologize to your wife?'

Clifford stumbled out, on his own now. The promenade was crowded, people pushing and shoving him. He told a few of them to 'fuck off,' and another few he said a gracious 'excuse me' to. Finally he found the door that led to the elevators and stairs. There were too many people waiting for the elevator, so Clifford headed for the stairs.

Milt – Day Four
I didn't win the three-hour spa package, but I did win a smart phone. Jean and I both already had iPhones, so this wasn't that big a deal. Maybe I could sell it to someone, I thought.

When my phone rang, I saw it was of course Jean's number calling, so I picked it up and said, 'Hey, buddy, having a good time?'

I was answered by a voice much deeper than my ten-year-old son's. 'Mr Kovak?'

'Who's this? Where's my son?'

Jean was by my side in a microsecond. 'He's OK, Mr Kovak. But we have him and some of his friends in custody. If you could come to A level, room 403, please.'

And the bastard hung up. We grabbed Jean's scooter and headed for A level.

The sign on the door of room 403 said security. I rapped with my knuckles and opened the door at the same time. Inside, I saw my son and Early, plus the two girls, Janna and Lyssa. Also present were Mike and Lucy and Lyssa's mom, Esther.

'What's going on?' I demanded.

'Milt! You gotta do something!' Mike all but shouted. To the small man standing by the desk in a semi-naval-looking uniform, he said, 'This is Milt Kovak! He's the sheriff of . . . of some place! Milt?'

'Prophesy County, Oklahoma,' I said, extending my hand to a guy who looked way too much like Barney Fife – if Barney had had a blond crew cut and a square jaw. 'Could you tell me what's going on, please?'

'Your children . . . I believe the expression is "rolled" a drunk,' he said, arms crossed over his chest, staring daggers at the terrified children.

'No, we didn't!' my son said, standing up.

'Sit down, John,' I said. He sat. He rarely hears me call him John. When I do, he knows I mean business.

To Barney Fife, I said, 'That doesn't seem plausible, Mr?'

'Gunther Heinrich,' he said, and I noticed a slight accent. 'Chief Heinrich. And it is more than plausible, Mr Kovak. The drunk in question is the one who captured them.'

There was a plate-glass window looking into another room, wherein sat a man in bedraggled clothes and messed-up hair, holding his head in his hands. 'That him?' I asked.

Heinrich nodded once.

'Mind if I talk to him?' I asked.

'Yes,' Heinrich said. 'I do mind. This is not your jurisdiction, *Mr* Kovak,' he said, stressing the 'Mr' so as to let me know I wasn't sheriff of his bailiwick.

'My son, and these other children, have the right to face their accuser,' I said.

'In a court of law,' Heinrich said.

'Court?' Esther said. 'Oh, God, no! I can't afford that! I used up our savings to go on this damned cruise!' She glared at Lyssa, who hung her head.

I turned to my son. 'Tell me what happened.'

'We left the children's pavilion and we were going to go to Janna's cabin and we took the stairs because there were too many people on the elevator and we saw that guy on the landing on his back and his mouth was bleeding and he was making weird noises and we tried to help him but he grabbed us and started calling us names and said we stole from him but we didn't!'

When he stopped to take a breath, the other three, who had been holding theirs, breathed with him.

'That's what happened, Sheriff Kovak,' Janna said. 'God's honest truth!'

'You were supposed to stay at the children's pavilion!' Lucy said.

'Not now, Luce,' Mike said. 'I'm with Milt. I want to hear what this guy has to say. How do we know he's not some pervert trying to manhandle these kids? We don't know that, do we?'

Barney, I mean Heinrich, turned abruptly and went to a door that led into the room where the accuser sat. He spoke to the man and the man stood up and followed him out the door.

'Yeah,' he said, pointing at the kids, 'those are the punks who ripped me off!' Looming over *my* son, he said, 'Where's my money?'

I quickly got between the drunk and Johnny Mac. 'Back off!' I said.

'Please, Mr Dunne,' Heinrich said. 'Have a seat over here.' He pointed to a chair clear across the room from the children. It was a small room, but it was still as far away from the kids as Heinrich could put him. Dunne turned and did as he was told. 'Now, Mr Dunne,' Heinrich continued, 'could you tell me what happened?'

'Yeah. I won nearly $5,000 at blackjack, and was headed up the stairs to my room, when these four came up behind me and knocked me down and one of them kicked me in the back of my head! Then all I could feel were these little hands all over me, digging in my pockets!' He stopped for a minute and said, 'I think the kick in the back of the head made me woozy, but when I came to, they were still picking at me, so I grabbed the little shits!'

'I'm willing to search my two boys for the money. Lucy? Esther?' I asked.

They both nodded. Looking at Heinrich, he nodded his consent. I went to my son first and patted him down. In his pockets I found a dirty tissue, seventy-five cents in assorted coins, his lucky shark's tooth he'd bought in Galveston and my wife's phone. Early was carrying yellow and blue crayons, two dollar bills and a toy soldier.

Early turned all shades of red. 'Oh, God! Oh, shit!'

'Early!' Jean said.

Early began to cry. 'I didn't steal it, really! I'm not sure how it got in my pocket!'

All the adults looked at each other, confused. 'What are you talking about?' I asked.

'That!' he said, pointing at the toy soldier. 'It belongs at the children's pavilion. But I swear I didn't steal it! It was an accident!'

I took the toy soldier and handed it to Heinrich. 'I hope you don't throw the book at him. Do you have dungeons on this ship?'

Well, that made Early cry in earnest, and my wife ended up going to him and sitting down with him by her side, and cooing to him. Johnny Mac looked at me with such fear in his eyes it made me want to vomit.

'It's OK, boys. Nothing's going to happen to you,' I said.

'The hell it isn't!' Dunne said, standing up. 'I want these little shits arrested!'

And then Jean McDonnell, doctor of psychiatry, wife of Milt Kovak, mother of John McDonnell Kovak, stood up. 'You call my son and this boy' – she was still holding on to Early – 'little shits one more time, and I'm afraid I might have to take one of my crutches to your skull.'

'OK, now,' Heinrich said. 'Mr Dunne, sit down. Ladies,' he said, addressing Lucy and Esther, 'how goes the search?'

Lucy held out her hand, which contained two hair clips and one of those fancy hair rubber bands, and Esther produced what my wife called a scrunchy, and that was it. Girls don't use their pockets like boys do. That's why God invented purses, I guess.

Dunne jumped up again. 'They hid it someplace!' He moved toward the children and I had to physically restrain my wife by getting in between them.

'Sit down, Mr Dunne!' Heinrich said. 'I will not tell you again!'

'He admits he blacked out,' I said. 'If I'm to believe my son – which I do – I think Mr Dunne here got mugged by somebody, passed out, then woke up when these children tried to help him.'

'That's certainly conceivable,' Heinrich said. 'Please, ladies and gentlemen, take your children back to your cabins while I deal with Mr Dunne.'

Jumping up yet again, Dunne demanded, 'You're not going to just let them go?'

'This is a ship, Mr Dunne. We know where to find them. They're not getting off anytime soon.'

I nodded at Heinrich and opened the door to let everyone out.

Meanwhile, Back In Prophesy County

Emmett's next interview was with Grady McDaniel, Dave's 'pinko, liberal' son. He wasn't at his home, but Emmett got his work address from Dave and headed there. Grady McDaniel had a storefront office not far from the courthouse. His name was stenciled on the frosted-glass front door, with the letters MSW behind it, which Emmett discovered later stood for 'Master of Social Work.' Beneath the name it read: Marriage Counseling, Children's Advocacy, Mediations, Notary Public. Emmett figured he might walk dogs, too, but there wasn't enough room on the door to mention it.

Emmett opened the door and walked in. There was a small front office without a receptionist, just a desk with a sign that said, 'Please sign in and ring bell.' So he did and took a seat in one of four chairs against the wall.

By Emmett's watch it was almost five minutes before the door behind and to the right of the reception desk opened and two people came out. One was an older woman with tissue in hand and red eyes. Emmett figured she was there for therapy of some sort. The other, he assumed, was Grady McDaniel. He was about Emmett's height – five-eleven, maybe six feet – with a slender body, curly brown hair, a seventies-style mustache, his mother's turquoise eyes, and was wearing blue jeans and a western-style pearl button shirt and motorcycle boots.

After seeing the woman to the door, he turned to Emmett. 'May I help you?' he asked.

Emmett stood and extended his hand. 'Emmett Hopkins from the sheriff's department,' he said.

'Right!' Grady said, shaking his hand vigorously. 'About that asshole Darby Hunt, right?'

'That's right—' Emmett started but Grady had grabbed his arm and was leading him toward the door he and the woman had just come through.

'Yeah, I've been getting calls right and left. Come on in my office so we won't be disturbed. Jeez, what a nightmare, huh? First the asshole gets out, and then someone goes and shoots him? Well, I guess we should have seen this one coming, huh, Emmett?'

The room Grady McDaniel ushered Emmett into was an average-sized office with a desk, chair, sofa, bookcase and comfy chair. Emmett took the comfy chair while Grady sat at his desk chair. The walls were strewn with dreamcatchers and pithy slogans.

'I mean, you and I should know better than the average lay person that something like that could happen, don't you think? He was *not* a well-liked man, needless to say. Generally hated and despised by one and all, wouldn't you say? I mean, my dad alone could have killed him with just his thoughts!' Grady said and laughed. Then sobered. 'I by no means meant to imply that my father had anything to do with what happened to Darby Hunt. But the entire family was enraged that he got out without any warning. Something needs to be done about that, don't you think, Emmett? I mean, the next of kin of a victim or the victim themselves if they're alive needs to be notified that a felon is being released if it affects their very lives, and of course this did! The man threatened my entire family in court—'

'Mr McDaniel—' Emmett blurted out.

'Grady, please, you call me Mr McDaniel and I think—'

'Grady!' Emmett all but shouted. He got some silence. 'I take it in your line of work you don't get to talk much, huh?'

Grady McDaniel lowered his head and Emmett couldn't help but notice his shoulders shaking. Shit, he thought, I made the pinko-liberal cry!

When Grady looked up, there were tears all right, but the man was laughing. 'Oh my God! I did it again! My wife tells me I do that at home. And you're right, Emmett, I don't get to talk much in my work life. I do a lot of listening. I'll try doing that now,' he said, and made the universal sign of locking his mouth and throwing away the key.

Emmett laughed back. 'I can see how that can happen, Grady. OK, here's the thing. Where were you the night before last, around eight-thirty?'

'Having sex with my wife,' he said. 'Sorry to be overly familiar, but there you have it. We're trying to get pregnant, and the book said that that day and that time were optimum for the best results. Then she had to lie on the bed for fifteen minutes with her feet in the air.'

'And while she was lying on her back with her feet in the air, where were you?'

'Right there with her, rubbing her shoulders. We're in this as a team, my wife and I. I've ordered a "Prego-Dad" pack off the Internet.'

With Emmett's look of bewilderment, Grady said, 'It looks sort of like a flak vest, but with inserts to add weights. It's supposed to simulate a woman's womb. It goes on like a corset, tying at the back, and as the mother gains weight, you add weights to the Prego-Dad so you have the same feelings she has. There's even an option you can get that simulates kicking when the time comes for the mother.' He beamed at Emmett. 'I got that. It was extra but I think it'll be worth it.'

'Pinko-liberal' was a misnomer, Emmett decided. This guy was pure 'crunchy-granola.' Remembering Jasmine during her pregnancy, he figured Grady would be a dead man the first time he complained of back pain.

Trying to keep Grady on tract, he asked, 'Any of your kin that you've talked to before or after Darby Hunt's death – did any of them seem overly upset? Like they might want to cause him harm?'

Again, Grady laughed. 'Well, yeah! They all did! And they all wanted to cause him harm. Or,' he said, finger on chin, 'to be more specific, wanted harm to come to him. We are not a violent family, Emmett.'

'And yet your brother is a cop. As one myself, I know an understanding of violence in others, as well as ourselves, is necessary. Have you seen Steve in town recently?'

Grady was shaking his head before Emmett got all the words out. 'No. It's been a while. I haven't talked to him about this at all. Steve and I don't have a lot in common. He may have talked to our cousin, Beth. They were much closer growing up than Steve and I ever were.'

'So who's been calling you?' Emmett asked.

'My mom, mostly. She and I are pretty tight. And my aunt Lisa, and her son Malcolm.'

Shit, Emmett thought, I forgot all about Malcolm. Early twenties, still young enough to be a hothead. 'So tell me about Malcolm.'

'Well, let's just say I'm not the only one in the family who doesn't subscribe to the "USA – Love it or Leave it" philosophy.'

'So Malcolm is also what your father would call a pinko-liberal?'

'Jesus. Is he still referring to me as that?' Grady shook his head. 'Well, better than what he called me last election. That doesn't bear repeating. But no, Malcolm isn't exactly political. He's just gay.'

'And that bothers them?' Emmett asked.

'Of course. They are true blue Oklahoma assholes. The men anyway. And not just the McDaniel men. My aunt Lisa's husband, Roger, Malcolm's dad, is a homophobe, too.'

Emmett wondered about that. Seemed like Beth Atkins was tight with her adopted father, and yet Emmett would be surprised to find out she wasn't gay. It wasn't just her clothes but her demeanor – everything about her. Had she not come out of the closet? Should he keep his mouth shut? Yep, mouth shut, he decided.

'Does your cousin Malcolm seem like he could have done this?'

'Malcolm?' Grady said, shaking his head. 'Malcolm came out when he was ten or twelve. I mean, if somebody wants a case study of nature vs nurture when it comes to homosexuality, they should look at Malcolm. I think he knew he was different way before he talked to his folks about liking boys more than girls.'

'I take it that didn't go down well?' Emmett asked.

Grady shook his head. 'Roger moved out after that. Took about a year for him to come to grips with it, and the fact that Aunt Lisa wasn't going to throw Malcolm out. He moved back in, but he and Malcolm have been estranged ever since. Malcolm and his boyfriend live together, and Roger refers to Jeff as "Malcolm's roommate."'

'Just because Malcolm's gay doesn't mean he can't be violent—' Emmett started, but Grady, as was his habit, interrupted.

'Oh, no, I didn't mean to imply that. It's just that Malcolm's very small – average height, I guess, around five-eight, but very slight of build. He got beat up a lot in high school.'

'It doesn't take a lot of strength to pull a trigger,' Emmett said.

Grady laughed. 'My dad took Malcolm hunting when he was about twelve, after he'd come out to his parents and his dad had moved out. Aunt Lisa hadn't told the family about it, so my dad just felt sorry for the kid not having his dad around. He took him hunting. Dad shot a rabbit and Malcolm burst into tears. Dad said he'd barely hold the rifle and refused to shoot it. So no, I don't think Malcolm could have shot Darby Hunt.' He was shaking his head and laughing. 'Jeez, my dad was pissed about that. "Ruined a perfectly good day of huntin'," he said. Then he found out Malcolm was gay, and it was like, "I told you so. Told you that boy was queer." Which, of course, he didn't. He never would have accused his own nephew of something so "terrible!"'

Emmett noted that the aforementioned was accompanied by a plethora of finger air quotes.

'Do you know where I can find Malcolm during the day?' Emmett asked.

Again Grady laughed. 'Yes, actually. He works for my father in the paint department.' Leaning in to stage whisper, and again with the air quotes, '"You know, them gays are good with colors."'

Emmett couldn't help it – he laughed. Standing up and heading for the door, he said, 'Thanks, Grady. I appreciate your time and the information.' He stopped and turned back. 'Off the top of your head, who do you think killed Hunt?'

'Off the top of my head? His mother. Of course, she should have done it in utero and saved us all a lot of heartache.'

* * *

Dalton had been thinking about it a lot. The whole gun thing had put the house of his dreams on the back burner, but now that he had his service revolver back, it was time to think about the future again. Him and Holly, and their home. Of course, she hadn't seen it yet, and he wasn't about to buy a house without her seeing it first. It was going to be her house too, after all. But he had a lot to think about before he did that. Like, did he do that first, then go buy a ring and propose? Or did he buy the ring first, show her the house and propose to her there?

He was so ready for his life to begin. And he knew it was going to be great, now that he'd found Holly. He'd never met a woman like her. She was what they called a free spirit, and he couldn't think of a better mother for his children than a free spirit. Not that he was saying anything bad about his own mama. She definitely wasn't a free spirit, but she'd still been a good mother. He didn't blame her for him not getting out on his own, or not having a girlfriend, or any of the other stuff. If he was to blame anyone, it would be his daddy, for up and dying on them when Dalton was only fourteen. He'd had to be the man of the house after that. And the man of the house just didn't get up and walk out.

But his mama had been talking about selling their house, about moving in with her recently widowed sister who lived in a big, fancy house in Bishop. His mama had been going to his aunt Martha's church every other Sunday now for about two months, so she was meeting new people and making new friends over there. His angel was definitely looking out for him, having all this come together at the same time. And his aunt had a live-in maid, so his mama wouldn't have to suffer, not having him around to do the cooking and cleaning and the laundry and such. She always made a joke that he'd make a good wife someday, but he figured with these skills he would make an *excellent* husband!

Now all he had to do was get up the nerve to take Holly to the house.

Milt – Day Four

'There's the most obvious question,' I said to the two boys sitting side by side on the twin bed I'd been sleeping on during the cruise. Jean sat on her twin bed while I loomed in the small space between the two. 'Why did you leave the children's pavilion without calling us first?'

'Ah . . .' Johnny Mac started, then looked at Early, who said, 'Ah . . .'

'Spit it out, boys. It's obvious you did it. You were caught, in a manner of speaking, on the staircase at the other end of the ship. You said you were going to Janna's cabin. Who told you that you could do that? Did Janna call her mother?'

'Ah . . .' Johnny Mac tried. Early just shook his head.

'Ah ha!' I cried in make-believe glee. 'I have a negative response! Janna *did not* call her mother. Did Lyssa call hers?'

Again Early shook his head while my son glared at him.

'Now I call this progress. Two negative responses!' I turned to my wife. 'Aren't my interrogation skills amazing?' I asked her.

'Indeed,' she said, giving the boys her stone-lion-outside-the-library stare.

'And I think we can all agree that neither you, Early, or your friend Johnny Mac called either of his parents. Can we agree on that?'

Since I was speaking directly to Early, he said, 'Yes, sir. We didn't call.'

'Now back to my first question: why didn't you call?'

My son stood up, almost knocking me down. 'Because you woulda said no! That's why!'

Well, that stopped me in my tracks. So I said a rough, 'Sit down!' Johnny Mac obliged and I sank onto the bed next to Jean.

'What was your plan, John?' Jean asked. 'Were you going to rush back to the children's pavilion when I called you to say we were on our way?'

Johnny Mac looked stonily at the wall. Early said, 'Yes, ma'am, that was the plan.'

Johnny Mac glared at Early. 'You have betrayed me for the last time!' he said, stood up and walked into the other part of the suite, climbing to the top bunk.

'Johnny Mac, get your ass back down here now!' I said, ready to rush into the other room and try some of my daddy's belt therapy on him. Jean saw me loosening said belt and said, 'Not on my watch.' To Johnny Mac, she said, 'Right now, John McDonnell Kovak.' Whoa, three names. He knew he was in trouble.

He sighed and climbed down. 'Early is not betraying you,' Jean said. 'He's actually acting responsibly, although, like you, he hasn't done so until now. Did the girls talk you into this?'

'Don't you dare blame Janna!' Johnny Mac all but shouted.

'Watch your tone, boy!' I said, trying to think what other punishments my parents used: the belt, a switch, a hairbrush, all used unsparingly on my backside. Looked like Jean was gonna put the kibosh on any of that.

'Was this the first time you've done this – left the children's pavilion – or have you done this before? Like the night you said the pavilion closed at one a.m. but the sign says it closes every night at ten p.m.?' Jean asked.

Neither boy said anything.

'I hope you realize that neither of you are going anywhere without your dad or me with you,' she added.

Johnny Mac sighed. Under his breath I heard him say, 'That sucks.'

'I heard that,' I said.

He just sighed again. He gets that from his mother. 'I'm wondering, though,' I said to Jean, 'if we checked the pavilion records if we would see whether they ever checked in?'

'Should we look into that, John?' Jean asked.

Our son stood up again. In a defeated voice, he said, 'Do what you will. I'm going to bed and I'm not getting up until we reach Galveston.' And with that he was off to his part of the suite, climbing the latter to the top bunk.

'May I be excused?' Early asked. We said yes and he crawled into the lower bunk.

Milt – Day Four

We forced the boys into nice clothes and made them eat dinner with us in the dining room. They went with the steak and French fries again, while I basked in the glow of an appetizer of bacon-wrapped, goat-cheese-stuffed scallops, a Caesar salad and a main course of lamb kabobs with pearl onions, button mushrooms and yellow peppers with a side of risotto. For dessert Jean and I split something called a chocolate volcano (a three-inch-high chocolate cake with a chocolate ganache in the center, vanilla ice cream on the side, and all of it drizzled with a dark chocolate sauce and topped with brandied pecans). The boys both had just plain ice cream, although I don't think that was coordinated since they didn't speak during the entire meal.

Then we forced them to go to a kid-friendly Vegas-style show in the big auditorium. Afterwards I let Jean and the boys go in our suite while I stayed outside to call home. Emmett picked up on the second ring.

''Bout damn time you checked in!' he said by way of a greeting.

'I'm on vacation,' I said for what seemed the umpteenth time.

'OK, I've only got one more person to interview and he doesn't look promising. Everybody has a half-assed alibi and the same half-assed motive.'

'Hell, Emmett, revenge is always a strong motive.'

'Yeah, but there's not one of them that stands out, know what I mean? They *all* hated his guts, they *all* wanted him dead, and most of 'em had the means and the opportunity. I mean, how hard is it to get your hands on a rifle in Oklahoma?'

'Did you ever find out what caliber?'

'Yeah, thirty-thirty Win.'

'Hell, that could be anything,' I said.

'Yeah, lot of rifles use thirty-thirty.'

I sighed. 'Don't know what to tell you, Emmett. Just keep plugging away. That's the only way to do it. At least for me.'

'Yeah, you always were a plodder. Me, I like the more effective miraculous brainstorm.'

I laughed. 'Yeah, well, you hold your hand over your ass and wait for that, 'k? I'm gonna join my wife,' and with that I hung up.

We made an early night of it and were all in bed by ten p.m. At around eleven there was a knock on the door. Jean and I had both been reading but the boys didn't move, which was a good indication they were actually asleep.

I got up, put a robe on over my shorts and T-shirt and went to the door. Mike Tulia stood there. 'What's up?' I asked him.

'Step outside?' he said, making it sound like a question. I did. When the door closed behind me, he said, 'Josh Weaver is missing.'

'Who?'

'Vern's oldest kid,' Mike said. 'Vern just called me. Said he couldn't find him anywhere. He called security and they're looking for him, but I told Vern you and I would help too. That OK with you?'

I was tired but I had to admit I also had a little cabin fever. Our cabin was so small it didn't take long for the fever to take hold. 'Sure,' I said to Mike. 'Let me get some clothes on.'

I went back into the cabin where Jean lay on her bed, pillows stacked behind her as she read, although the book was now on her lap. 'Who was that?'

'Mike,' I said quietly. 'Josh Weaver's missing. Mike volunteered him and me to go look for him.'

'Well, that was nice of him,' and yes she said that sarcastically. 'I thought that was what security was for. Other than for arresting small children, of course.'

I decided to ignore that. It was her kid, too, after all. At this point she wasn't going to see the law and order part of it like I did. 'Security is on it, but Mike promised Vern.'

'That you'd look for him?' she said.

'Come on, honey—'

'Don't honey me,' she said, her whisper fairly loud. 'Mike Tulia's daughter is more than likely the one who got John into this whole mess! Just what did she plan on doing with my son up in her cabin? Answer me that!'

You know, you can give a person all the high-faluting education in the world, a whole medical degree in psychiatry, but mess with a woman's kid and the mama lion will win every damn time.

'I'll be back as soon as I can,' I said, buttoning up my shirt. I was out the door before she could utter another word.

Mike and I headed up to the promenade deck, checking out the shops and the casino. We saw Chief Heinrich's men going into the different entertainment venues and decided to let them disturb the entertainers and patrons rather than us. When we found nothing in the shops or casino, we headed to the open-air pool area, me taking the port side (I think) and Mike the starboard (I think). Nothing. We headed to the food court which was mostly empty, and on to the children's pavilion, not suspecting he'd be there, but we had to check. He wasn't there. We headed out to the deck that went around the food court.

Mike stopped and looked out at sea. It was black as pitch. 'You don't think he fell overboard, do you?' he asked me.

I shrugged. 'I dunno. Hope not,' I said.

'Can you imagine?' Mike said, his voice soft. 'A kid like him out in that?' He pointed into the blackness. 'Bobbing up and down, not being able to see anything, just this ship fading from sight?' Mike shook himself. Looking at me, he laughed nervously. 'I think this might be my last cruise.'

'I hear you,' I said, staring out at the blackness. I could feel my skin crawling from the thought of a boy, my boy – out in the blackness, alone, treading water, waiting—

'I wouldn't put it past the little shit to be hiding,' Mike said, breaking into my painful thoughts. 'He's given Vern nothing but hell ever since he divorced his mom.'

'Where would he hide?' I asked.

'I dunno. Where would you hide?' he asked.

I thought about it, then pointed to a door. 'That says employees only. Think Josh would obey that?'

'Hell, no,' Mike said.

So we ignored the sign too and went in. Stairs immediately headed down several flights until we reached a long, narrow, unadorned corridor with lots of doors on either side. Probably crew quarters. Another door near the stairway led – by the sign – to the engine room. We tried opening it, but it was locked.

'So what do you suppose Josh would do when confronted by a locked door?' I asked Mike.

'Give up. The kid doesn't have a lot of drive.' We looked down the long corridor. 'Think we should try some of these doors?' Mike asked.

I shrugged. 'In for a penny,' I said, and headed to the doors on the left, while Mike took the doors on the right. They were definitely crew cabins and few of them were locked. I could see spare navy uniforms in open closets. And truth be told, most of the rooms I found were God-awful messes. Of course, when did they have time to clean their own cabins when they were always waiting on us hand and foot?

Mike had found several open doors before he hit the jackpot: an enraged young lady.

'What the hell do you think you're doing?' she yelled. 'This is my private room! Are you a passenger? It's not enough that I slave for you day and night, you have to come down here and what? Do you think you can seduce me? Or are you a rapist?'

All this time, Mike was backing up and trying to apologize.

'I'm really sorry! I didn't think anybody—' Mike tried, to no avail.

'Oh, my God! You're not alone!' she screamed upon seeing me. 'Rape!' she yelled at the top of her lungs. 'Rape!'

I held up both hands in surrender. 'Miss, wait now, miss—'

But she yelled that word again. Mike and I looked at each other and took off running for the stairs leading up.

We got to the brisk night air of the deck and both sighed heavily. 'Jeez, what was with that broad?' Mike asked.

'You do have a way with words, don't you, Mike?' I said.

'What?' he asked in apparent innocence.

'Hens? Broads? What next? Bimbos? Dames? Floozies?' I said.

'Gee, Milt, did I hurt your feelings? You on the rag, boy?'

'See, there you go!'

'OK, I'm not a she-man, all right? I'm a man's man! I like to hunt and fish and watch the cowboys and fart in my living room!'

'Hell, I like all those things, too, including farting in my living room' – I like it, I just didn't do it anymore since Jean and I got married – 'but you just don't call women—'

At that moment we must of hit a minor tsunami 'cause the ship rocked heavily, knocking me and Mike up against the wall. Across from us was one of the life boats. When the ship hitched, an arm, presumably attached to a body, fell out from under the tarp covering the life boat. And the arm wasn't moving.

SEVEN

Milt – Day Four

Mike and I were surrounded by four security personnel, plus Chief Heinrich, the head steward, and somebody from the bridge whose rank I didn't get. We all stared at Josh Weaver's uncovered body. By the marks on his neck, the fact

that most of his tongue was hanging out, and my years as a professional lawman, I deduced he'd been strangled. Unfortunately even
Mike, a tool and die guy, deduced the same thing, so I didn't get
all uppity about it. We were all staring when the door down to the
crew quarters opened and the irate young lady from only a few
moments earlier came barreling out.

'Chief Heinrich!' she cried. 'You got them! Thank God! They
tried to—'

She stopped in mid-sentence, I suppose because people moved
enough for her to see poor old Josh lying there with his tongue
lolling out.

'Oh,' she said. 'Is he dead?'

No one answered her 'cause at that moment Vern Weaver came
rushing down the deck with Crystal running behind him. I'm a
happily married man, but that didn't keep me from noticing that
when Crystal ran, especially wearing nothing but a silky-looking
short nightie and a matching silky-looking short robe, her D cups
hardly moved. Her legs were longer than I thought humanly
possible, and her red hair flowed behind her like she was in a
shampoo commercial. I couldn't help wondering if the fact that
her D cups didn't move meant they weren't real. That would be
a real shame, because they were awful pretty peeking out of that
flimsy nighty.

'Josh!' Vern yelled. The crew made way for him and he grabbed
his son and pulled the boy to his chest. I started with an 'Ah,
Chief,' thinking about all the forensics he was messing up, but
Heinrich just glared at me so I shut up and watched Vern cry over
his son. Crystal came up behind Vern and hugged his back, making
sounds like she was bawling her eyes out, but the lady had some
heavy mascara on and I didn't see it smudge. I'm just saying – for
what it's worth.

I tapped Mike on the shoulder. 'You should stay for Vern, but
I'm just in the way here,' I said. 'So I'm heading back to my
cabin.'

Mike nodded his head and moved to his partner, patting a free
shoulder. I walked back to our cabin, wishing I had Jean's scooter
'cause I was dog tired and didn't feel like walking the length of
the ship to get to bed. So to keep my mind occupied while I made
my way, I had to wonder, who would want Josh Weaver dead?

The kid wasn't the best-looking, brightest, friendliest, nicest or any of the other 'est's' you could think of, but that was hardly a reason to choke him to death. He and Vern had been at each other, but no more than any other father and teenaged son. Something I had to look forward to, I thought with a little trepidation. I was thinking about the people we knew who knew Josh. The Tulias, Esther Monte, her daughter and her shipboard romance, Lance Turner, and Rose Connelly and her boys and in-laws. Why would any of them want him dead? The only people even close enough to the Weaver family to care would be the Tulias – Mike, Lucy and Janna. I ruled out Janna purely because she wouldn't have the strength to put Josh in the life boat. Could probably rule out Lucy for the same reason. Not to mention neither one had hands big enough to have left the bruising I had seen on Josh's neck.

But the most likely scenario was someone I didn't know. Josh, as a teenager, probably roamed the ship at his leisure, so probably met a lot of people, including kids his own age. With the personality he appeared to have, it was likely he'd rubbed the wrong somebody up the wrong way.

I'd have to ask the boys in the morning what they'd thought of him the few times they'd been around him.

Johnny Mac – Day Five

Johnny Mac woke up feeling good, until reality came crashing down on him. He'd lost his best friend and any chance of making Janna his girlfriend. He'd pissed off his mom and disappointed his dad. And he was stuck in this cabin or eating nothing but fancy food until the ship docked which, thank God, would be sometime the day after tomorrow. Another two days to get through, he thought.

'You boys awake?' his dad called from the other room.

He heard Early say, 'Yes, sir,' and thought *suck up*, then said, 'Yes, sir,' himself.

'Come on in here a minute, boys, we need to talk,' his dad said.

Johnny Mac sighed deeply and crawled down his ladder, avoiding eye contact with his former best friend. This is not going to be fun, he thought to himself. Of course, nothing as of late had been a bit of fun.

They went into the other room and took seats together on his dad's hastily made-up bed, Johnny Mac knowing his dad had made it himself – it sure wasn't a professional job.

'Where's mom?' Johnny Mac asked, rubbing sleep out of his eyes.

'In the bathroom, getting dolled up,' his father answered. Then he sighed kind of heavy like, and Johnny Mac figured something else was coming down on his head.

'Boys, something really bad happened last night,' his dad said, and Johnny Mac braced himself for what was to come. Did they steal something really big this time? Roll another drunk? Because he knew it was them – Josh and some of the others.

Then his dad said, 'Josh Weaver was killed last night.'

For the first time in almost twenty-four hours, Johnny Mac and Early looked at each other. 'Shit!' Early said.

'Watch the language, Early,' Johnny Mac's dad said.

The boys looked at each other again, silently asking each other, 'Do we tell? Is it time?'

Johnny Mac nodded at Early and said, 'Dad, there's something we need to tell you.'

Meanwhile, Back In Prophesy County

Dave McDaniel's paint and body shop was on his way to work, so Emmett dropped by there first. Dave was in the small front office with a customer when Emmett walked in.

'Be right with you, Emmett,' Dave said.

Emmett walked over to a wall that had pictures of a race car that he remembered Steve telling him about. Steve and his dad had built it when Steve was in high school, with the hopes of racing it one day. When the customer left, Emmett asked Dave, 'You and Steve ever race this thing?'

'Officer, I refuse to answer on the grounds that you'd lock my ass up and hide the key.'

Emmett turned back to the counter and laughed. 'I meant on a legitimate race course.'

'Naw. Never could qualify. Still got it, though.' He pointed with his thumb to the bays behind him. 'Take it out for a spin occasionally. Wanna go with me next time?' Dave said, grinning.

'Think you can speed your ass off on the back roads if you got a sheriff's deputy with you?'

'It had crossed my mind,' Dave said.

Emmett grinned. 'You bet your ass. Give me a call. Meanwhile, I need to interview your nephew, Malcolm. Understand he works here?'

'Yeah, just a minute.' He opened the door to the bays and said, 'Leonard, go get Malcolm out of the paint room and tell him to come to my office.'

Dave pointed to a door at the back of the small lobby area. 'My office is right in there,' he said. 'You can use that to talk to him.'

'Thanks,' Emmett said as a young man opened the door from the bays. He had a painter's mask hung around his neck and was wearing paint-spattered coveralls and heavy gloves which he was attempting to take off. As Grady mentioned, he was about five-eight, very thin, with straight black hair and brown eyes he kept focused mostly on the ground.

'Malcolm, this is Emmett Hopkins from the sheriff's department. He needs to ask you some questions about Darby Hunt,' Dave said. 'Just answer them truthfully then get back to work, 'k? I have to go pick up a part and I'll be back in fifteen.'

Dave went out the front door and Emmett ushered Malcolm into Dave's inner sanctum. It was nothing to write home to mom about. Not much bigger than a walk-in closet, it smelled of grease and body odor and was hip-deep in paperwork and car parts. Emmett took the chair behind the desk and Malcolm pulled up a straight-back chair across from him.

'Yes, sir?' Malcolm said, his focus again downward and his demeanor timid.

'Don't mean to bother you, Malcolm,' Emmett said, 'I'm just interviewing everybody in the family about Darby Hunt's murder. You know anything about that?'

'He's dead,' Malcolm said.

'Yeah, he is. You know who killed him?'

Malcolm looked up, the brown eyes wide. 'No, sir!' he said, his voice a little less timid. 'I surely do not.'

'You hunt, Malcolm?'

'No, sir.'

'You know anybody who hunts?'

Malcolm looked up again and the look on his face seemed to

indicate he thought the question stupid, which upon reflection, Emmett had to agree with.

'Anybody using anything taking a thirty-thirty Win cartridge?' Emmett added, to make himself seem a little less asinine.

Malcolm shook his head and looked down again.

'What did you think about Darby Hunt?' Emmett asked.

Malcolm shrugged. 'I didn't. Think about him, I mean.'

'So when you heard that the guy who eviscerated your aunt was getting out of jail and coming back to Prophesy County, the man who had threatened your entire family, you didn't think about that at all?'

He shrugged. 'Well, yeah, I guess.'

'So what did you think?'

He looked up again at Emmett. 'That it was bad?' he offered.

Emmett nodded. This kid probably didn't kill Darby Hunt. And so far he hadn't found anybody who probably did.

Milt, Day Five

Before Johnny Mac could say anything, there came a knock on the door. I sighed and went to answer it. Mike Tulia – again. This time his daughter Janna was with him and she was red-eyed, snotty-nosed and hiccuping sobs.

'Sorry, Milt,' Mike said, 'but Janna insists on seeing your son and she won't stop crying until she does.'

'I don't see that as my problem, Mike,' I said, ready to close the door.

Janna burst into renewed tears as my wife stepped out of the bathroom. 'Let them in, Milt,' she said, and I had to wonder if she was going to bitch slap the defenseless little girl. You know, after what she'd said the night before.

I opened the door wider and Janna ran into the room and right up to Johnny Mac who stood up, turned a deep purple, and patted Janna on the back. 'It's OK,' he said.

'No, it's not!' Janna cried. 'Someone killed Josh! They're coming after us next!'

'What the f—' Mike started.

And I said, 'Huh?' just about the same time.

Early stood up, a panicked look in his eyes. 'Why?' he demanded. All of us talking at the same time.

'OK!' Jean said from her sitting position on her bed. 'Everybody shut up and sit down!'

Jean has this way about her – we all sat down and shut up.

'John, you and Early were going to tell us something earlier. Is what Janna is saying connected to what you were going to tell us?'

'Yes, ma'am,' Johnny Mac said.

'Then the three of you can tell us what it is, but be polite and don't talk over each other. Decide who speaks when and tell us.'

Both Janna and Early looked at Johnny Mac, so he started. 'Josh was bad,' he said, and the other two nodded their heads. 'He kept playing these games where he wanted us to basically steal stuff. Like at the pool –' He looked at Janna, who took up the saga.

'Yeah, he said it was a game, but he had us grab stuff that people had left behind at the pool, and the one with the most stuff won. When Johnny Mac told him that was stealing, he said he'd put it all back, but I don't think he did.'

'And then,' Early said, 'when we got to Georgetown, he wanted us to steal from a store—'

'All at a different store—' Janna interjected.

'Yeah,' Early concurred. 'But I didn't. And neither did Johnny Mac.'

'No, Early was really cool about it,' Johnny Mac said, grinning at his former, now again, obviously, best friend. 'Dad, he used the money you gave him and bought something, threw away the bag and told Josh he stole it!'

'But I have the receipt,' Early said.

Janna's eyes got big. 'Really?' she said, looking at Early with those big blue eyes. 'I wish I'd thought of that.' She hung her head. 'I sorta stole something,' she said, her voice not much more than a whisper.

Mike went up to his little girl and pulled her into his arms. 'I'm so sorry, baby – I made you hang out with that asshole! Why didn't you tell me what he was doing?'

He put her back down and she said, 'Because he would have done something bad, either to me, or you or Mama. He was really mean, Daddy.'

'What about you, John?' his mother asked.

Johnny Mac blushed and shrugged his shoulders. 'I ended up

at a jewelry store and the money Dad gave me wouldn't buy anything in there. So I stole a pen off the counter top and ran.'

'Where's the pen?' I asked.

Johnny Mac's blush grew a deeper shade of red, and I saw Janna reach for his hand. 'Josh threw it on the ground and stomped on it.'

'Who all was involved in this?' Jean asked.

All three kids looked at each other then back at Jean. Johnny Mac stood up. 'We're not stool pigeons, Mom. We won't rat out anyone else.'

'Was Lyssa involved?' Jean asked.

'Lyssa and her mom weren't with us that day,' Janna reminded her.

'How about Josh's little brother, Ryan?' Mike asked.

There was no response.

'What about the two Connelly boys?' Jean asked.

No response.

'Do you think one of them may have killed Josh?' I asked.

All three jumped up. 'No!' they all shouted at once.

'Well, somebody did. Was it one of y'all?'

'Now, hold on, Milt—' Mike started, but I stayed him with an outstretched arm.

'Was it one of y'all?' I repeated.

'No, Dad,' Johnny Mac said. 'None of us did it.'

'Then who do you think did?' I asked.

The three looked at each other, turned their backs on us grown-ups and did a whispered side bar. Finally Johnny Mac, as spokesman, said, 'We think it was probably that man who accused us – that Mr Dunne. He found out who really did it, which would be Josh, and killed him. Which is just mean, we think!'

'Yeah, that's pretty mean,' I agreed. 'OK, you guys go in there,' I said, indicating the boys' part of the suite, 'while us grown-ups talk out here.'

They did, rather eagerly, I'd say, leaving me and Jean and Mike sitting on Jean's bed.

'Well, if Josh was doing this and getting the kids involved, I'd say his brother Ryan was definitely in on it,' Mike said.

'And Lyssa,' Jean said. 'I've rarely seen your daughter without Lyssa.'

'That's true,' Mike said.

'That leaves the Connelly boys,' I said. 'Unless there are other kids we don't know about.'

'Too bad they won't talk,' Mike said, indicating our kids in the next room with a nod of his head.

'I learned to throw guilt from a Southern mama,' I said. 'Hide and watch.'

I went into the boys' part of the suite. All three were sitting on the bottom bunk, their feet hanging over the edge.

'Hey, y'all,' I said. 'Look. There's only one thing we can do. We have to go to the ship's security chief about what you told us, and the problem is that without knowing what other kids were involved, I'm afraid he's going to have to gather up all the kids on this boat, which means we might have to stay aboard longer than we planned. Not to mention that all the poor kids who had nothing to do with this will suffer.'

Johnny Mac held up one finger then they all turned away from me for another whispered conference. They turned around and Johnny Mac sighed loudly. 'OK,' he said. 'Yeah, Ryan, Josh's brother, was there every time, and the Connelly boys were there at the pool, but not in Georgetown.'

'What about Lyssa?' I asked.

The boys looked at Janna. 'She was at the pool with us, but not with us in Georgetown, and definitely had nothing to do with Mr Dunne because she was with us. We didn't do that, Sheriff Kovak. Honest to God!'

'Thank y'all for telling me. It's best that we get this all out in the open.' I patted Janna on the head as I left to go into the larger part of the suite. But I had to admit, my son had good taste in little women.

Milt – Day Six

I went down to A level to the security office and went in to see Chief Heinrich. He was on the phone and indicated that I sit and wait – I did as indicated.

'We'll dock in Galveston the day after tomorrow,' he said into the phone. 'Should we hold everyone aboard ship until—' He listened then said, 'I see. Yes.' He listened again, then said, 'Of course, we will continue our investigation aboard ship—' Again he listened, and finished with, 'Very good. I'll see you then.' And hung up.

To me he said, 'Mr Kovak, how may I help you?'

'Got some info you might be interested in,' I said. And proceeded to tell him what the kids had told us about Josh Weaver and what he'd been up to.

'The little shit!' Heinrich said, halfway under his breath.

'Not the first time I've heard him called that,' I said.

'Do you know where he kept his – what should I call it? Booty?'

'I think an interview with Josh's brother Ryan might be in store,' I said. Then asked, 'So who was that on the phone?'

'The Galveston police,' he said. 'The coast guard will be boarding when we dock, as will the police.'

'And we all have to stay aboard while this is going on?' I asked.

'I'm afraid so. No one can leave until everyone has been interviewed. It may take quite a while. Five hundred souls, you know.'

'Well, four hundred and ninety-nine,' I said, by way of being accurate.

'You have a macabre sense of humor, Mr Kovak,' he said.

I shrugged. He wasn't wrong. So then I brought up what I'd come here for in the first place. 'I'd like your permission, Chief Heinrich,' I said, 'to gather up the parents of these kids to tell them what was going on. I'm pretty sure Vern Weaver didn't know what his son was up to, or both sons for that matter. I know the others didn't.'

'And why would you think I'd allow you to do this, rather than do it myself?'

'Well,' I said, 'coming from me it wouldn't be so scary. Like you mentioned, on this cruise I'm just another passenger, whereas you're the authority. And maybe I can have a room that isn't, you know, like in your security area? One of the small venues on the promenade level?'

Chief Heinrich smiled, sorta. It was more like a grimace, but I think he meant it as a smile because he said, 'You are very funny, Mr Kovak. To think I could give you access to *anything* on the promenade level! Most people on the ship have no idea about the boy who was killed, and we want to keep it that way until we dock in Galveston. That is what the captain wants, and that is what I will do. So,' he said, standing up behind his desk, 'there is a small conference room on this level you can use, but I will be in attendance.'

I stood up also. I moved forward and held out my hand. Heinrich took it and shook it and told me the room number of the conference room. I left the room feeling a trifle smug. Always ask for more than you want, 'cause then you might just get what you need. To paraphrase those most genteel Englishmen.

Milt – Day Six

We compromised and went to the buffet/food court for lunch. The food was good but not the fancy-pants stuff I was used to. I had some gigantic crab claws with a tub of drawn butter, peel-and-eat shrimp with a really good red sauce, some corn on the cob, coleslaw, potato salad, baked beans, a couple or four deviled eggs and a pitcher of beer. For dessert I got some chocolate-chip cookies, a piece of apple pie and a slice of red velvet cake. And some vanilla ice cream to be shared between the apple pie and the red velvet cake. My wife looked at my plate and just shook her head, mumbling something under her breath about a heart attack on a plate, but I wasn't really paying attention.

The boys' plates were heaped high with corn dogs, pizza slices, corn on the cob, French fries and mac and cheese. Jean had a nice green salad. The woman has no idea of good food.

Most of the tables were like picnic tables with bench seating. It took some doing, but we found a table with chairs for Jean.

Once we were all settled, Jean asked me, 'So what did Chief Heinrich say to your idea?'

'He wants to be there, but I get the impression he's OK with me running it. He gave us a conference room in the security office. And, honey, I'm gonna need you to be there. You know, in case anyone goes nutso about this, or maybe you can check people out and see who looks guilty.'

Using her head as a pointer, she indicated the two boys. 'And them? We aren't going to actually leave them alone?'

'Good God, no!' I said. 'They'll come with us. I want all the kids there.'

'Why?' she asked, liberally dosing her salad with at least a half an ounce of red wine and vinegar dressing.

'They might know more than what the boys and Janna told us.

I'd think some of them, probably at least Ryan, had something to do with Clifford Dunne getting mugged.'

She nodded her head. 'Good point,' she said.

Heinrich had given the appropriate stewards semi-formal invites to pass out to the parents of the appropriate kids to meet in the conference room at two p.m. Me, Jean and the boys got there about one-thirty. I'd had the boys bring some toys with them and then put them in a corner while Jean and I set up. We sat at the conference table and made a list of the points I wanted to cover: when she might step in here or there, what we wanted Heinrich to say, etc. Heinrich joined us at about one forty-five, and we handed him a short little intro for him to read. He looked at it and handed it back.

'If you don't mind,' he said, looking from me to my wife and back again, 'I've been talking for myself for some forty-odd years now. I see no reason to change at this late date.'

Oh, crap, I thought. He's planning on taking over. I looked at my wife and shrugged. I must have had a hangdog look about me, 'cause she patted my hand.

At about one fifty-five the people started showing up and I had the boys come sit with us – Early next to me and Johnny Mac next to his mom. First in the door were Mr and Mrs Connelly Sr, followed by Rose and her two boys, Trip and little Jacob; about a minute later Vern Weaver and his Crystal, along with a depressed-looking Ryan, Vern's younger son, showed up, with Mike, Lucy and Janna right on their heels. At two oh five, the door opened yet again and Lyssa came in followed by a giggling Esther and Lance Turner, smiling down at his conquest. Why he was here I wasn't sure.

After they took their seats under the steely eye of Chief Heinrich, he stood up and said, 'I know you are all aware of the murder of Joshua Weaver. Some new information has come to light. Ferreted out by Mr Kovak, or should I say, Sheriff Kovak of Prophesy County, Oklahoma, for those of you unaware of this.' By the looks on the faces of those assembled, the only ones not aware of this were the senior Mr and Mrs Connelly. 'After checking Sheriff Kovak's credentials, I've discovered he is much more familiar dealing with murder investigations than I am. Therefore, I will be turning this meeting over to him. Sheriff?'

You could have knocked me over with a feather. He sat down and I stood up. 'Thank y'all for coming,' I said. 'The first thing I need to tell y'all, and Vern, I do apologize to you in advance, but it seems like Josh was playing some mean games with the younger ones. And it looks to me like all the kids present were involved to some extent.'

Vern just shook his head and looked down at the table. However, Baker Connelly Sr stood up. 'My grandsons were not involved with that young man at all. They had nothing to do with this and we're leaving.' He practically yanked his wife up by her arm, then shouted, 'Rose!'

Rose sighed big time. 'I don't think so, Dad,' she said. 'The boys and I will stay here. Maybe you should take Mother back to the cabin.'

'I said now, young lady!' Connelly shouted.

Without raising her voice, Rose simply shook her head and said, 'No.' Both her boys looked at her with surprise and, dare I say it? Respect.

For some reason, Lance Turner found this exchange to be very funny, laughing out loud at one point, while Esther Monte tried to shush him.

'Linda!' Connelly said to his wife and stormed out of the room, his wife following behind him.

'I'm sorry for the interruption, Sheriff,' Rose Connelly said. 'Please continue.'

I nodded my head at her and went on. 'In a nutshell, Josh was trying to get these kids to steal for him. I don't know how much he got out of it, except what he got for rolling that drunk from the casino the other night. Ryan? Were you with Josh then?'

Ryan was desperately shaking his head, when his dad took his hand, kissed it and said, 'Boy, just tell the truth. It'll be all right.'

Tears sprang to Ryan's eyes. He looked over at Rose's boys then raised his head to look me in the eyes. 'It was just me and Josh,' he said. 'Josh made me hit the guy in the back of the head, and when he fell on the stairs I started going through his pockets and found a lot of money. But Josh took it all.'

Rose's youngest child, Jacob, the seven-year-old, began to cry in earnest. Rose bent over her boy. 'Honey, what's wrong?' she started, but Trip, Jacob's older brother, grabbed his arm and twisted it. Rose didn't miss that. She grabbed Trip's hand off the younger boy and threw it away from her. 'What are you doing?' she demanded.

'Nothing!' Trip answered.

'Jacob, what is it?' she asked the younger boy again.

'Ryan didn't do it all by him—'

'Shut up, you little shit!' Trip screamed.

Rose stood up and yanked her eldest up by the scruff of his neck. 'You were involved in this?' she demanded. 'And you included your little brother? What is the matter with you?'

'Just trying to have some fun on this stupid boat! I never wanted to come on this trip! I wanted to go to Disney World! But Grandpa said no! So you just did what you always do – whatever he says!'

'And that's your excuse for mugging a man and stealing his money? You were bored?' She sorta screamed the last part.

Trip had the grace to hang his head, while Jacob just cried harder.

Heinrich stood up. 'May I ask how old is Trip?'

Rose let go of her son and sat down, bringing little Jacob into her lap. 'He's eleven,' she said.

'Too young to be arrested on-board ship. I will ask, however, that you keep him sequestered in his room. We will have his meals brought to you, and when you and your younger son need to go about the ship, one of my security personnel will stand outside your door.'

Trip looked up with wide eyes. Rose looked at her son then back at Heinrich. 'That will work out well,' she said.

At this point my wife stood up and asked Rose to join her outside. I said, 'I'll keep an eye on your boys.'

'Thank you, Sheriff Kovak,' she said, giving Trip another look.

'Ryan's eleven, too,' Vern said. His son looked at him like he'd been stabbed in the heart. 'You did the crime, boy, you gotta do the time.'

'The same arrangement,' Heinrich said.

Esther Monte stood up. 'Well, my baby wasn't involved in any of this, so I guess we can go.'

My two boys and Janna all started staring at the table. I touched her arm and said, 'Please sit down, Esther. There's more.'

Esther looked at her daughter and said, 'What the hell did you do?

'Lyssa,' I said, 'it has come to my attention that you were part of the group that stole the things people left at the pool one night. Part of one of Josh's games. Isn't that right?'

Lyssa stared hard at Janna and the boys, but not one of 'em lifted their heads. 'Yes, sir,' she finally said in a small voice.

'Lyssa! You stole something?'

'Esther, please. It's my turn. You can have her after I'm done,' I said. 'Lyssa, what did you steal?'

'I found some sunglasses and gave them to Josh. But when y'all were in Georgetown, at that first island we stopped at, Janna told me they stole things from stores and that Ryan won because he got the most expensive thing!'

Ryan jumped up, but his dad pulled him down. 'Take your lumps, boy,' Vern said. 'Better to learn it now.'

Lyssa looked at Ryan and said, 'I'm sorry.'

Lyssa sat down and her mother said, 'It'll be OK, honey,' with her arm around Lyssa's shoulders. 'But you and I are going to have a long talk.'

'Ryan?' I said. He looked up at me.

'Yes, sir?' he said.

'Do you know what Josh did with the things y'all stole? And what was it you stole?'

'I took a souvenir shot glass. And no, sir, I don't know what he did with most of it. He really liked the sailing ship Early stole—'

'I didn't steal it!' Early said, jumping to his feet.

I used my hand to indicate he sit back down. 'For the record, Early's the only one who actually didn't steal anything—'

'But he gave Josh that neat sailboat!' Ryan said, standing up. Vern pulled him back down.

'Early used the money I gave him and bought that sailboat and stuck the receipt in his pocket. He gave me the receipt so I can vouch for his truthfulness. However, Janna and Johnny Mac both stole small things. As did Ryan, it seems. I don't think Josh made a lot of money off that particular crime wave. So, Ryan, you were saying?' I said.

'That ship is next to his bed,' Ryan said. 'The other stuff he threw away, I think. I know what he did with Johnny Mac's thing. It was a ballpoint pen and Josh ripped it out of his hand and threw it on the ground and stomped it until it broke! He liked to mess with Johnny Mac because he thought he – Johnny Mac, I mean – was a goody two-shoes.'

I saw Vern Weaver, his head down, shaking it side to side. This had to be really hard on the blustering old fool. I took a chance at looking at Crystal. She was checking her nails.

'What about the money he got from the guy you mugged?' I asked.

Ryan shrugged his shoulders. 'Don't know,' he said. 'I didn't see him hide it, but he must have. It's certainly nowhere I can see.'

'So you looked?' I asked.

Ryan turned red. 'Well, not hard or anything. I mean, I just glanced around—'

Heinrich stood and left the room for a moment. Through the windows of the conference room that looked out to the lobby area of the security site, I saw him talking to two of his men who quickly went out the door. I figured they were headed for the cabin Josh and Ryan shared to look for Clifford Dunne's $5,000. I doubted they'd find it there. I'm pretty sure Ryan tossed the room once he heard his brother was dead. Of course, he might have waited a decent interval, but I sorta doubt it. Then again, he might not have had time, as I understood he was now bunking with Vern and Crystal, as Vern didn't want him alone right now.

Jean and Rose came back in the room and took their seats.

'OK,' I said. 'I'm mostly through. I just wanted to tell y'all that these two,' I said, indicating Johnny Mac and Early, 'are confined to only going places where we go.'

Lucy stood up and said, 'Sounds like a good idea.'

'Mom!' Janna said, aiming the baby blues at her mother.

Lucy laughed. 'Not working!'

And Mike said, 'Not even on your dad.'

The other parents all agreed and started filing out.

EIGHT

Meanwhile, Back In Prophesy County

Emmett headed for the sheriff's department, thinking that now he'd finished interviewing everyone in his county that had anything to do with Darby Hunt's late wife, maybe he should interview more of Hunt's own family? Maybe some of them felt he was a bad influence and decided to kill him. Then Emmett sighed inwardly. With Billy Hunt dead from drunk driving and Shorty Hunt in jail out in California for whatever, who in that family would think Darby was such a bad influence? Wouldn't hurt to call some of 'em, just in case.

Maybe he'd go by and talk to Hunt's mama, see what she had to say. He shuddered at the thought. That mean old bat was liable to pull a gun on him before he opened his mouth. Probably blamed him anyway for her son getting shot.

Which led him to wonder if there was anyone left from the old days still in police work who would take offence at Darby Hunt getting out? He knew Milt had been around, but Milt's alibi for the night of the shooting was pretty good; Bill Williams was still around, and the deed had been done in his county. And he was the first one to know that Darby Hunt had been let out.

He shook his head. Naw, he thought, Bill didn't get real caught up in his cases. Most of it was like water off a duck's back with Bill. Dead bodies were just the price of doing business when you were in law enforcement, he heard Bill say once. So unless there was something really personal about Cheryl Hunt's murder – like she was his sister or daughter or cousin or something – he doubted Bill would get his knickers in a knot over it. But, just to be on the safe side, Emmett pulled his squad car into a parking lot and pulled out his cell phone. Another reason, he reckoned, to get one of those bluetooth things. He dialed Lisa Atkins' number.

When she said hello, Emmett said, 'Miz Atkins, this is Emmett

Hopkins with the sheriff's department again. Real quick: is Bill Williams, sheriff of Tejas County, any kin to y'all?'

'Not that I know of,' she said.

'Ex-boyfriend of your sister's or anything?'

'Cheryl started going with Darby Hunt in junior high and never went out with anyone else.' There was a slight sob on her end of the phone. 'Never knew a gentle hand from a man. Not ever.'

'Ma'am, I'm sorry. Thanks for the info.' He hung up quick, not wanting to hear her cry, started the car and headed for the shop. Once there, he checked in with Holly and headed back to his – Milt's – office. And dialed Milt's cell phone.

'I'm sorta busy,' Milt said when he answered.

'I got nothing,' Emmett said.

'Yeah, well I've got my own dead body here.'

'No shit? But you're not sheriff on the boat, Milt.'

'I'm just helping out the security chief here. So, what's up with Hunt?'

'I talked to everybody and their brother, literally, and can't see anyone sticking out. I mean, all the McDaniels had reason to kill him, but most of them have an alibi, and those who don't just don't seem the type.'

'So you got the McDaniels and who else?' Milt said.

'Well, there's a bunch of them. Including Hunt's daughter. And then there's Hunt's girlfriend—'

'He had a girlfriend?'

'Yeah, I told you! The principal at Petal's school!'

'Oh, right. That sucks. I just don't understand women who go for convicted felons. Especially ones who killed or raped women.'

'Doesn't make a lick of sense to me either!' Emmett said.

'You talk to Bill Williams? See if anybody on his end knows anything?'

'Yeah, I guess I should do that. And speaking of Bill, did he seem unduly upset back when Cheryl Hunt got killed?'

'Unduly? Not so I noticed. I went over there when it happened, since Bill arrested Darby on the spot and Darby was a resident of my county, but Bill just seemed relieved that nobody in Cheryl's family had let the bastard get away. Why?'

Emmett shrugged, even though he knew Milt couldn't see him.

'Just a thought – you know, sometimes law enforcement gets too involved, maybe something personal—'

'Naw, not Bill. But speaking of personal, your heart just doesn't seem to be in this, Emmett,' Milt said.

'Well, now, if anybody deserved killing, it was old Darby Hunt,' Emmett said.

'We just uphold the laws, we don't write 'em and we don't get a say, you know what I mean?'

'Yeah, I know what you mean, but that doesn't mean I have to enjoy myself,' Emmett said, said bye and hung up.

He got the papers Bill Williams had faxed over to him and got the list of Darby Hunt's relatives. Crossing off Billy and Shorty still left a whole gob of them. Getting out a phone book, he looked up some of the names and discovered one of the Hunts, Josiah, was a preacher man, pastor of the LIOB Baptist Church, not affiliated, according to the yellow pages ad, with the Southern Baptist Church. After talking to their leader, Emmett had a feeling that would be a relief to Southern Baptists everywhere. He called the number and Josiah himself answered. 'LIOB,' he said.

'Pastor Hunt?' Emmett asked.

'You got him,' the man said.

'This is Emmett Hopkins, head deputy of the Longbranch Sheriff's Department—'

'You're calling about my ne'er-do-well cousin Darby, I betcha,' he said.

'Yes, sir,' Emmett said.

'It all come from his mama's side,' Josiah said. 'She's Milsted, and them Milsteds are a bad lot. Bad to the bone.'

'So you think it was all Darby's fault that Billy drove drunk and got himself killed, and Shorty's in prison in California for being stupid?'

Josiah laughed. 'Well, now, those two *were* bad apples, Deputy, I ain't gonna argue that.'

'Why I'm calling, Pastor—'

'Just call me Brother Josiah, Deputy.'

'Just call me Emmett, Josiah,' Emmett said. 'So, I thought being a preacher you might be able to tell me about your kin and if any of 'em might want to kill old Darby.'

'Well, now I heard somebody killed Darby. And I'm figuring

it was God's will. But as for this branch of the Hunts, I'm saying probably not. Both Billy's daddy and Shorty's daddy are dead, and Billy's mama, too. Shorty's mama's still with us, but she's a sweet little ol' thing, wouldn't hurt a fly.'

'What about Vivica?' Emmett asked, thinking of the female cousin Milt had mentioned who was as big as the boys but twice as mean.

'Oh, now we don't tolerate her kind round here,' Josiah said. 'Them's that lie down with their own sex and all that, like Jesus said.'

Emmett was pretty sure Jesus never said any such thing, but he wasn't going to argue with this dumbass bigot. 'So where is she?'

'Last I heard she had a cattle ranch in Montana, her and some other sinful woman. And they're having babies too. If they lived around here, I'd take those poor children away from her, you can guarantee that!'

'Anybody else in the family—'

'Well, now there were four brothers, who begat eight sons. Darby was his daddy's only child, and my daddy had two girls, and three more boys, including me. Both my older brothers died some time ago. Shorty has a brother, but he lives in Arkansas, and Billy had a brother, but he was in the car with Billy when it crashed. He didn't die, but he might as well have. He's been lying in his mama's living room for almost twenty years now, on life-support. I'd pray the God Lord take him home, but I think my aunt would hold on to him so tight either he'd stay here or she'd go to heaven with him.'

'So that's it?' Emmett asked.

'Yessir, that's all.'

'Did you kill Darby?' Emmett asked, a little desperately.

Josiah laughed good-naturedly. 'Sorry, Deputy. Don't mean to disappoint, but no, I didn't kill ol' Darby.'

'By the way, Josiah,' Emmett said, 'what does LIOB stand for?'

'Literal Interpretation of the Bible, Deputy! Every word of that good book is pure truth and should be accepted as such. And those that don't won't be rising come judgment day!'

Emmett thanked the preacher man and hung up.

Time to call Bill Williams in Tejas County. He hoped to hell Bill had heard about Hunt's murder through the grapevine, because he sure as hell hadn't called him to tell him about it. Emmett, he said to himself, stop thinking about Petal and get serious about this. Okey dokey, he answered himself. Will do.

Dalton sat at his desk in the bullpen and stared at Holly's back. He couldn't keep the smile off his face. She was as cute as a mongrel pup, he thought to himself.

He'd talked to Jamie Smith over at the Longbranch First National, the lady who'd loaned him the money for his car, and she'd cleared him for the amount of the house, less his down payment. Since Dalton lived with his mama, and only paid some of the bills (she didn't ask for rent), he'd been able to sock away a goodly amount. Enough for a down payment and a nice diamond, with some left over to start a college fund for his and Holly's first child.

The down payment was big enough that his monthly payments, even with taxes and insurance, would be well within his means. When he first heard the realtor lady say how much the house was, he thought he'd never be able to swing it but, here it was, right here on his desk, in black and white. He could do it. With enough left over from his paycheck for all the rest – like utilities and insurance and his one credit card, and groceries and such. Holly's paycheck could be used just for fun. Until she got pregnant and quit her job, of course.

Hands shaking, Dalton picked up the phone on his desk and called Holly's extension. She was less than a yard away from him, but he thought she'd think this was funny. And he loved making her laugh, even when he didn't mean to.

Holly looked at the readout on the phone, turned to look at Dalton and laughed as she picked up the receiver.

'How may I help you, Deputy?' she asked in a mock-serious voice.

'You wanna have dinner tonight? There's something I want to show you.'

'Sure. What do you want to show me?'

'It's a surprise,' he said. 'Where do you want to eat?'

'How about my place? I'll stop by the grocery store on the way home.'

'Why don't we do that together, after the surprise,' Dalton said, unable to wipe the smile off his face.

'Sure,' she said. 'Why not?'

Milt – Day Six

We had a lot of work to do before the ship docked in Galveston. Jean took her scooter and the boys up to the pool level for them to go swimming, while I stayed in the security area to work out what to do with Chief Heinrich. We sat in his office, coffee mugs in front of both of us, the chief leaning back in his big old leather chair while I tried to get comfortable in a small visitor's chair that at least had arms.

'Do you think there is a possibility that Clifford Dunne had anything to do with the boy's death?' the chief asked me.

'I thought he thought the younger kids did it. Did he change his mind?' I asked.

Heinrich shook his head. 'Not that I'm aware of.'

'You think we should talk with him?'

Heinrich appeared to think about that for a moment. Then he shrugged his shoulders and sat his chair up closer to the desk. 'Can't hurt,' he said, then hit a button on his phone and said into it, 'Clive, find passenger Clifford Dunne for me, please. Bring him to my office.'

'Yes, sir,' came the disembodied voice of Clive, who had an English accent that went well with his name.

'What else?' Heinrich said, looking at me. 'I was serious when I said you had more experience with murder investigations than I have. I've been a ship's security chief for twenty-five years, and in all that time I've never had anything even close to a murder.'

'What's close to a murder?' I asked.

He thought about that for a moment. 'Assault, I'd say. Rape or a serious beating. Not on my watch.'

'Well, I gotta say you've been lucky. Dealing with all these people on vacation, all the booze floating around, all the pretty women in bathing suits.'

'I'm not saying it hasn't happened,' he said. 'I am just saying it has not been reported.'

I nodded my head. 'I hear what you're saying. Lot of women don't want to report it, especially if they drank a little too much and were flirting – they think it's their fault. One thing I've already been teaching my boy is when a girl says no, you stop what you're doing. Girls need to know it's not their fault, but boys need to be taught that no means no.'

'That's true,' he said.

'I saw you send some guys out during the meeting. I assume it was to check the Weaver boys' cabin for Dunne's money,' I said.

'Yes,' Heinrich said. He looked up at the window of his office to see the two men he'd sent come in the door. 'And I believe we are about to get the answer to that.'

One of the men came in and saluted Heinrich. I thought that was carrying the faux navy stuff a bit far, but what do I know?

'Chief,' said a swarthy guy with a heavy accent. All I can say is it wasn't Mexican. That accent I recognize. This was different. 'We searched the cabin and found ten dollars in the boy's wallet, nothing else.'

'Thank you, Papademetriou,' Heinrich said and Papa-whatever saluted again and backed out of the door.

'Papa-what?' I said.

'Papademetriou,' Heinrich said. 'He *is* from Athens.'

'As in Greece?' I said.

'Yes,' Heinrich said. 'Now, we know that Josh Weaver did not hide the money in his cabin. Where else would he hide it?'

'Damned if I know,' I said. 'Where else could he? Not like he had free reign of the ship—'

Heinrich made a rude sound. 'Well, he certainly seemed to think he did!'

A buzzer sounded on his desk. He hit the button he'd been talking to Clive on and said, 'Yes?'

'Chief? I have Mr Dunne for you,' Clive, or another English accent, said.

'Send him in,' Heinrich said.

We both stood up when the door opened and a sailor-suited security guard let in Clifford Dunne. He looked a little more respectable today, wearing Bermuda shorts and a Polo shirt. He was also wearing black wingtips with white socks pulled up to his knees. I said respectable, I didn't say good.

'You find out who robbed me? You got my money?' Dunne said as he entered.

'Please sit down, Mr Dunne,' Heinrich said, indicating the chair next to me. 'I'm not sure you met Mr Kovak formally when you were accusing his children of having robbed you.' Dunne made a noise that wasn't pleasant. Heinrich went on: 'But other than being the father of one of the boys, he is also the sheriff of a county in Oklahoma, taking a vacation with his family.'

'Well, wooptifuck,' Dunne said. 'Why'd you have me dragged down here to hear this?'

'Sheriff Kovak is assisting me with the murder,' the chief said.

That shut Dunne's mouth for almost thirty seconds. Then he said, 'Murder? What murder?'

'The boy who actually robbed you was found dead,' Heinrich said.

'Ha!' Dunne said. 'Good for him! You find my money?'

'Not yet, no,' Heinrich said. 'But the question has arisen regarding the possibility that you may have taken matters into your own hands.'

'Do what?' Dunne said, looking slightly perplexed. Then, having obviously worked through what Heinrich said, continued, 'You think I— What the fuck? Are you out of your mind?' he said, jumping up. 'I'm the victim here! I'm the one who was hit on the head, knocked to the stairs, robbed and left for dead!'

'I don't think anyone wanted to kill you,' I said. 'You were moaning pretty good when the younger children found you. And, by the way, saved your ass.'

'Or were fixing to rob me more if I hadn't stopped them!' Dunne said, turning on me.

'Sit down, Mr Dunne!' Chief Heinrich said in a very stern voice. Hell, I would have sat down to that voice. So did Dunne. 'We are not forgetting that you were a victim. But that does beg the question: did you ever meet or see Josh Weaver?'

Dunne was already shaking his head. 'Who's that? Is that who died? Was he the kid who robbed me? How old was he? Because I remember little hands—'

'The little hands you remember may have been from when the little kids were trying to help you—' I started, but Dunne interrupted.

'No! I distinctly remember little hands going in my jacket pocket and pulling out the money!'

'The boy who died was fourteen, but he did have younger children helping him,' Heinrich said. 'Those were probably the smaller hands.'

'How old were those boys?' Dunne asked.

'Eleven,' Heinrich supplied.

Dunne was shaking his head. 'No, I've got a ten-year-old girl, and her hands aren't as small as the ones stealing my money. These were tiny hands!' Dunne said.

Heinrich and I looked at each other. The younger Connelly kid – Jacob. He was only seven. Between Josh and Jacob's older brother Trip, the two must have bullied the child into it. I thought I might ask Jean to have a get together with the young boy.

Heinrich stood up. 'That will be all, Mr Dunne. Thank you so much for coming by.' He moved to the door and opened it. To Clive he said, 'Please see that Mr Dunne gets back to his cabin.'

Clive said, 'Yes, sir,' just as Dunne said, 'Forget it! I don't need a guide!' And stormed out of the security office.

Meanwhile, Back In Prophesy County

So Emmett drove the twenty-something miles to Tejas County to see Bill Williams in person. He called first to make sure Bill would be there and got there just in time for lunch.

The Tejas County Sheriff's Department had moved out of the small downtown area of Elucid, the county seat of Tejas County, to a new building in what they called 'the metroplex,' which wasn't much more than a strip mall with the sheriff's office at one end and the county food bank at the other, with a couple of county welfare-type places in between. Emmett noticed that he passed a nice-looking Mexican food place on his way to Bill's shop.

'You had lunch?' Emmett asked after he and Bill shook hands.

'Not yet. You like Mexican?'

'Does the Pope shit in the woods? That place I passed on my way?' Emmett asked.

'That's the one.'

They headed out in Emmett's car, although the Mexican restaurant wasn't more than a couple of city blocks away. Once inside, menus perused, orders taken and sweet ice teas laid down, Emmett said, 'Guess you heard about old Darby Hunt?'

'That he got himself wacked? Yeah, I heard that. Was expecting a call from you,' Bill said.

Emmett felt himself flushing. 'Sorry about that. Haven't been in charge in a long time, sort of got the better of me.'

'So who're your suspects? Other than the entire McDaniel family, of course.'

Emmett shook his head. 'He had a girlfriend, and then there's his family, but that's about it. I was wondering about her family here in Tejas County?'

Bill shook his own head. 'You mean Cheryl's? Never was much of a presence. The senior McDaniels moved here after their kids were grown, but they're both gone,' he said.

'Anybody else you can think of?'

'Well, now, seems Cheryl had a girlfriend, you know, best friend kind of thing, who lived here with her husband. She was pretty shook up over the whole thing, threatened Hunt right back at the trial – when he threatened her family.' He laughed. 'I remember it like it was yesterday. Little thing, maybe five-two, ninety pounds dripping wet, blonde and blue. Hunt starts his crap and she comes flying out of the gallery, her husband trying to catch her, and she says, "You're a dead man! I'm gonna kill you myself!" And then she called him names I'd blush to repeat.'

'Hell, Bill! She sounds like a winner!' Emmett said.

Bill shrugged. 'Her and her family moved to Oregon about a year after. Saw her mama at the Piggly Wiggly the other day, said Dora has five kids now and is as big as a barn.' He shook his head. 'Shame, when you think about it.'

'What? Her getting fat, or not being around for me to accuse?' Emmett asked.

Again Bill shrugged his shoulders. 'Both,' he said. 'So what's with the girlfriend? And why do women do that, anyway?' Bill asked. 'I mean, there are plenty of meanass men out here free as a bird if they want a bad boy.'

'Yeah, well, maybe these women just want the allure of a bad guy, not the real thing,' Emmett said. 'When they're behind bars they can't hurt you, right?'

'Right,' Bill said.

Which made Emmett think: was that it? Was Reba Sinclair worried, now that her beloved was out, that he'd start the same crap with her that he had with his wife? That her life was in peril? Did she decide to strike first? Was the principal of Petal's school an excellent shot?

'You're paying, right?' Emmett said as he got up and threw

some ones on the table. 'For the tip. Gotta get back to my county.'
And with that, he was out the door, figuring Bill could use the
walk back to his shop.

Milt – Day Six

When I got to our suite, Jean and the boys were back from swimming and had changed clothes. The boys were playing some game
that involved ninjas (the one word I heard), and were secure in
their part of the suite, so I sat next to Jean on the bed.

'Heinrich and I figured out that the younger Connelly boy –
Jacob, I think?'

Jean nodded her head. 'Yes, Trip's the older one.'

'OK, Jacob. Anyway, he's the one who actually took the money
out of Clifford Dunne's jacket pocket.'

'Oh, Lord,' Jean said.

'Yeah,' I agreed. 'Maybe you should have a talk with him?'

'I'll call Rose this evening,' Jean said. 'Maybe we can talk after
dinner.'

But before she could make that call, we got a call on the ship's
phone from Lucy Tulia, inviting us to the dining room for the
early seating at a large table with everyone involved, except, she
said, the senior Mr and Mrs Connelly.

So we got the boys dressed in something a little nicer than
shorts and T-shirts, Jean put on a sundress and I wore a jacket,
and we went to the dining room. We were escorted to a huge round
table. We weren't the first. Esther Monte, her new, for want of a
better word, boyfriend, Lance Turner, and her daughter Lyssa were
all seated, as were Vern and Crystal Weaver; his son Ryan was
sequestered in their cabin. The four of us sat down, with Early
taking the seat next to Lyssa and Johnny Mac taking the seat on
the end with me and Jean in the middle. I was slightly curious
why he didn't sit next to Early, when the Tulias showed up and
Janna ran straight for the chair next to Johnny Mac. The grin he
gave off went from ear to ear. I swear the boy was advanced for
his age – only ten and already in love. I'd have to keep a strict
eye on him to make sure there was no kissing going on. Way too
young for that!

Mike and Lucy parked next to their daughter. A few minutes
later, Rose Connelly showed up with her youngest son, Jacob,

filling the table. Her older boy, like Vern Weaver's youngest, was sequestered in his cabin. We busied ourselves with looking at the menu and ordering. Lance got up and headed for the restrooms, and the senior Mr Connelly came in to say something to Rose. As he left, I noticed he whispered something in Esther's ear. She didn't seem to like it but did not reply.

There were always some of the same things on the menu – like steak, shrimp cocktail, Caesar salad, etc., but the main items changed every night. That night I ordered bacon-wrapped shrimp with water chestnut and jalapeño for an appetizer, a soup of lobster bisque instead of a salad, beef Wellington with a side of broccoli gratin, and poached pears for dessert. Though I got to say, the strawberry shortcake that Johnny Mac and Janna shared looked mighty tasty.

It had been decided on the phone that we'd let the kids go to the children's pavilion, but that one of the parents would escort them there and that the sitters would be told the kids were not to leave without a parent. Mike and I were elected to do the honors.

It took about fifteen minutes to get them there and get back to the dining room.

On the way back, Mike said, 'So, Milt, what do you think?'

'Huh?' I said.

'About all this crap – Josh being murdered, our kids being taught how to steal—'

I shook my head. 'I think our kids handled it pretty well,' I said. 'Early was pretty smart in spending his money and lying to Josh and, although Johnny Mac said he didn't have enough money to buy anything in that jewelry store, my take is he didn't think about it. But he did steal the only thing in the store that cost less than a dollar, and that toy that Janna took was practically a give-away, little more than a dollar. So I think their upbringing paid off, is what I think, Mike. As for Josh's murder, I don't know if it had something to do with Clifford Dunne's five thousand or not. Maybe Dunne found out it was Josh – how I don't know and it seems unlikely – or somebody else found out Josh had that kind of money on him and wanted it for themselves.'

Mike was nodding his head. 'Reasonable deductions,' he said and grinned at me. 'Sorry,' he said, 'but I feel sorta like Watson to your Sherlock.'

'Sorry, no cocaine on me,' I said.

By the time we got back to the table, a new bottle of wine was being passed around. We got there just in time. Everyone was in high spirits, except poor old Vern. Crystal was paying little attention to him, instead flirting with Esther's date, Lance.

After Esther's third glass of wine, she said, 'Crystal, honey, I think you'd be doing more good taking care of your husband rather than trying to romance *my* shipboard romance!'

Crystal bristled and Lance laughed, leaning over and kissing Esther, who laughed with him.

'You OK, baby?' Crystal said to Vern.

'I'm fine, honey,' he said, patting her hand. 'I think maybe I'll go back to the cabin.'

'You want me to go with you?' Crystal asked. Her tone was saying, 'No you don't, no you don't.'

'Naw, honey, you stay. I'm gonna be fine, just need a little alone time.' Vern stood up and wandered off.

To the rest of the table, Crystal said, 'He'll be OK. This has just been a real shock to him.'

Esther and Lance were still sucking face when I said, 'Anybody come up with any ideas about who might have done in poor old Josh?'

'Poor old Josh?' Lucy said. 'I don't think that's appropriate, Milt. I think it should be "that little shit Josh."'

'Now, honey—' Mike started, but Lucy was having none of it.

'He was trying to get our kids to steal! He did get some of them to!' she said, looking at Rose.

Rose sighed, tears coming to her eyes. 'Milt told me earlier that they've figured out from talking to the man who was mugged—'

'Clifford Dunne,' I said.

'Mr Dunne, that Jacob was the one who actually took the money, egged on or bullied into it by Josh and my son Trip. Jacob stopped sucking his thumb when he was three. I caught him yesterday morning and this morning with his thumb in his mouth when he was still asleep. I couldn't understand why until this all came out.'

Lucy reached over and took Rose's hand. 'I'm so sorry. I wasn't trying to accuse you or your boys—'

'But they did it,' Rose said. She lifted her head high and said,

'My father-in-law has told me that when we get back home he plans to take a more active role in the boys' lives. Turn them into good little soldiers. I guess I'll be moving out.'

We were all turned to Rose, hearing the shocking news, when there was a sound from across the table. Lance Turner was holding his throat and making a retching sound.

'Lance?' Esther said. 'Lance, are you OK? Baby, what's wrong?'

He tried to stand up, hit the table, backed into his chair, knocking it over, then collapsed on the floor. Everybody ran to him and Jean said, 'Move out of the way. I'm a doctor. Milt, call for the medics.'

She got down on the floor and ripped Lance's shirt open. Some kind of froth was emitting from his mouth. Jean checked his pulse. Then she leaned forward, as if to smell his breath.

'Please, would someone help me up?' I was still on the phone so Mike and Lucy got her to her feet. 'Esther!' she said.

'Don't stop!' Esther cried. 'Make him better! Do CPR!'

Jean grabbed Esther's hand. 'I'm sorry, Esther. He's dead. Which wine glass was his?'

'What? Dead? No, he can't be dead!'

'Which wine glass was his?' Jean insisted. 'Esther! It's important! Which wine glass was his?'

Esther shook her head, then looked at Jean. 'Which wine glass?' She looked around the table. 'This one,' she said, starting to pick it up.

'Don't!' Jean said. Then she grabbed one of the cloth napkins still on the table and picked the wine glass up herself, holding it to her nose.

I finished my call and asked her, 'What is it?'

'Cyanide,' she said.

I leaned down to smell the glass. 'Bitter almonds,' I said.

Meanwhile, Back In Prophesy County

Emmett radioed in to Holly and got a home address for Reba Sinclair, the principal at the Christian school. She lived within walking distance of the school, on Pine Bluff Drive, where there were no pines and not a bluff in sight. Her house was a typical seventies ranch, a three-bedroom MIL plan, with red brick veneer and newly painted white trim. It had a small front porch with hanging baskets of plants drooping from the eaves and big potted plants taking up

most of the floor space. He made his way gingerly to the front door
and rang the bell. He could hear movement inside the house, so
waited. It only took a minute or two for the curtain on the glass of
the front window to move slightly and expose one of Ms Sinclair's
myopic blue eyes. Seeing him, she opened the door.

While at the school she'd been wearing a cream-colored suit,
skirt to the knee, buttoned to the throat, sensible shoes. Her home
attire was a tad different: Daisy Dukes and a tube top, and barefoot.
One look and he could see why Darby Hunt might be interested;
the woman may have been unattractive from the neck up, but damn
if she didn't have a body by Buick, Emmett thought.

'Deputy?' she said, hand on jutted-out hip, obviously aware of
Emmett's observation.

'Ma'am, a few more questions, if you don't mind,' Emmett said.

'But I do mind,' she said, and started to close her door.

Emmett put out his foot to stop the door from closing. 'Ma'am,
I'll be happy to wait out here while you call your lawyer to
come over, but one way or the other, you and I are having a
talk tonight.'

Reba Sinclair sighed heavily but let up her pressure on the door.
Emmett wiggled his toes, hoping to get the circulation going again.
Like her former future mother-in-law's house, the front door led
directly into the living room. Emmett couldn't help noticing that
the room was like Reba Sinclair herself: good bones, but
unattractive. It was a big room with a nice fireplace and mantel,
and an alcove above the mantel, which was empty. The room was
brown on brown with some beige thrown in for, he supposed, color.
Everything was old and all but used up, and the place smelled kind
of funny to Emmett's way of thinking.

The living room held a brown couch in that nubby material he
hadn't seen around since the eighties, a matching love seat and
arm chair, and three matching Formica-topped tables – two end,
one coffee. There were no pictures or anything else on the walls;
no books or magazines on the tables, not even an ashtray. And
that wasn't the smell. It wasn't stale cigarette smoke. It was something worse than that – a sad smell, a smell of failure, of dreams
lost. He couldn't put his finger on it, but it made him itchy –
uncomfortable, ready to leave. Instead he sat down on the sofa as
Reba Sinclair indicated.

'What do you want?' she asked him, perching on the tip of the arm chair. 'I thought I answered all of your questions.'

'Well, ma'am, it's an ongoing investigation, so new questions keep coming up,' Emmett said, realizing she had legs about seven miles long and shapely to boot. He tried looking elsewhere, and settled on her face.

'Such as?' she asked, lips pursed, back ramrod straight.

'Such as, do you know any of Mr Hunt's wife's family who live here in Longbranch?'

'No! Why would I?'

'I don't know that you would, ma'am. I'm just asking. His daughter's a school teacher, perhaps you've met her?'

'Didn't I just say I hadn't?'

'I suppose you did,' Emmett said, wishing he'd thought a little bit longer about things before he'd hightailed it over here. 'Did Mr Hunt ever talk to you about them?'

'Only to say they all hated him. Had since he and Cheryl were kids! He said Cheryl fell down one time and broke her nose, and they blamed him for it. So every time she got a boo-boo, she'd say it was him!'

Emmett felt his hands tightening on the clipboard in his hand. 'You wanna see the pictures of her the last time she got out of the hospital?' he said through clinched teeth.

'Ha!' Reba Sinclair said. 'He told me she faked some photos! She was very devious.'

'But he didn't deny killing her?' Emmett asked.

'The poor baby just had more than he could take! All the things she was saying about him, the way the family acted and the lies they told! And then taking his little girl away from him! It looked like the judge was going to grant Cheryl total custody – with Darby only getting *supervised* visitation! Now how would you take that, Deputy? Would you just sit still for that type of injustice or would you perhaps go just a little bit nuts and act out?' She squared her shoulders and looked off into the distance. 'That's what happened to my Darby. He said he just lost it. Didn't even know he'd done it until it was all over. He said it was like watching someone else doing that, not him.'

Jeez, Emmett thought, how many times had he heard that one? And the thing was, sometimes it was true. Didn't make the perpetrator any less guilty, though. But this time? With Darby Hunt? Naw, he knew exactly what he was doing – just like every other time he hurt her.

Well, he thought, in for a penny, in for a pound. 'Ma'am, I'm just wondering if maybe when he got out, you two got together and he wasn't the man you thought he was—'

'I haven't even seen him yet, Deputy!' she said in a high, loud voice. 'I sent him those presents and he was going to come see me, tonight, as a matter of fact. Tonight we would have consummated our eighteen-month love affair.' She put her face in her hands and began to sob.

Emmett didn't truck with bawling women, so he excused himself and headed back to the shop. Wondering if he actually believed her – or anyone else in this case, truth be known.

Once back at his – Milt's – desk, he picked up the phone and called the state police, asking for the whereabouts of Steve McDaniel, Dave McDaniel's oldest son who used to work for Emmett at the police department in Longbranch. After a bit of a runaround, he was finally put through to Steve.

'Goddam,' Steve said, 'is this really Emmett Hopkins of Longbranch, Oklahoma?'

'In the flesh,' Emmett said, then, 'well, maybe not the flesh, but it's my voice.'

'Getting too literal for me, Emmett. How the hell are you? Calling about Darby Hunt, I betcha,' Steve said.

'I'm fine. And, yeah, I'm calling about Darby Hunt.'

'I didn't kill him,' Steve said. 'If I coulda guaranteed I'd never get caught, I'da done it in a heartbeat, but can't get any guarantees on murdering somebody. Even somebody as evil as Darby Hunt.'

'You think somebody in your family did it?' Emmett asked.

Steve hooted with laughter. 'Jeez, Emmett, what a question! If I did, you think I'd tell you? No, I don't think somebody in my family did it, and you wanna know why?'

'Why?' Emmett asked.

''Cause nobody in my family is that stupid. That asshole gets killed, and who're the first people you look at? My family, that's who!'

'Your cousin Malcolm didn't seem all that bright,' Emmett offered.

'Malcolm? Shit, Emmett, he's a little light in the loafers, but there's not a mean bone in that boy's body. He's a good kid with a homophobe for a dad. Don't make him out to be a murderer, for God's sake! Actually, he's the least likely in my family to do it, and I don't believe we're living an Agatha Christie novel here,' Steve said.

'Huh?'

'Don't you read? Agatha Christie, the great English mystery writer? It was always the least likely suspect who did it.' He sighed at Emmett's ignorance. 'Anyway, Malcolm didn't do it.'

'OK, who's the most likely suspect?' Emmett asked.

'Well, me, of course!' Steve laughed. 'Look, Emmett, it's been a blast talking to you and all, but I got a shit-pile of work here. Good luck. When you find the hero who did this, let's pin a medal on him, OK?' And with that, he hung up.

Dalton needed to go do a security check at the little mall in Jasper. One of the stores' alarms had gone off in the middle of the night but when Anthony had responded to the alarm (he'd been on-call), nothing was out of the way. Emmett told Anthony to go on home and that he'd have it checked out the next day. Well, today was the next day and Dalton was the one doing the checking. He wasn't crazy about this particular chore, since he wasn't that up on electronic things, but he'd do it, and stay on it until it was done right, even if it took a day or two.

Once at the mall – a square of shops opening on to an open-air courtyard with a fountain, with parking at the back of the stores – the first thing Dalton saw was a jewelry store. With that incentive, he was able to fix the problem with the alarm in less than an hour, and five minutes later was standing in front of a cabinet full of engagement rings.

'She's got real small hands,' Dalton said in answer to the clerk's question of what size his soon-to-be fiancée wore. Dalton looked at the ring of ring sizes, comparing them to his own large hand. He'd looked at her fingers entwined with his enough to know exactly what size they were. He picked it out first try. Then the clerk, a woman even older than his mother, wanted to know what size diamond.

'Well, I want it big enough to show off, but not so big it looks showy, you know?'

'How's this?' the clerk asked, holding up a one-and-a-half-karat pear-shaped solitaire already set in a gold band. 'Very traditional,' she said.

Dalton peaked at the price tag. 'Maybe a one karat, forget about the half?' he suggested to the clerk. 'She's not traditional, and she doesn't wear a lot of gold. Mostly she wears silver.'

'How about this?' the clerk said, pulling out a baguette one karat. 'This is platinum rather than silver, but they match in color.'

It was really beautiful, Dalton thought, but it just wasn't Holly. And then he saw it. It was in another case, the one next to the engagement rings. 'That one!' he said.

The clerk raised her eyebrows. 'This one?' she said, going to the next display case and opening it. She put her hand on the ring and Dalton nodded. 'Son, this isn't a traditional engagement ring—'

'Holly's not traditional,' he said, smiling at the clerk. 'She's one of a kind.'

The clerk smiled back. 'Well, so is this ring. It was made by the owner's son and it's been in that display cabinet for five years.' She brought it out and handed it to Dalton. Pointing out each facet, she said, 'The center stone is a two-karat ruby, and the surrounding stones are emeralds and diamonds, with opals and other precious stones.'

The stones were in a mound shape, with smaller stones cascading down the silver band. 'This is it,' he said.

The clerk told him a number, and he didn't even flinch. The number was higher than the one-and-a-half-karat diamond, but it didn't matter. This was the one.

NINE

Milt – Day Six

Chief Heinrich had Lance Turner taken down to the medical facility and put in the one locker they had for a possible dead body. Unfortunately he had to share accommodations with Josh Weaver. Jean and Lucy went to get the kids from the children's pavilion. Lucy had volunteered to take Lyssa to their cabin with Janna, while Jean had volunteered to take Rose's youngest,

Jacob to our cabin with Johnny Mac and Early so that Rose could go to Esther's cabin with her. Esther was pretty broken up.

I went with Heinrich to interview Esther, and it wasn't pretty.

'I'm so sorry to bother you at a time like this,' Heinrich said to a still-sobbing Esther, 'but we need to talk.'

Esther used half a box of Kleenex to stop the flow, hiccupped a few times and finally said, 'Whatever.'

Rose sat beside her, her arm around Esther's shoulders.

'Did you see anyone put anything in Mr Turner's glass?' Heinrich asked.

Esther shook her head.

'Was there anyone in a position to do so?' he asked.

She shrugged. 'Me, I guess, and Crystal on the other side of him. She was flirting with him something fierce!' she said, lifting her face up to glare at the chief. 'She probably did it because he wanted to be with me and not her!' Which brought on the sobs again. Then she turned on me. 'And your wife! She could have saved him if she tried! She didn't even try! What kind of doctor is she anyway? Not to even try!'

I started to speak in my lady's defense, but Heinrich put a staying hand on my arm and said, 'When Doctor Kovak' (not what she goes by, but I let it slide), 'smelled the cyanide on Mr Turner's breath, she knew CPR would do no good. Actually, it could have done harm to her – if the poison was on his lips, she could have been poisoned herself. But there would be no way of reviving him from this poison. Do you understand, Mrs Monte?'

Esther gulped in air, steadied herself and said, 'It's Ms Monte. And no, I don't understand. Why would someone do this? What did he ever do to anyone to merit this? He was such a nice guy! You know how hard it is to find a nice guy nowadays? Impossible! Right, Rose?'

Rose just patted her back.

'What did you know about him, Ms Monte?' Heinrich asked.

'Oh, hell, call me Esther. It's easier.' She shrugged and was silent for a moment, then said, 'I don't know. Not much, I guess. He was from Baton Rouge, Louisiana, he said. Never married. Said he was an engineer.' Again she shrugged. She looked up at Heinrich. 'I guess that's not much, huh?'

'It's a start, Esther. Thank you,' Heinrich said, standing up. I followed suit.

As we headed toward the door, Esther said, 'Milt, I'm sorry for what I said about Jean. I didn't even know she was a doctor until she said it when – when . . .'

'No problem, Esther. You get some rest,' I said, and Heinrich and I headed out and back down to the security suite.

He gave Clive Lance Turner's name, his hometown of Baton Rouge, and asked him to do a computer search for next of kin. Then we went in Heinrich's office and took our usual spots.

'So what do you think?' Heinrich asked me.

'Well, I think Turner's dead and somebody killed him, and if this isn't connected to Josh Weaver's murder I'll eat my hat.'

Heinrich's eyebrows rose. 'You don't wear a hat,' he said.

'It's an expression,' I said. 'It means I'm pretty sure this is connected to Josh Weaver's murder.'

'Ah. Yes, as do I. Do you suspect Ms Monte?'

'Esther?' I thought about it then shook my head. 'Naw. Can't see it. I don't think she had anything invested in this guy. I think she's more upset by being that close to a murder victim than it being a guy she may or may not have been sleeping with.'

Again the eyebrows. 'You don't think she was sleeping with him?' he asked.

'Well, kinda hard when you got a little girl with you. And as I understand it, they've got just one of the small cabins.'

'But Turner, I'm sure, had his own cabin.'

'Yeah,' I agreed, 'but that would mean leaving her daughter alone late at night.'

Heinrich gave me a condescending smile. 'It has been known to happen aboard ship, my friend. Often and with gusto.'

I could feel myself turning red. I don't think of myself as naïve, but I think I just came off that way. I'll admit I was a little embarrassed. In an attempt to save face, I said, 'Well, whatever, but I still don't see Esther as our bad guy. If we go with the theory that Turner's and Josh's deaths are linked, why in the world would Esther kill Josh?'

'Because she found out before we told her that he had been tricking her daughter into stealing,' Heinrich said.

'OK, well, write down her name on our suspect list—'

'Do we have a suspect list?' Heinrich asked, sitting up in his chair.

'Well, if you haven't started one I'd suggest you do so now,' I said.

It was his turn to turn red with embarrassment. I felt vindicated.

We were saved from any more one-upmanship by Clive coming in with a laptop. 'Chief!' he said in his English accent. 'I found a Lancelot Turner out of Baton Rouge, Louisiana, USA, who was an engineer. But, sir, he died in 2004.'

He turned the laptop around to show Heinrich and me. There was a picture of Lancelot Turner of Baton Rouge, Louisiana, USA, who was an engineer, and who died in 2004 – a fiftyish African American with a bright smile.

Johnny Mac – Day Six

Johnny Mac's mom told the three boys, Johnny Mac, Early and little Jacob, Rose's son, that Jacob was staying with them because his mother was helping Lyssa's mother with something. They took the information at face value and went in the suite to play with the toys Johnny Mac and Early had brought with them on the ship. Johnny Mac and Early were getting a little tired of the same old toys, but they were all new to Jacob, who was happy as a clam and only needed the bigger boys to tell him what something did or how to make it do what it did. The bigger boys were happy to oblige.

They'd been playing for about fifteen minutes when Johnny Mac's mom got a phone call. She talked for just a minute, then came in their part of the suite and said, 'I have to go out for a bit. You three stay right here. Do you understand?'

'Yes, ma'am,' all three boys said, almost in unison.

Johnny Mac's mom pointed her index finger at them and said, 'Stay!' Johnny Mac gave her a look and she laughed as she walked out the door.

'What's wrong with your mom's legs?' Jacob asked once she was gone.

'She had polio when she was a kid,' Johnny Mac answered.

'What's polio?' asked Jacob.

Johnny Mac shrugged. 'I dunno really. It's something they used to have a lot back in the olden days, but now it's all gone.'

'So what she has isn't catching?' Jacob asked.

Johnny Mac sighed. 'No!' he said. 'That's just dumb!'

'Well, I didn't know!' Jacob said rather loudly.

'So, Jacob,' Early said. 'I'm real sorry Josh and your brother made you do that – stealing that money, I mean.'

Jacob, who had confessed his participation in the mugging of Clifford Dunne to the other kids while at the children's pavilion, looked down at the toys so the two older boys wouldn't see the tears that stung his eyes. He shrugged his shoulders. 'Not your fault,' he said.

'I know,' Early said. 'I'm just sorry they did that to you.'

'Me, too,' Johnny Mac said.

'It was awful,' Jacob said in a small voice. 'The guy smelled awful and there was throw-up on his clothes and snot and boogers, too. He was really gross. And I think he peed himself.'

'Ooo,' both boys said in unison.

'That's seriously gross,' Johnny Mac said.

'Absolutely!' Early agreed.

'Not only that, but I knew it was wrong,' Jacob said, his voice showing the signs of tears being shed. 'My mom taught me and Trip both not to steal, but Trip thought this whole thing was just a big joke! I don't think it was funny. 'Cause now Josh is dead and I think it's my fault!'

Johnny Mac and Early looked at each other, then Johnny Mac said, 'Why do you think that?'

'Because I said his name real loud! Him and Trip were making fun of me, him mostly, and I said real loud, 'Josh Weaver! You stop laughing at me!' And I think the drunk guy might have heard me. When he got sobered up, I bet the man remembered what I said and went after Josh.' Jacob began to cry.

Johnny Mac put his arm around Jacob's shoulders and started with what was now his old standby, 'There, there.'

Early said, 'Johnny Mac, you think we should tell your dad this?' Which just made Jacob cry all the harder.

'He'll arrest me!' he managed to get out between sobs.

'No, he won't,' Johnny Mac said. 'Even if that drunk man did hear you and he *did* kill Josh, it's not your fault! You had nothing to do with Josh getting killed. Whoever killed him is responsible for all of it, plain and simple.'

Early looked at his friend with admiration, and Jacob looked up with hope in his eyes. 'You think?' Jacob asked in a small voice.

'Absolutely!' Johnny Mac said, with all the confidence of a young man who was the son of a steely-eyed sheriff.

Milt – Day Six

Jean called me from Esther's cabin. 'I called in a sedative to the clinic on A level. Could you pick it up and bring it to Esther's cabin on your way back?'

'Sure. You left the boys alone?' I asked.

'I didn't have a choice,' she said, a little defensively, I thought. 'Rose called and said Esther wouldn't stop crying.'

'OK, I'll come back now. I'll get the pills and bring 'em to you, then go see the boys.'

'Well, you'd better. I'm sure one of them is dead by now,' she said in her most sarcastic tone of voice. Then she stopped herself. 'Oh my God. I'm sorry. I can't believe I said that!'

'It's OK, babe, I'm on my way,' I told her, hung up and said to Chief Heinrich, 'I gotta go take care of business. I'll be in my cabin if you need me—'

'Wait!' Heinrich said, jumping to his feet and almost knocking over Clive and his laptop.

'What?' I said, my hand on the doorknob.

'Exactly! What now? Turner wasn't who he said he was! The plot, as they say, thickens! So what do I do now? Remember, this is what you call your bailiwick, Kovak, not mine! I run a tight and smooth-sailing ship. I do not solve murders!'

'Get him fingerprinted and send the fingerprints to the FBI database. Might take a while to get results. Ask them to also run a sheet on whoever the prints belong to; kill two birds with one stone that way. My boys are alone so I gotta get to my cabin. Oh, do you have my cell phone number?' He didn't so I gave it to him, then headed out of the security area.

The clinic was at the other end of A level, so I went down there – I could have walked half of Longbranch in the same time! – got the pill; there was just one – and headed to Esther's cabin. She was on the other side of the ship from us, but it was starboard to port, not bow to stern, so it wasn't that far.

Jean opened the door when I knocked on it. 'Here you go,' I said, handing her the little packet with the pill in it.

'Thanks, honey,' she said. 'And I'm sorry about that crack—'

'Forget about it,' I said, leaned inside and kissed her lovely mouth. 'I'm off to find the boys now.'

I left and headed to the port (or the starboard, I have no idea, but I like to pretend that I do) side of the ship, and to our suite. The boys were sitting on my bed, lined up like little peas in a pod, their legs dangling off into space.

'Hey, guys,' I said upon entering the suite.

'Boy, Dad, am I glad to see you!' Johnny Mac said, jumping down from the bed and coming to take my hand. 'Sit here,' he said, indicating Jean's bed. I sat and Johnny Mac went back over to sit next to little Jacob, who was sitting in the middle of the two bigger boys. 'Jacob has something he needs to tell you about, Dad. Just listen, OK? It's not Jacob's fault, and I think you'll understand that once you hear the whole thing, 'k?'

'OK,' I said, wondering what new horror awaited.

Jacob took a deep breath and said, 'When Josh and Trip were making me take that money from that man, Josh was teasing me and—' He looked at Johnny Mac, who nodded his encouragement. 'And I said something like, "Josh Weaver, you stop that." I'm not sure exactly what I said, but I know I used his whole name.' And then he clammed up.

I nodded my head for him to go on, but nothing happened. Finally I said, 'Is that it?'

'Yeah,' Johnny Mac said, stretching the small word out to at least two syllables. 'That means that man, Mr Dunne? He could have heard Jacob say Josh's *whole* name and so he went after Josh for his money, and Josh wouldn't tell him where it was, so Mr Dunne stabbed him!'

'Then shot him!' Early said.

'Then chopped off his head!' Jacob offered.

'Well,' I said. 'That's good, boys. I'll give this information to Chief Heinrich.' I stood up but the boys still sat on my bed. I sat back down. 'Was there something else?' I asked.

'You gonna call him?' Johnny Mac asked.

'Who?' I asked.

'Chief Heinrich!' Johnny Mac said.

'You mean now?' I asked.

'Well, yeah! This is a good lead, right?' Johnny Mac said.

I looked at the three eager faces. 'You're right son, this is a good lead. And I think it deserves more than a phone call. Let's go down to Chief Heinrich's office and tell him about this in person!' I said, hopefully getting myself out of my son's tiny doghouse.

And so off we went.

Meanwhile, Back In Prophesy County

Emmett picked up the phone and dialed the number for Darby Hunt's home. His mother, whose name was listed on Darby's release papers as 'Elizabeth,' (he remembered Mrs Atkins saying Beth wanted to change her name since she was named after the old bat) answered on the third ring with a resounding, 'What!'

'Mrs Hunt, this is Emmett Hopkins with the sheriff's department—'

'You killed my boy!' she screamed and hung up the phone.

Emmett sighed and sat back in his, or Milt's, swivel chair. Well, that hadn't gone well, he thought. He squared his shoulders and said out loud, 'Nothing to it but to do it,' got up and yelled down the hall to Holly, 'I'm headed to old lady Hunt's house. If I never come back, Holly, you're in charge until Milt returns.'

'Hot damn!' he heard his civilian aid say then giggle. For some reason, Emmett figured she wasn't taking him seriously.

He got in his squad car and headed to the defunct subdivision where Elizabeth Hunt lived. Fancy name, Emmett thought, for such a cranky old bitch. He got out of the car, walked up to the porch and rang the bell. There was no sound of movement from the inside. He knocked with his fist. Still no sound of movement. Then from behind him he heard the unmistakable sound of the cocking of a shotgun. He turned slowly around, his hands well away from the forty-five caliber that rested on his hip.

'Hey, Miz Hunt,' he said to the old lady whose body was balanced against her walker, but whose shotgun was snug tight to her shoulder and chin. 'How you doing?' Emmett asked. He was watching her trigger finger. 'Sorry about your boy, but you know we had nothing to do with that. I'm trying to find out who shot him, is what I'm doing.' Eyes on the trigger finger. 'I was hoping you would talk to me about that horrible night, when Darby got shot—'

The finger moved and Emmett hit the deck. The blast blew over his head, taking out a shrub and some brick veneer. She was in the movement of unloading the other barrel when Emmett hit the walker, sending Elizabeth Hunt over backwards. The buckshot went into the air, and Emmett pulled the old lady under the eaves of the house as it came back down to earth. She was hitting him the entire time he was trying to keep her from getting hit by the buckshot.

'You son-of-a-bitch!' she yelled. 'I'm gonna kill you! You killed my boy, now I'm gonna kill you! I'm a good mama!'

Emmett managed to cuff her and call it in. Then he sat down at the open door of his squad car and just watched as she screamed expletive after expletive in his direction. His worse-case scenario regarding Darby Hunt's mama had come true. And he'd lived through it. He grinned. 'Way to go, Emmett,' he said out loud.

Milt – Day Six

Chief Heinrich and Clive were both sitting in the outer office, staring at the fax machine. Nothing was happening in that arena. So I said, 'Excuse us, Chief, but Mr Connelly here has some more information he'd like to share.'

Heinrich stood up and turned to the boys, crossing his arms at his chest. 'Yes, Mr Connelly?'

Jacob looked at Johnny Mac, who nodded encouragement, whispering, 'You can do it, Jacob!'

Turning back to Heinrich, Jacob recited his earlier confession. Heinrich looked at me. 'I think we might want to bring Mr Dunne back in for questioning.'

I gave a stern face. 'In light of this new information, I think we should haul his ass in here and interrogate him,' I said.

Heinrich looked at Jacob. 'Will you be willing to do a line-up, Mr Connelly?' he asked.

Again Jacob turned to Johnny Mac, who again nodded. Back to Heinrich, the boy puffed out his chest and said, 'You bet, sir!'

Then we headed back to the cabin for bedtime.

Milt – Day Seven

The next morning was our last full day at sea, and our last day to figure out who killed Josh Weaver and Lance Turner before the coast guard and Galveston police boarded the ship. I wanted to find out if they were killed by the same person, or to discover if there were two killers aboard. I couldn't imagine that they weren't killed by the same person. If there *were* two killers, maybe Gypsy Cruise Lines should think about doing psychological profiles of their passengers before letting them on-board.

But the two different methods of dispatch had me wondering.

Most killers find a method they like and stick to it, but Josh was strangled and Lance was poisoned. Strangling – even a fourteen-year-old – takes strong hands, and by the marks around Josh's neck, big hands – a man's hands. Poisoning, on the other hand, was historically a woman's method of murder. Lance had been seated at the table between two women: Crystal Weaver and Esther Monte. Crystal had been flirting with Lance and ignoring her heartbroken husband whose son had just been murdered – heartless but not homicidal. Esther, on the other hand, had been fairly loud in landing her flag atop Mount Lancelot – or whoever he was, since we now knew he was not Lancelot Turner, engineer, of Baton Rouge, Louisiana. But if either woman was at fault, where in the hell did they get cyanide on board a ship in the middle of the Caribbean?

Maybe Esther had meant the poison for the flirty Crystal rather than her new hunk Lance. Or – and I liked this – Esther found out Lance was not who he said he was and had done something to uncover who he really was and what he was after. Like maybe he was a private detective undercover as a passenger to find dirt on Esther for something. Esther had said she'd used all her savings to come on this trip – how did I know this was true? What did any of our group really know about each other? With the exception of the Weavers and the Tulias? And I just had their words for that. The only thing I really knew about Esther was that she had a daughter named Lyssa. There was no doubting Lyssa was her daughter – they were practically doubles. I think I could accept on face value that she was from Atlanta, because she told us this in front of Lyssa and most kids would say, 'Atlanta? No, Mom, we're from Cleveland,' if it had been a fib.

But did Esther ever mention where she worked? What if she worked in a bank? Embezzled a million bucks, bank was about to find out so she jumped on this ship to . . . to . . . What? Sail to Puerto Rico, a US territory that didn't even need an extradition treaty? If so, why didn't she stay there? Hell, why would she get back on the ship after being safely delivered to the Cayman Islands? Surely there were small islands around the Caymans without extradition treaties with the US. And besides, if the Caymans were such a good place to stash money, maybe they didn't have an extradition treaty themselves.

This wasn't working.

OK, Crystal. Obviously a gold-digger, because I couldn't possibly see love-at-first-sight on her part, and it was pretty obvious Vern was loaded. But why would she kill Josh? He seemed to be accepting her now, even though they'd had problems early on. And what about Lance? I wasn't buying Esther's theory that Crystal was jealous of her and killed Lance over that; and even if that were true, wouldn't Crystal kill Esther and not Lance? And besides, let's face it, Esther was a nice lady, and not bad-looking, but between the two – and I'm speaking strictly as a man here, not as a human being – Crystal had her beat hands down. OK, mostly it was her outward appearance – OK, it was definitely ALL her outward appearance, even if my wife did say Crystal was stuck in the seventies with what Jean called 'her Farrah do.' Whatever, the long red tresses looked good to me. I'm pretty sure the breasts weren't real, but that hardly stopped most men – some even encouraged their women to get boob jobs – from drooling over a flashy woman like Crystal. It didn't make sense that Crystal would kill Lance.

I decided I needed sustenance and woke up the family for breakfast. I decided on quantity over quality and took the boys to the buffet line at the food court, while Jean took a book with her to the dining room – with a wide smile on her face.

So I got about four eggs scrambled, with hash browns, seven rashers of bacon, four sausage patties and four sausage links, a thick slice of ham, a waffle, two pancakes, biscuits and gravy, and some fruit – to make it a healthy breakfast. The boys plowed through their own version of a healthy breakfast that consisted of a lot of stuff that needed a whole lot of syrup. Then the three of us headed to the children's pavilion.

I signed the boys in and then the three of us sat at a table in the indoor part of the pavilion and played card games – mostly Uno, which to me was just a fancier version of the old Crazy 8 we used to play as kids. I was down three games (we'd only played three – Johnny Mac won one and Early won the other two) when Mike came in with Janna and Lyssa. I was glad to see him. I stood up, surprised my knees still worked after sitting for so long on the kiddy chair at the kiddy table. Mike said Lyssa had spent the night as her mother was still upset and needed some alone time. I knew that Rose had come by rather late last night to get Jacob, and I had helped her carry the boy back to their cabin. One of the girls took my seat, the other the fourth unoccupied seat, and they proceeded to wipe the boys' butts with their gamesmanship (or would that be gameswomanship – I try to stay current, but sometimes it's hard), while Mike and I stepped out into the food court, grabbed some coffee and took a table.

'So what the hell's going on, Milt?' Mike asked.

I shook my head. 'You got me,' I said. 'I don't get it. Somebody kills Josh, then kills Lance? Why? And why use two different methods of murder?'

'Damn, I hadn't thought about that!' Mike said. 'But you're right! They did! I mean, Josh was strangled, right?' I nodded. 'And then Lance was poisoned. That's not common, right? To use two different forms of murder like that? Right?'

'Right,' I said. 'That's not the norm.'

'So does that mean there are two killers?' Mike asked.

I shook my head. 'I don't see how that's possible. On a ship this size? How could there be? They've got to be connected.'

'You think Esther did it?' he said, his body language saying I only had to agree for him to pounce on the idea.

I shrugged. 'She had the opportunity, but why would she do it? They seemed to be getting on fine—'

'No, now, did you hear her?' Mike said. 'She got kinda loud with old Crystal when she thought Crystal was flirting with him.'

'Crystal *was* flirting with him,' I said. 'And in that case, wouldn't she try to poison Crystal, not Lance?'

'I guess,' Mike said, slightly dejected.

I stood up. 'You can stay with the kids?' I asked. 'I've got to go talk to Heinrich.'

'Yeah, I've got this shift,' he said, and I headed down to security.

Milt – Day Seven

Either Heinrich washed his uniform a lot, or he had a bunch of those navy uniforms he wore, because the one he had on today was so bright I needed shades when I walked into his office.

He stood and shook my hand as I approached his desk. 'Sheriff, glad you could join us again today.'

'My pleasure,' I said. 'Did you ever get back word on our Lance's fingerprints?'

He turned the top piece of paper on his desk around so that I could see. Front and center was our Lance's smiling face staring back at me. It said: 'WANTED: Joseph Mooreland Kinder, aka Ken Mooreland, aka Joe Moore, aka Jose Mendicino, aka Lando Josephs; for the crime(s) of embezzlement, three counts; extortion, three counts; assault and battery, two counts; attempted murder, one count. Wanted for questioning in: Harris County, Texas; Montgomery County, Maryland; Queens County, New York; Marin County, California.'

'Esther doesn't know how lucky she is,' I said.

'Yes, it appears someone did her a favor,' Heinrich said, a bit of something in his voice.

'And you're saying?' I asked.

He shrugged. 'I'm just wondering why someone would do Ms Monte such a huge favor.'

'Well, to be fair, I kinda doubt this had anything to do with Esther.'

'I would never before have considered you naïve, Sheriff Kovak,' he said.

Kinda pissed me off. 'I don't consider myself naïve either, Chief Heinrich,' I said.

'No? Let me see: First she didn't do it, then she's a virgin—'

'Hey now!' I said, standing up. 'I never said that – I didn't even imply that! For Christ's sake, the woman has a nine-year-old child! All I said was I wasn't sure if they'd done the nasty yet. And I'm still not sure. Unless you've asked her, Chief? What did you say? "Oh, Ms Monte, by the way, were you doing the horizontal mambo with the dead guy?"'

'No, Sheriff,' he said, standing up himself, 'I said, and I quote, "Were you and Mr Turner intimate?" to which she replied, "Yes, we were."'

'Well, OK then,' I said, sitting back down.

'Yes,' Heinrich said, taking his seat back.

So we sat there not staring at each other.

'So what am I being naïve about this time?' I asked him.

He shrugged his shoulders. 'Maybe I'm just being too aggressive. I was implying that Ms Monte killed Kinder herself.'

'Kinder? Oh, Lance. Right.' I shrugged back. 'I just don't see it,' I said. We were quiet for a moment. Finally, I sighed a big one. 'You think we're at each other's throats because neither of us has any idea who killed Josh Weaver or Lance Turner, and we don't even know if they were killed by the same guy or not?'

'Has to be the same guy,' Heinrich said, looking desperate.

'Then why two methods of murder?' Damn, I kept harping on that. Why was I harping on that? Did it mean something? If so, what the hell did it mean?

Heinrich shook his head. 'Convenience?' he offered.

'How so?' I asked.

He shrugged. 'All he/she had when he/she killed Josh was his/her own hands, but when it came time to kill Lance, he/she had somehow gotten his/her hands on the poison.'

I swear to God I'd never heard a person actually talk like that – the whole his-slash-her business. But I just said, 'How? Where? Did you check with your clinic? Do they keep cyanide in stock?' I asked.

'Yes and no. Yes I checked with them, and no they don't keep cyanide on hand.'

'So what are the uses for cyanide, other than killing somebody?' I asked.

Heinrich shrugged. 'I remember in the past, when the drug Laetrile was being used as a cancer cure, it came out that the same ingredients in cyanide were also used in Laetrile.'

I nodded. 'Yeah. That sounds familiar. And I remember when I was a kid I used to love to eat peach pits, and my father made me stop, said they'd poison me. That's cyanide, right?'

'I believe it is in the pits of many fruits, peaches and apricots, and others.'

'So why would someone have cyanide on-board ship?'

He shook his head. 'This I do not know.'

'So now, should we tell Esther Monte who Lance really was?' I asked, since I was thinking we should.

Heinrich shook his head. 'I would rather hold off on that for now,' he said. 'Until I'm more sure that Ms Monte is not somehow involved in this man's death.'

My turn to shake my head. Pushing myself up, I said, 'I'll bet you ten bucks she's not.'

He stood up and held out his hand; I took it to shake. He grinned.

'I accept your bet,' he said. I didn't have the heart to tell him I wasn't serious, but by the grin on his face, I think he might have already figured that out.

TEN

Meanwhile, Back In Prophesy County

Emmett called Dalton to come to Darby Hunt's former residence and allowed him the pleasure of getting the old biddy into his squad car. Emmett followed Dalton to the station.

'Put her in the interrogation room,' he told Dalton. 'And make sure she's secured – as many restraints as appears necessary.' This was a formidable woman, and he didn't want her breaking through her restraints and going for his jugular.

'Yes, sir,' Dalton said as he helped the old lady navigate with her walker and her cuffed-together wrists. At this point, Emmett didn't care how bad it looked; the woman was a menace.

He went to his office and sat down at his – Milt's – desk and called Holly on the intercom. 'We got anything harder than coffee around here?' he asked.

'No, but I can put some chocolate in your coffee – double the caffeine?' she suggested.

'Sounds better than nothing,' Emmett said and disconnected. Then sat there dreading the interview to come. She wouldn't tell him squat, he knew that. Even if she knew who killed Darby, she wouldn't tell him. There had to be a way to play her. He envied Milt that skill – that innate knowledge he had on how to play a person to get the right information. Emmett had never been good at that. As police chief of Longbranch, he'd left that kind of stuff to his staff. He'd gotten the job of police chief straight out of the academy. He'd been an MP in the army, gone to the academy and was the oldest graduate of his class. Those two things had led the desperate city council of Longbranch, who'd been without a chief for nearly a year, to recruit him. He'd remained police chief for twenty-something years. Until all hell broke loose.

So, no, he didn't have that skill. That skill of playing a perp, of getting the information needed by a few key questions dropped in the right spots. Unfortunately, neither did Dalton, who was the only deputy in the office at the moment. Nita didn't come in until the late shift, and Anthony was out in the west part of the county trying to figure out why anyone in Oklahoma would want to rustle sheep.

Holly came in with his doctored coffee and he took a sip. Hum, he thought, not bad. He drank the rest of it, sighed so deep his toes tingled, and stood up. Time to face the beast, he thought.

The Prophesy County Sheriff's Department interrogation room was next to the break room, across the bullpen from the wing where his and Milt's offices were located. He crossed in front of the bullpen, where he got a hearty salute from Holly, to the hall that led to the cells, and straight to the interrogation room.

Elizabeth Hunt was sitting in a straight-back chair, her walker between the chair and the table, leaning her head on the padded arm of her walker.

'Ma'am,' Emmett said as he walked in.

No response.

'Ma'am?' he said a little louder.

Still no response.

Oh, shit, Emmett thought. She's up and died on me.

'Ma'am?' He tried again, this time touching her arm.

She reared back like a bucking bronco and shouted, 'Don't you touch me!'

Emmett went around the table to sit opposite her. 'Miz Hunt, we need to talk,' he said.

'I ain't talking to the likes of you!' she spat out. 'You killed my boy!'

'No, ma'am, I didn't kill your boy. We don't know who did, but we're trying to find out—'

'Bullshit! You killed him! I saw you! You did it!' she shouted.

Uh oh, Emmett thought. Maybe she's not playing with a full deck. 'Miz Hunt, do you know what day it is?' he asked.

She glared at him. 'What's that got to do with the price of tea in China?'

'Just answer, please, ma'am.'

'What was the question?'

'What day is it?'

'The day after you shot my boy! That's what goddam day it is, you asshole!' She touched her nose. 'You trying to kill me, too?' she shouted. 'Where's my oxygen?'

'Ma'am? You're on oxygen?' Emmett asked.

'Goddamit! I can't breathe! Where's my oxygen?' she shouted, her breathing getting more agitated.

Emmett ran to the door and opened it, calling to Holly, 'We got any oxygen around here?'

'Not that I know of,' Holly said, jumping up from her seat. 'You need an ambulance?'

'Yeah, do that now.' Turning, he called, 'Dalton!'

Dalton high-tailed it to where Emmett stood in the doorway. 'Can you get back in Miz Hunt's house?'

'Yes, sir. Door's still open, I reckon.'

'Go in, look for any oxygen equipment and bring it back here, got it? And move!'

'Yes, sir!' Dalton said, and jogged off to the exit and his squad car.

Dalton had barely gotten out of the parking lot before the ambulance pulled in. Holly was in the room with Mrs Hunt so Emmett ran outside to show them in.

When they got back into the interrogation room, Holly had the old lady breathing more calmly, although she was still wheezing a bit. The paramedics got her on oxygen and started their business.

'We need to explain to these boys that she ain't going to the hospital!' Emmett told Holly.

She nodded. 'I'll handle it,' she said. And Emmett knew she could. Even dressed as she was – hair in two small ponytails on the top of her head, each ponytail a different color with one red and one blue, full gothic make-up, a Grateful Dead T-shirt tied in a knot at her waist and black leggings under a pink tutu – the girl commanded respect as well as attention. And then there was the whole lust factor. The paramedics would listen to her for one of those three reasons, and Emmett didn't really care which one.

Johnny Mac – Day Seven

Johnny Mac was really impressed with Janna, as though he hadn't already been impressed enough. She was beating the snot out of Early in Uno. Every time she threw down a draw two card in front of him she laughed, and Johnny Mac couldn't help beaming at her. He failed to notice the unhappy looks coming his way from Early.

When the second game Janna won was over, Lyssa, who hadn't been paying that much attention, said, 'I want to go see my mom.' Her voice was dejected.

Early said, 'I was real sorry to hear about Mr Turner. He seemed like a nice enough guy.'

Lyssa shrugged. 'He was OK, I guess. And yeah, it's sad. But I'm worried about my mom. I really want to see her.'

'Then why don't you?' Johnny Mac said.

Lyssa looked at Janna, who said, 'My mom said Lyssa needed to stay away for a little while. But if it was my mom, I'd want to go see her, too.'

Johnny Mac looked out the glass walls of the children's pavilion at Mr Tulia, Janna's father, drinking coffee and working at what looked to Johnny Mac like a crossword puzzle. And he had an idea.

'Janna, why don't you go keep your dad busy, while Early and I sneak Lyssa to her mom's cabin?' Johnny Mac said.

Janna grinned. 'I'd rather be the one sneaking her in, but as he's *my* dad, I guess I'm the one to keep him busy. And I know just what to do! Watch for this signal,' she said, pulling at her earlobe. 'When you see me do that, haul butt!'

Milt – Day Seven

So, OK, I wasn't going to mention to Esther Monte that Lance wasn't who he said he was, or tell her who he actually was, but that didn't mean I couldn't interview her again. By this time, she should be somewhat calmed down, I thought. So I knocked on her cabin door.

She opened it, still in her nightgown, with a robe hastily thrown on but not tied, the flimsy material showing a little more of Esther Monte than my wife would have preferred. Her hair was sticking out in several directions, mascara was smeared on her face, globs of stuff at the inside corners of her eyes, and that white stuff that cakes on your lips when you drool during sleep – all around her mouth. Being a manly man, I didn't gag.

'Sorry if I woke you, Esther,' I said.

'What?' She shook her head. 'I guess.' She turned and walked into her cabin. I followed. 'Rose gave me a sleeping pill last night, or early this morning. I think it was more for her benefit than mine.' She smiled weakly. 'She's a good woman, that Rose. Barely knows me and yet she stayed up with me half the night.'

'Yeah, she seems like a real nice woman,' I said. 'Want me to get you something to drink? Some coffee?'

'Oh, God, yes!' she said. She handed me the phone. 'Order some, please. And some toast. I'm hungry but I can't see myself getting dressed enough to go to the dining room for breakfast.'

I called the room service number on her phone, ordered a coffee and a glass of sweet iced tea, and toast. When they questioned the existence of sweet tea, I simply said, 'Iced tea and several packets of sugar, please.'

Yankees and foreigners know nothing about sweet tea, one of the wonders of the modern world. For those of you who remain uninformed, sweet tea is when you put the sugar in the tea pitcher while the tea is still hot from steeping, stir it till the cows come home, then serve it over ice. It's a kind of sweet you can't get just pouring sugar into a glass of already iced tea.

While we waited, I asked her, 'Are you feeling better this morning?'

She sighed heavily. 'I guess,' she said. 'I still can't believe he's dead.' She looked up at me with large, dark brown eyes swimming in tears, and said, 'Why? What did he ever do to anyone? He was nice to everybody! He was even nice to Rose's in-laws, for Christ's sake! And he treated all the kids like they were his own! He adored Lyssa. I really thought – I mean, I thought—' She gulped back a sob. 'I thought I'd finally met the one!' And she burst into tears and fell face-first onto my last clean shirt. To my shame, all I could do was think about the mascara and eye-boogers and the mouth gunk.

When the knock came at the door, I managed to extract her and stand up to answer it. I'll admit I was weak enough to glance down at my shirt. It was a God-awful mess.

At the door was the steward with our order. He brought in the tray and laid it on the small dressing table. 'My condolences, Ms Monte,' he said, which just got her started up again.

I whisked him out of the cabin and sat back down on the bed

and began patting her back. 'Esther, you gotta buck up. There are questions that have to be answered.'

Rubbing her eyes with her fists, like a little kid, she finally looked up at me and said, 'Like what?'

First I handed her the cup of coffee and some sweetener and added sugar to my tea, stirring it with my finger since the steward hadn't seen fit to bring an iced-tea spoon – or any utensil for that matter.

Finally answering her question, I said, 'Like, did anyone have a problem with Lan—'

'I just told you! He was nice to everybody! And everybody loved him!'

'Well, somebody didn't!' I said. She looked at me like I'd just stepped on her puppy. Which I suppose I sorta had. 'I'm sorry, Esther, but the man's dead. And somebody poisoned him.'

'Could the poison have been meant for someone else?' she asked. 'Like Crystal?' Then her eyes got real big. 'Yes! Can't you just imagine how many people want to kill Crystal? Like Lucy Tulia, for one!'

'Lucy?' I said. 'Why in the world would Lucy—'

'Because Crystal was after her man, that's why!' Esther said.

'What makes you say—'

'Because I saw Crystal coming on to Mike! And I heard him flirting back, that's why!'

'When was this?' I asked her.

'Right before Josh went missing,' she said. 'You and Jean had gone to your cabin early – I think Jean was sick of us, and who could blame her?'

'Oh, no, I don't—'

'Please,' she said and gave me a look. I shut up. 'Anyway, Vern and Crystal had gone back to their cabin, which just left Lucy and Mike and Rose and me. We three ladies went to the bathroom together—'

'Yeah!' I interrupted. 'Why do y'all do that?'

She gave me another look, which I guess I deserved, and went on, '—which left Mike alone. I was the first one to come out and Mike wasn't at the table. Then I heard his voice by the entrance to the club right there?' she said, and I nodded to show I knew where she meant. 'And I looked and saw Crystal with him. Vern must have gone to sleep and she'd snuck out. Her back was to the wall, her arm was extended around Mike's neck, one knee up rubbing his thigh, and he was leaning forward, one arm supporting himself against the wall, and the other, well, it appeared to be wandering.'

'Shit,' I said.

'Yeah, I know,' Esther said. 'I was hoping that like you and Jean, those two were an exception to the rule.'

'What makes you think Jean and I are?' I asked out of curiosity.

'Have you ever seen the way the two of you look at each other?' she said, then laughed slightly. 'I guess not. Hard to see the look on your own face.'

I nodded. 'Glad you noticed. I think we are definitely an exception to the rule. So,' I said, clearing my throat, 'did they notice you?'

'Not until I said, "Cut it out!" in a loud whisper. I could see Lucy and Rose coming out of the bathroom.'

'So what happened?'

'Mike turned white and moved away and Crystal just laughed, patted his junk and moved away. The girls didn't see her.'

'Patted his junk?' I repeated.

'It means—'

'I know what it means. It just seems kinda—'

'Gross? Yeah. Even Mike seemed taken aback by it.'

Well, shit, I thought. I was not happy. Now I was going to have to interrogate Mike, and I had begun to think of him as a sorta friend. Shit.

Meanwhile, Back In Prophesy County

Since Holly seemed to have such a calming effect on Elizabeth Hunt, Emmett decided to let her do the interview. Back in the closet where they kept the stationery was also where they kept all the seldom-used equipment they'd purchased over the years. Emmett remembered, when he first signed on with the sheriff's department, Milt showing off some of the goodies stored there. One of the goodies was a communication system: a mic and an ear bud. So when Dalton was back with Mrs Hunt's canister of oxygen and her cannula, Emmett made him sit with her while he took Holly to the bullpen.

'This,' he said, showing her the ear bud, 'goes in your ear so you can hear me. What I want to do is give you questions to ask her; and then you repeat them to her. And I'll hear the answers through the interrogation room's audio system.'

'You go in the break room and talk in the walkie,' Holly said, 'so I can see if I can hear you.'

He nodded and moved to the break room. Staring out the window in the door, he pushed the button on the hand-held walkie and said, 'If you can hear me hold up three fingers.'

Looking through the glass-topped door of the break room he could see her with three raised fingers. 'If you can hear me, give me the one finger you'd like to use the most.'

Grinning, Holly held up her middle finger.

'Well played, Miss Humphries,' he said into the walkie. 'Well played.'

Johnny Mac – Day Seven

Johnny Mac, Early and Lyssa went to the outdoor part of the children's pavilion and waited until the pavilion babysitter was looking the other way, then jumped over the fence onto the deck. They scurried around the deck to a door which led to the food court, which was quite close to the corridor that led to the pool area. Janna's dad's back was to them; she glanced their way, then quickly back to her dad, and tugged on her earlobe. They hustled through the door and into the pool area, home free.

The kids hurried through the pool area, down the long promenade to the elevator that took them down two floors to the doorway that led to their cabins. They were quiet and watchful as they made their way towards the cabin Lyssa shared with her mom. So quiet that they were able to hear a conversation going on at the open door of a cabin a few doors away. They slowed on hearing it.

'I love you,' a man's voice said.

'I love you, too, baby,' a woman's voice said.

Lyssa whispered, 'That's Mrs Weaver!'

'That's not their cabin,' Johnny Mac whispered back.

'I know!' Lyssa whispered again, wiggling her eyebrows.

Crystal Weaver must have heard them, because the door to the cabin closed with her on the outside. 'What are you little hellions doing out on your own?' she said, grabbing Johnny Mac by his shirt front. 'I thought your daddy was going to keep y'all under lock and key? Does he even know y'all are off on your own *again*?' She fairly shouted it all, spittle flying everywhere.

'Let me go!' Johnny Mac said, pulling away from her grasp on his shirt.

'Oh no you don't, you little bastard!' she yelled, and grabbed him by the arm.

Lyssa jumped on Crystal's back and began hitting her with her fists. On seeing this, Early gained the courage to try a fairly ineffective karate chop to the arm Crystal was using to hold onto Johnny Mac. As ineffective as it would have been in any other situation, Crystal was not a terribly physical woman, and it was enough – added to the monkey on her back – to make her let go of Johnny Mac and begin swatting at Lyssa, who had begun pulling her hair. The red tresses came off in Lyssa's hands and she fell to the ground.

All this happened just about the time Johnny Mac's father, the sheriff, rounded the corner from Lyssa's mom's cabin.

Milt – Day Seven

I heard all sorts of noise coming from around the corner and coulda sworn some of the voices sounded like kids. I had a bad feeling as I rounded that corner. And I was right. A well-stacked blonde with short, spiky hair stood over Esther's daughter Lyssa, while Early and my son tried to pick the little girl up. Lyssa had something fuzzy in her hands that I didn't immediately recognize.

'What's going on here?' I said to the blonde. She turned to face me, and I recognized her. 'Crystal?'

'I thought you were going to keep these brats locked up? Look what they've done!' she said, touching her head as a tear sprang to her eye.

'Dad! Listen—'

'Don't even start, John!' I said. 'Lyssa, is that Mrs Weaver's . . . ah, hair?'

'Yes, sir,' she said as Early got her to a standing position. She handed me the wig, which I handed to Crystal.

'Thank you,' Crystal said, another tear falling from her eye.

'Ma'am, I suggest you go on to your cabin now,' I said to Crystal, 'while I deal with these children.'

'I hope you do!' she said and stalked off.

I turned to the three kids and pointed in the direction of our suite. 'Our cabin now!'

With both boys holding Lyssa's hands the three charged off, with me following at a slower pace. They were waiting for me at the door, which I unlocked and opened for them to enter. I pointed to Jean's bed. I wanted to sit on my bed, which was closest to the sliding glass doors and meant that the glare would be behind me, giving me a good view of the three miscreants, but giving them a more obscured view of me.

'Why in the hell did you grab Mrs Weaver's wig?' I asked. I mean, I was curious.

'I didn't!' Lyssa exclaimed.

'See, Dad—'

'I'm not talking to you, John,' I said. I never call him John, or at least rarely do it. Only when I'm seriously pissed at him. I could see his whole body slump.

'Early,' I said. 'Please tell me why you were out of the children's pavilion.'

'No, sir,' he said.

I looked at him in surprise. He'd been such a great stool pigeon up to now.

'Why not?' I asked.

'My name is Early Rollins, sir. I don't have a rank, and I don't have a serial number, sir.'

'It's all my fault,' Lyssa said.

Both Johnny Mac and Early said, 'Don't!'

But she just shook her head at them. 'I wanted to see my mom. I was real insistent about it and I talked Early and Johnny Mac into taking me back to my cabin—'

'Why didn't you go by yourself?' I asked, which I thought was a reasonable question.

Lyssa just stared at me. She didn't seem to have an answer for that.

'Dad?' Johnny Mac ventured.

'Yes?' I said.

Johnny Mac took a deep breath. 'OK,' he said. 'Early and I told Lyssa we'd go back with her. We talked Janna into keeping her dad busy and, when the babysitter wasn't looking, we hopped over the fence onto the deck.' He took another deep breath. 'It was all my idea and all my fault.'

'Well,' I said, 'I hope you're ready to give up your plans for college.'

'Huh?' he said.

'Just kidding,' I said. 'But when we get back home you're grounded for a month, and I'm serious about that.'

He sighed. 'Yes, sir,' he said.

As I started to get up, Lyssa said, 'Don't you want to know what we found out about Mrs Weaver?'

I settled back down. 'Other than her being a blonde, you mean?'

Lyssa waved her hand at me, a gesture I'd seen her mother use a dozen times on this cruise. 'Oh, that's nothing compared to what we heard!'

'OK,' I said. 'Give.'

'Well, we saw a lady's backside sticking out of an open cabin door, and then we heard this male voice say, "I love you" and she – Mrs Weaver – said, "I love you, too, baby." Just like that!'

'How did you know it was Mrs Weaver?' I asked.

'I recognized her voice,' Lyssa said. 'And I told Johnny Mac who it was, but I whispered and he whispered back, but still she must have heard, because she turned around and the man she was talking to – the man who *loved* her' – (and here she made a face and exaggerated the word 'love') – 'slammed the door to the cabin and she started screaming at us—'

'And then she grabbed my shirt,' Johnny Mac picked up the narrative, 'but I pulled away, and then—'

'She grabbed Johnny Mac's arm—' Early said.

'And then I jumped on her back—' Lyssa said.

'And starting hitting her and I karate-chopped her arm—' Early said.

'And she let me go!' Johnny Mac said.

'But then she started hitting at Lyssa—' Early said.

'And I started pulling her hair,' Lyssa said. Then all three calmed down. And Lyssa finished with a big grin. 'And that's when her wig came off in my hand and I fell down.'

I sighed. I didn't know what I was going to do with these kids. They were ignoring orders from their parents, running wild on the ship, pulling people's wigs off and all sorts of stuff. Standing up,

I said, 'You boys stay here. If either of you step out that door,' I said, pointing at said door, 'the next bed you see will be in one of Chief Heinrich's holding cells.' Turning to the girl, I said, 'Lyssa, I'll walk you to your mom's cabin.'

With that, I left the suite, hoping I wasn't going to have to break Jean's cardinal rule and beat my son.

Milt – Day Seven

I didn't have the heart to tell Esther Monte what her daughter had been up to. I just knocked on the door, said, 'Somebody wants to see you,' and ushered Lyssa in and shut the door behind her. Then headed back to the cabin. Halfway there I ran into Mike Tulia and his daughter Janna.

'Jeez, Milt! They got away. With the help of a co-conspirator!' he said, giving his daughter a dangerous look.

'I found them,' I said. 'The boys are in the cabin for the rest of the cruise and Lyssa is with her mother.'

'Yeah, well, I'm taking this one to her mother! Lucy's the disciplinarian in the family.' He looked down at Janna. 'You're in for it now, girl,' he said.

Janna did not look happy.

'Meet you at the bar in half an hour?' I said to Mike.

'No sweat. Make it fifteen,' he said, and headed off towards their cabin.

Since I had the boys and Jean and I were separated, she had her phone on her, so I called, wondering where she was. She picked up on the third ring. 'Umm?' she said.

'Where are you?' I asked.

'Having a massage at the spa. After this I'm having a facial.'

'I didn't win it for you at bingo, so now I'm paying for it?'

'Exactly!' she said with a laugh.

'OK. That's good. I've still got some business to take care of. The boys snuck out of the pavilion again, but I found them and they're currently under house arrest.'

I could tell by her voice that she'd shaken off the masseuse and was half sat up. 'Are they OK? Who's watching them?'

'They're fine, and no babysitter this time. I told them if I caught them out again, I'd have Chief Heinrich put them in his holding cells until we got to Galveston.'

'God, you're a mean man,' she said, her voice – and presumably her body – calming down.

'Enjoy yourself,' I said and hung up. Now I had to deal with Mike, and it wasn't going to be fun.

I made it to the bar and ordered a light beer. My jeans were getting a little tight; I figured it was from the regular beers I'd been drinking aboard ship. It couldn't have anything to do with my dining-room antics – the food was free; therefore, no calories.

Mike joined me in less than the allotted fifteen minutes. 'Jeez, these kids! I don't know what to do with the little shits!' he said.

'I told mine that one more incident and I was having Heinrich put them in a holding cell,' I said.

Mike shook his head. 'One of the girls would just find a way to break them out.'

I laughed, then sobered. 'Listen, Mike,' I said. 'I heard something I need to confirm with you.'

'What's that?' he asked, being handed a full-bodied bottle of Corona with a lime wedge on top.

'I heard it through the grapevine that you and Crystal spent some alone time together.'

Mike choked on his Corona. 'Shit. That's no grapevine, that's Esther, right?'

'Yeah. She mentioned seeing the two of you together.'

Mike sighed big time. 'We weren't "together" together, if you know what I mean. Crystal snuck back to the bar after Vern went to sleep, pulled me into that foyer to the comedy club and got frisky.' He sighed again. 'OK, I thought about it. She was coming on to me big time – God only knows why – and I thought about it – a lot. But then I kept thinking about what you said, you know?'

I frowned. 'What did I say?' I asked him.

'You know, about losing everything for a piece of ass. And it's true. Just because she's got a nice outside doesn't mean the sex would be any better than what I've already got. 'Cause what I've already got is pretty damn good. And just when I was thinking that, along comes Esther and makes it look like I only stopped because I got caught. And I swear, Milt, that's not the case.'

'So you haven't been seeing her before this trip?'

The look on his face was total confusion. 'Huh?' he said. Then, 'Shit, no! I didn't even meet her until the morning of the cruise. Lucy and I stood up for them at the wedding. I knew she had to be a knockout, 'cause why else would Vern dump his wife of twenty years? I mean, he and Lois always seemed really tight.' He shook his head. 'See? Perfect example of your theory about losing everything over a piece of ass! He lost custody of his boys, he lost his house he'd paid millions for, and he lost his best friend – Lois. All for plastic boobs and a red dye job.'

I looked at Mike with new respect. 'It's not a dye job, it's a wig,' I said.

'No shit?' He laughed. 'I wonder if Vern even knows that?'

I held up my bottle of Bud Light and said, 'Here's to our wives; may they always have us by the balls.'

He grinned and clinked his Corona to my Bud Lite. 'Amen, brother,' he said.

ELEVEN

Meanwhile, Back In Prophesy County

The break room doubled as the observation room, so no one was allowed to use the soda machine while a suspect was being interrogated. Emmett put the 'in-use' sign on the glass window of the break room, popped a dollar in the soda machine and got himself a Dr Pepper, turned on the sound from the interrogation room and sat down at the break table. Holly was already talking to Mrs Hunt.

'So sorry about your oxygen, Miz Hunt,' she said. 'I wish we'd known!'

'I tried to tell that sheriff of y'alls, but he wouldn't listen to me!' the old biddy said.

Holly laughed. 'Well, you know men!' she said.

'Don't I, though. Hell, Darby was just like his father. That man had a lump of coal for a heart, I'm telling you the truth.'

'Good,' Emmett said into the walkie. 'Keep her talking about her husband.'

'So what happened to your husband?' Holly asked.

Elizabeth Hunt grinned like the Cheshire cat. 'I killed him,' she said.

'I'm thinking her elevator don't go to the top floor,' Emmett said.

'How so?' Holly asked, with a quirk of her head.

'Fed him to death! The man did love a breaded and fried pork chop! Mashed 'taters, chicken-fried steak, fried chicken, rice casserole, macaroni and cheese. Sometimes all in the same meal, come a Sunday. We used to do it up grand come a Sunday,' the old woman said.

'Sounds delicious,' Holly said, although Emmett could tell she was gagging just a little bit. The girl was like a vegetarian or something.

'You know it. But Darby comes home and he won't eat a thing. I fix him all the things that used to be his favorites – butter beans and ham hock, collards, five-layer chocolate cake, but he wouldn't eat a damn thing! Just sits there and picks at his food, like mine wasn't good enough for him after he been in the pen. You think the food in the pen's any good?'

There was silence for a moment, then Holly shook herself. 'Oh! You're asking me?'

'You're the one I'm talking to, aren't I, for God's sake!' the old woman said.

'Well, I'd guess that the food wasn't that good in the pen,' Holly summed up.

'Damn straight!' Mrs Hunt said, puffing out her chest. 'I even made him cheese enchiladas!' She leaned forward and said, 'I got a friend, Miranda, she's from Mexico. She taught me how to make 'em. They're real good. Want me to make you some?'

'Sure!' Holly said with more enthusiasm than Emmett figured she meant. 'Did Darby like the cheese enchiladas?'

'Hell, no!' his mother said. 'Stuck his nose right up at 'em. Accused me of trucking with Mexicans. I said as how I only had that one friend, so that would be trucking with "a" Mexican, not "Mexicans!"' She laughed heartily at this. 'After he came home he was right mean about coloreds. You know, all of 'em: black ones, Mexicans, Jews and A-rabs. Couldn't abide them A-rabs. Heard a lot about that once he got home, I can tell you that!'

'So bring up his death,' Emmett said in Holly's ear. 'See if she has any idea who might have killed him.'

'I was so sorry to hear about Darby's death,' Holly said.

'I wish he'da married you,' the old woman said, patting Holly's hand. 'You'da made a better wife that that damned Cheryl, always with the stuck-up ways. Never did like that little bitch!'

'Well, ma'am, I wasn't even born back then,' Holly said.

''Course you were!' the old lady said.

'Don't argue with her,' Emmett said in Holly's ear. 'She's a taco short of a combination plate, remember? Just let her rant on and let's see what happens.'

There was a barely discernible nod of Holly's head. 'So who do you think shot him? Did you see anybody outside that night?'

The old lady shook her head. 'Didn't see nothing 'cept what was on the TV. We were just sitting there watching the TV, one of my favorite reality shows – the one where they dance?' Holly nodded her head. 'I like that one. They wear real pretty clothes. We were just watching that then the whole front window plumb blows out! And I turn to my boy' – her face got red and she began to tear up – 'to say how somebody broke out the window, but my boy, my Darby, he's lying back in his chair and there's a hole right between his eyes. Right between his eyes!' She screamed the last part and began to bang her head on the table.

Holly ran around the table and grabbed her head. 'Oh, Miz Hunt, don't do that! Please! I'm here, it's gonna be all right. Please, Miz Hunt!'

The old lady turned and buried her face in Holly's Deadhead T-shirt, and began to cry. Holly patted her back and looked up at the mirrored wall, behind which Emmett sat. She didn't know where he was, yet she was staring right at him. Funny how that works.

Johnny Mac – Day Seven

'This has been a weird trip,' Early said.

Both boys sat on the bottom bunk in their part of the suite, Transformer figures in hand.

'Yeah,' Johnny Mac said. 'But kinda fun, too.'

Early grinned. 'Yeah. And, well,' and here Early's face grew red, 'I kinda like Lyssa.'

Johnny Mac nodded. 'Yeah,' he said. 'She's nice.'

'I mean,' Early said, his face darkening, 'like – like. Ya know?'

Again Johnny Mac nodded. 'Me, too. I mean, Janna.'

'Yeah?' Early said.

This scintillating conversation was interrupted by a knock on the door. Both boys looked at each other, then at the door, then back at each other and jumped up, running to open the door. Janna and Lyssa were on the other side.

'Hey,' Johnny Mac said with a big grin, echoed by Early.

'Hey,' both girls said in unison.

'Y'all wanna go spit in the ocean?' Janna asked.

The grin left Johnny Mac's face. 'Can't,' he said. 'My dad threatened to have us locked up in security if we got out again. And I think he meant it. How did y'all get out?'

Janna shrugged. 'My mother made me promise I wouldn't leave the cabin. She keeps doing that, although it rarely works.'

'Mine took sleeping pills and is out like a light. She has no idea where I am. Can we come in?' Lyssa asked.

Johnny Mac and Early looked at each other, shrugged, then Johnny Mac said, 'That would probably be against my dad's rules. But,' he said, and grinned, 'I got a deck of cards. If y'all sit on that side of the doorway and we sit on this side, we can play cards!'

Everybody grinned at this solution so Johnny Mac ran into the bunk-bed area and came back with a deck of cards.

'Anybody know how to play Crazy Eight?' he asked. 'It's just like Uno, 'cept the take two cards are the twos, and the change suit card is an eight. Wanna try it?'

'Sure,' Janna said and sat down, Lyssa following suit.

The boys sat down on their side of the door jamb, but on sitting down Johnny Mac found something poking him. He reached in the pocket of the shorts he'd pulled out of his dirty clothes that morning, and found the note he'd discovered under the door days ago.

'Oh, shit!' he said. 'Look at this! I forgot all about it. What with two murders and everything!'

Everyone stared at the note: *You breathe a word about today and you'll be sorry. Sure would be a shame if your mom had an accident! Don't tell anyone about this note or anything else, or oops, SHE FELL DOWN THE STAIRS, OFFICER.*

'Where did you get this?' Janna asked.

'It was under the door when we got back here one night,' Johnny Mac said. He looked at Early. 'Which night was it?'

'It was the night after we were in Georgetown,' Early said. 'See where it says, "You breathe a word about *today*—" *Today* must be that day in Georgetown.'

'Yeah, I think you're right,' Johnny Mac said.

'Then it must have been written by Josh!' Lyssa said.

'No,' Janna said. 'That's not Josh's handwriting. It's too . . . neat. You could barely read Josh's writing. I know – he sent me a note one time and it took me and my mom both to figure out what it said.'

'Why was he sending you a note?' Johnny Mac asked, wondering why a teenager would be sending a little kid like Janna a note. He wasn't jealous, he told himself, it was just wrong.

'We were all going to their lake cabin for the weekend and he sent a note through his mom – this was before Crystal, of course – for me to bring my scooter.'

'You have one of those electric scooters?' Lyssa asked.

'Yes, and I love it! But the roads around the lake cabin are dirt and—'

'Ladies!' Early said. 'This note, OK?'

'Oh, right,' Janna said. 'OK, so Josh didn't write this. And I know Ryan didn't either—'

'It looks like a woman's handwriting to me,' Lyssa said.

'It does!' agreed Janna.

'We need to check out Josh's cabin,' Lyssa said. 'See if we can find anything incriminating.'

'Don't you think the ship's security people have already done that?' Johnny Mac, as son of a sheriff, pointed out.

'Probably, but they weren't looking for notes *written by a woman*!' Janna said.

'Exactly!' Lyssa agreed.

'Didn't Josh share a room with Ryan?' Johnny Mac asked.

'Yes, but Uncle Vern moved him into their cabin when Josh died. The security people wanted that cabin closed off, and Uncle Vern didn't want Ryan in there by himself, you know, after what happened and all,' Janna said.

'I bet old Crystal loves that,' Early said with a big grin.

'Yeah, I bet!' Lyssa agreed, grinning back.

'So how do we get into Josh's cabin?' Johnny Mac asked. 'Especially with us not being able to leave this one.'

'We don't leave, the girls go,' Early said. 'And as to how – I think we need to call a steward. I have a hankering for a soda.' He was grinning from ear to ear, but Johnny Mac didn't have a clue as to why.

Milt – Day Seven

When Mike and I finished our beers, I headed down to the security office to talk to Heinrich. He was in his office staring at the computer.

'Anything interesting?' I asked.

He hit something, and said, 'No. You?'

'Well, maybe. Seems Crystal Weaver has a lover and he's on this ship.'

Heinrich's eyes got big. Made me feel good – I knew something he didn't! It's the little things that get us through our golden years.

'And I take it it wasn't Lance Turner,' he said, sitting back in his chair.

'Nope. Somebody we don't know about.' I told him about the kids' encounter with Crystal in the ship's corridor. 'However, the lady *does* get around! She went after Mike Tulia earlier in the cruise. He says he was gonna turn her down, even before he got caught,' I said.

'What makes you think the guy in that cabin wasn't Mike?'

'It wasn't his cabin. And the kids have been around Mike enough to have recognized his voice. They recognized Crystal's. And, besides, how would he get into somebody else's cabin?'

'There are some empty ones on the ship. Do you know what the cabin number was?' Heinrich asked.

'No, but the kids might. You want to go get 'em and see if they can find the place?'

'Sure,' Heinrich said, standing.

Johnny Mac – Day Seven

They were in luck – the steward was Louisa, the one they had the first couple of days and who was new and a little scatty. They needed that.

'Hi, kids,' she said, coming up to the open door. 'Y'all need to get in or out – can't have you blocking the corridor. It's not big enough for two people as it is.' But she said it all with a smile, which took the sting out of the reprimand.

The girls got up and went into the cabin with Johnny Mac, while Early got his soda from Louisa and then proceeded to hug her. Startled, she hugged him back and laughed. 'How sweet are you!' she said, not noticing him slipping the skeleton card out of her pocket.

'You've just been such a big help to us is all,' Early said and smiled.

She patted his head, waved at the other kids and took off. Closing the door behind her, Early turned to the others and held up the skeleton card.

'Oh my God!' Janna said, covering her mouth with her hands as she began to laugh.

'This'll get us into any room we want!' Early said.

'Good thing Josh is already dead – if he knew you had that, he'd be ripping off the entire ship!' Lyssa said.

Johnny Mac stood up and walked slowly up to his friend. He held out his hand and Early took it and the two embraced in a manly fashion. 'You're the bomb,' Johnny Mac told him.

Milt – Day Seven

Heinrich and I headed to our cabin where the boys were holed up. Thankfully they were right where I left them, playing cards on the bottom bunk of their part of the suite.

'Hey, guys,' I said upon entering the room.

'Hey, Dad!' Johnny Mac said with some enthusiasm, until he saw Chief Heinrich and froze in place.

I instantly knew what my son was thinking – that Heinrich was there to take the two of them to the brig.

I smiled and shook my head. 'Nobody's going to jail, boys, so lighten up.' I saw my boy breathe again. 'We need you to take us to where you saw Mrs Weaver when the whole wig thing happened.'

The boys looked at each other and Johnny Mac shrugged his shoulders. 'We can try, Dad, but all these halls look alike.'

'True enough,' I said, 'but I know where I was when I found y'all, so maybe we can figure it out from there.'

Both boys nodded and we headed out. I went to the door of Esther Monte's cabin and took off down the corridor I'd been on, and rounded the first corner. It sure did look exactly like every other corridor.

'OK, this is where I turned and saw y'all. How far up do you think you were?' I asked the boys.

Johnny Mac and Early jogged up a few doors then turned and looked at me, conferred, then walked towards me a door more, then another. 'About here, I think,' Early said.

Heinrich checked his roster of cabin occupancy. 'That room is occupied by a retired couple from Ohio,' he said. Scanning, he said, 'But the cabin one back is unoccupied.'

The boys turned and walked back to that door, looked back at us, conferred again and Johnny Mac said, 'Yeah, this could be it.'

Using his pass key, Heinrich opened the door of the unoccupied cabin. It was bigger than our cabin by about twice the size, had a king-sized bed, a real dresser and a bigger bathroom. The king-sized bed, however, was unmade and obviously used fairly recently.

'You got DNA capabilities aboard ship?' I asked Heinrich. He just stared at me.

'Figured you didn't.'

'Why would you need a DNA test, Dad?' Johnny Mac asked. 'I don't see any hairs or anything like that.'

The boy watched too many *CSI* shows, but even so, some things he didn't understand, thankfully – like certain fluids that I had no intention of telling him about.

'You're right, son,' I said. 'I don't see any hairs either. Why don't y'all wait in the corridor while the chief and I take a look around.'

Johnny Mac – Day Seven

Johnny Mac and Early had barely stepped out of the cabin, door still open, when Janna and Lyssa shot around the corner from Lyssa's cabin.

'Johnny Mac!' Janna cried out. 'We've been looking for you!'

'We got in and boy, did we find—'

'Shhhh—' both Johnny Mac and Early said, grabbing the girls and pointing into the cabin.

'What's going on, John?' Johnny Mac's dad said as he came to the door.

Johnny Mac smiled big at his dad. 'Look who found us!' he said.

'Hi, Sheriff,' Janna said with her sweet smile.

Lyssa gave the sheriff a finger wave.

'Aren't you girls supposed to be in your cabins?' the sheriff asked.

'Yes, sir,' Janna said. 'That's where we're headed.'

The two girls, hand in hand, turned tail and headed back in the direction of Lyssa's cabin.

'What were they talking about, John?'

'Huh?' Johnny Mac countered.

'They got in what? And what did they find?'

'Gee, Dad, I don't know. They were fixing to tell us, then you interrupted and scared them and they ran off.'

'You know, boy, I can tell when you're lying,' his dad said.

'Sir, I am not lying. They were going to tell us something, but you came to the door and it scared them and they ran off. I do not know what they were going to tell us. Do you know what they were going to tell us, Early?'

Early looked at Johnny Mac for a moment, then smiled big. 'No, Sheriff, sir, I do not know what they were going to tell us. And that's the truth.'

Johnny Mac's dad gave them the stink-eye for about a full minute, then walked back into the cabin.

Meanwhile, Back In Prophesy County

Emmett spoke softly into the walkie. 'Holly, get her cleaned up, give her a soda and see if she wants something to eat. I got more questions once she calms down.'

Again, the slight nod of Holly's head.

Emmett left the break room, taking down the 'in-use' sign as he did. Just in case Holly brought the old woman into the break room to pick out her own soda. You just never know.

He went back to his – Milt's – office, sat in his – Milt's – really nice swivel chair with the arms and the high back, and thought. Did the McDaniels do this? If so, which one? Or was it like that old movie Jasmine made him watch, that Agatha Christie thing, where they all did it? It wasn't like he didn't know who Agatha Christie was, like Steve McDaniel had implied; he'd seen all the movies. In the movie he was thinking about, all the suspects took a turn stabbing the bad guy, but old Darby Hunt just got shot the once. And, like his mama said, right between the eyes. Now it took a hell of a talent to break through glass and manage to shoot somebody right between the eyes. Emmett couldn't have done it himself. Hell, he didn't know anybody who could. It seemed to him that if someone in the McDaniel family was that good a shot he'd have heard about it. But who else was there? He wondered if Beth Atkins, Darby Hunt's daughter, had a boyfriend – or for that matter, a girlfriend, if his hunch was right – who felt the girl needed to be free from a dad like Hunt? Even though she'd been legally adopted by her aunt and uncle, old Hunt might have thrown a stink now that he was out.

Emmett picked up the phone and dialed Beth Atkins' home phone number. A machine picked up, and Emmett remembered she was probably at the high school, teaching. So to the machine, he said, 'Miss Atkins, this is Deputy Emmett Hopkins from the sheriff's department. If I'm unable to catch you at school, would you please return my call at either of these numbers.'

He rattled off the sheriff's department number and his cell number and hung up, then got the number for the high school and dialed that. A school secretary answered on the third ring. It must have been between classes, because the noise on her end of the phone was deafening.

'Sheriff's department!' Emmett said loudly. 'I need to speak to Beth Atkins.'

'Who?' the woman shouted at him.

'Beth Atkins!' he shouted back.

'Oh! She's doesn't have a class next period so she's probably headed for the teacher's lounge. Let me put you through there!' the woman shouted.

'Thanks!' he shouted back, then heard the blessed silence of the phone being transferred and ringing on the other end. When a woman picked up, Emmett said, 'Miss Atkins?'

'No, she's not in here right— Wait. Beth! It's for you.'

He heard the phone drop, then a new voice. 'This is Miss Atkins.'

'Hey,' Emmett said. 'This is Emmett Hopkins from the sheriff's department.'

'Yes? I thought I was through with you, Deputy,' she said, but there was no rancor in her voice.

'Just a quick question. I was wondering if you had a significant other in your life—'

'Who would kill my birth father for me?' She laughed. 'No, Deputy. I have no, as you say, "significant other" in my life right now, and I hope I'd have the sense to pick one who wouldn't kill a family member just because I didn't like them much.'

Emmett sighed. 'OK, ma'am, it was just a thought. Sorry to bother you.'

'No bother,' she said. 'Call me with crazy questions any time.'

'How about this one: did you know your dad – I mean, Darby Hunt – had a girlfriend?'

'No, I didn't, but I'm not surprised. There are all sorts of women out there with self-esteem so low they feel the need to get romantic with murderers. I understand serial killers get love letters from women all the time.'

'True enough, but you'd think an educated woman like Reba Sinclair—'

'Who?' Beth asked.

'Reba Sinclair. She's the principal—'

'I know who she is, Deputy.' There was a small silence, then Beth Atkins said, 'We need to talk.'

Milt – Day Seven

There wasn't much to see in the unoccupied cabin, except the unmade bed. Heinrich and I split up and I escorted the boys back to our cabin. Jean was propped up on her bed reading when we came in.

'Hey, guys,' she said with a big grin. I took a look at my wife. She has one of those faces that just make you wanna smile. Beautiful hazel eyes, a pert nose, a generous mouth with a smile full of straight white teeth like a toothpaste commercial, and freckles. I love her freckles. The woman I saw before me was my wife, all right, but something was wrong.

'What did you do?' I asked her.

Her formerly beautiful hazel eyes, now dimmed by all the gunk surrounding them, got big. 'What?'

I studied her face. It wasn't just the eyes. Her freckles were gone.

'Gosh, Mom,' Johnny Mac said, 'you look beautiful!' He threw his arms around his mother's neck and she hugged him back.

She did look beautiful, if your standard of beauty was a model in a magazine. My standards were a bit higher – I prefer *real* women. Ones with a little meat on their bones, a face you could see, wearing clothes that recognized their womanliness. I couldn't see my wife's face – all I could see was makeup.

'After the facial I decided to get a professional make-up job,' Jean said, looking at me with what seemed like a bit of fear in her eyes. Something I'd never seen before and hoped never to see again.

And I realized that, after eleven years together, my wife might not know what a beautiful woman she is. That all her years on crutches had taken their toll on her self-esteem when it came to her looks.

I removed my son and said, 'My turn.' I sat down beside her and kissed her. 'You look beautiful,' I said, touching her cheek. 'But I prefer the freckles.'

'Yes, but you're weird,' she said, smiling back.

'You look real pretty, Miz Kovak,' Early said.

'Thank you, Early! Now, tell me, where have you guys been and what have you been up to?'

So we told her about the unoccupied cabin and the unmade bed and that we really found nothing at all.

'No way for DNA testing?' she asked me.

'Mom! There wasn't any hair!' Johnny Mac informed her.

'Oh,' she said, looked at me, and then back at our son. 'Right. Of course.'

It was getting late and I was up for an early supper. Just as we were about to leave, the phone rang. I picked it up and heard, 'Hey, Milt, it's Mike.'

'Hi, Mike, what's up?'

'Esther's getting room service tonight. She doesn't feel like facing people right now. So Lucy and I are taking the girls to the buffet for dinner. Janna asked me to call you and see if the boys could join us. Believe me, I won't take my eyes off them for a second this time.'

'You'd better not,' I said. 'God only knows what damage they could do.'

'I hear you, I hear you!' Mike said. 'Besides, Lucy will be with me and she's a lot more trustworthy than I am.'

I laughed. 'Let me check with the boss,' I said, put my hand over the phone and said to Jean, 'Mike and Lucy are taking the girls to the buffet for dinner and want them to come,' I said, pointing with my head at the boys.

'Oh, please, Mom! Please! I hate that fancy food!'

'Yes, Miz Kovak, please!'

I cocked my head at her. 'Last dinner on-board,' I said. 'Romantic evening, just the two of us.'

Jean looked at the boys, then at me, then back at the boys. 'OK. But if you two do anything—'

'We swear, Mom! Don't we, Early?'

'Yes, ma'am, we swear!'

Into the phone I said, 'It's a go, Mike. I'll bring 'em to you at the buffet.'

Twenty minutes later I found Jean at our designated table, sipping a glass of wine from a bottle. 'How much did that cost us?' I asked.

'We have one free bottle of wine. This is it,' she said.

'Shit,' I said. 'Free? Good deal at twice the price.' I poured myself a glass and picked up the menu, looking for today's treat. Squab stuffed with wild rice and peeled grapes. Ah, shit, I thought. Peel me some grapes, baby! That was for me. When the waiter came, I ordered the squab, with a side of white asparagus, an appetizer of escargot (it was good the first time; what were the chances it wouldn't be good the second? Slim to none, I figured), a wedge salad with bleu (that's the way they spelled it) cheese, figs and pecans, and a dessert taco, which was like one of those taco shells they put salad in, except sugared and filled with flan and fresh fruit. That's what the menu said. I figured there was no way it was gonna be bad. I hadn't had anything on the ship yet that didn't make me wanna slap my mama it was so good.

After the waiter had gone, my made-up wife asked, 'Do you know what squab is?' She'd ordered the same thing, so I couldn't have gone off too bad.

'One of those little chickens, right?'

She grinned at me. 'No, honey, it's a baby pigeon.'

I was quiet for a moment. 'A pigeon?'

'Yep,' she said, taking another sip of wine.

'Like one of those flying rats that hang around in downtowns and shit on everything? Like that?' I asked.

'Yep.' She laughed at the expression on my face. 'Except these,

I'm sure, are from sterilized farms, and don't grow up, so how can they shit on anybody's downtown?'

'I'm gonna eat a baby pigeon,' I said under my breath, then took a big swig of my wine. 'Don't tell the boys.'

TWELVE

Johnny Mac – Day Seven

The boys heaped their plates and followed the girls to a table one over from Janna's parents. Her mom was facing them, so as to curtail any adventurous ideas. Janna, who was facing her mother, put on a phony smile, the one she used for her parents, and said, 'I bet y'all are anxious to hear what we found in Josh's cabin, huh?'

Sitting beside her, also facing Mrs Tulia, Johnny Mac smiled back. 'We sure are. If we keep smiling like this will our face muscles freeze up and we'll end up looking like Batman's Joker?'

'Just smile and nod, smile and nod,' Janna said. 'Anyway, we didn't find the money. We did find a slip of paper in a woman's handwriting—'

'It looked just like the handwriting on your note, Johnny Mac!' Lyssa said.

Janna shot her a look. 'Yes, it did.' She got her smile back under control.

'What did it say?' Early asked.

The two girls exchanged looks. Then, in unison, they said, 'Meet me at the usual spot, lover.'

Johnny Mac almost choked on a French fry. '*Lover?*' he exclaimed. 'Gross!'

'Does that mean he was *doing it*?' Early asked, not exactly sure what 'doing it' meant, but he'd heard his older brother say it and knew that that's what 'lover' meant. Maybe.

Janna frowned. 'I dunno.' She looked at Johnny Mac, who shrugged.

Lyssa sighed. 'God, y'all are such babies. Yes, "lover" means they were doing it. Now we just need to figure out who he was doing it with. Did anybody see him hanging out with any girls?'

'Just us,' Janna said. Then she and Lyssa looked at each other, grimaced, and said in unison, 'Ooo!'

'Maybe it's not a lady's handwriting,' Early said.

'It's pretty girly-looking,' Lyssa said.

'Yeah, I have to agree with Lyssa,' Johnny Mac said. 'It looked like my mom's handwriting. The way the letters sorta curled.'

Early nodded his head. 'You're probably right. And, I wasn't thinking. Since it said "lover" it had to be a girl, huh?'

Johnny Mac nodded his head, while the two girls looked at each other and rolled their eyes.

'Did you find anything else – interesting or not,' Johnny Mac asked. 'I mean, what might not have seemed interesting to you – as girls – might have seemed interesting to Early and me.'

'You mean being boys and all?' Janna said, with just a slight curl of the lip.

Johnny Mac was bright enough to catch the sarcasm. 'I wasn't being mean, Janna,' he said. 'There are just some things girls know more about than boys, and some things boys know more about than girls.'

'Like what?' Janna demanded.

'Don't y'all think we're getting off the subject here?' Lyssa said, echoed by Early's 'Yeah.'

Janna sighed. 'OK, Lyssa, what did we see that only a boy can interpret?'

Lyssa shrugged and closed her eyes. 'OK. We saw Early's boat that he bought sitting on the nightstand. Next to it was an empty root beer can. There was some change on the night stand, about thirty-seven cents. On the shelf over the bed were two baseball caps – one said, "Houston Oilers" and the other said "Jason's Bit BBQ." In the closet were hang-up clothes, obviously Josh's 'cause they were too big for Ryan. On the shelf above that was a box. In the drawers were boys' boxers and T-shirts and socks.'

She opened her eyes to find the other three staring at her. 'What?' she said.

'How did you do that?' Janna asked, awestruck.

'What? Oh, listing off everything? My doctor said I have total recall. It's a gift,' she said and smiled sweetly, hands folded in front of her.

'Cool,' Johnny Mac said. 'But what was in the box?'

'Box?' Lyssa asked.

'In the closet. On the shelf above the hang-up clothes,' Johnny Mac said.

'Oh!' Lyssa's face turned red. 'I forgot to look! Janna found that note in the second drawer – where he kept his shoes and belts and other crap – and I forgot all about the box!'

'We need to see what's inside that box!' Johnny Mac said.

All four turned and looked at Janna's parents – who were looking right back at them.

Meanwhile, Back In Prophesy County

Emmett made plans with Beth Atkins to meet her at the Longbranch Inn at around five p.m. In the meantime, he headed back to the break room to check out what was happening with Mrs Hunt.

The old lady had a Subway sandwich in front of her and a Diet Yoo-hoo out of the machine. And she and Holly were talking about quilting, a subject obviously dear to the old bat's heart.

'Now I'm into them crazy quilts. Where you don't have a real pattern? At least not one of the traditional ones,' she was saying. 'And you can make 'em real bright colors all over! I made two so far.' The look of pleasure on her face faded. 'Got no one to give 'em to now. Now that my boy's gone. They woulda made real good wedding presents.'

'Ask her how well she knew Darby's girlfriend,' Emmett said into the walkie.

Holly did. The old lady replied, 'She took me up to see him at the pen a couple of times, but I didn't know her well. She didn't talk much on the ride, and I usually got me some shut-eye. But she was nice enough. I mean, he got that motorcycle and that big-screen TV, didn't he? Now that's true love, donja think?'

'That's true,' Holly said.

'Ask her who all Darby'd seen since he got out. Anybody come to the house? He get any calls?'

Again the mere movement of Holly's head in acknowledgement. 'Did Darby have a lot of company once he got out?'

The old lady shook her head. 'No. Not even kin. My husband's brothers' boys used to be all over when Darby was young, but nary a one of 'em showed up when my boy got out!' She shook her head. 'I called 'em to go pick him up from the pen but they wouldn't do it! Trash, the whole lot of 'em, just trash. My poor boy had to take a bus home. And me! I had to drive to the bus stop in town to get him. I don't hardly drive at all anymore, but would that worthless Hunt bunch do a goddam thing to help me? Not so's you'd notice!'

'That's a shame,' Holly said. 'You'd think they'd be more accommodating, being kin and all.'

'Yeah, you'd think so!' the old lady said, tears starting in her eyes again.

Emmett said into the walkie, 'What about phone calls! Ask her about phone calls!'

'How about phone calls?' Holly repeated.

'I think that girlfriend of his called a couple of times. He'd always rush for the phone when it rang. Only rang like maybe two times since he got back. I don't get a lot of phone calls myself. Got no kin left. Not even my boy,' she said, put down her Subway sandwich and began to bawl.

'When she calms down,' Emmett said into the walkie, 'tell her we're confiscating her shotgun but not pressing charges for shooting at a deputy. Then get somebody – somebody *armed*, Holly, not you! – to take her home. Got that?'

She nodded her head and Emmett left the break room to head to the Longbranch Inn for his meeting with Beth Atkins.

Dalton wasn't much use that afternoon. His eyes were either on his beloved or on the clock, willing it to be five o'clock and time to leave. The ring was burning a hole in his pocket. Anthony had come in for his late shift at noon and Dalton wanted to tell him what was going on, but he figured he shouldn't. This was just between him and Holly and he should keep it that way.

Finally, five o'clock came and Dalton went up to Holly's desk. 'You ready?'

'I have to get Mrs Hunt back to her house,' Holly said.

'Anthony can do that,' he said.

'OK, that's good. Why don't you pick me up at my apartment in an hour? I rode my bike in today,' she said.

'Plenty of room for your bike in my car,' he said. He drove a Ford Explorer, four years old and paid for.

Holly laughed. 'You're really anxious to show me something, huh?'

Dalton grinned big and blushed. 'Yeah, I guess so.'

'OK, fine.' She picked up her purse and her bag she carried with a book and her lunch and other stuff in it, and headed first to Anthony's desk to ask him to take Mrs Hunt home, and then for the jail cells where she kept her bike. When she walked out to the lobby with it, Dalton took it and walked to the parking lot.

His hands were shaking. He hoped Holly wouldn't notice. He opened the back of the Explorer and put the bike in, closed it and got in the driver's side. Holly was already sitting in the passenger seat. She hadn't waited for him to open the door for her. That's just the way she was – real independent. When they went some place, she never would sit in the car and wait for him to come around and open her door. She always said she didn't know what she was supposed to do, just sitting there. Stare out the window? Do her nails? It made sense to Dalton. He always wondered about that, too.

But today he wasn't wondering about any of that, or worried that she'd opened her own door while he was putting her bike in the back. Right now his lunch was coming back on him and he thought he might vomit, he was that nervous. Would she like the house? What if she hated it? Well, he just wouldn't buy it then! he told himself.

'So where are we going?' Holly asked once he was in the driver's seat.

'Close to downtown,' he said, and started the car. His hands were shaking so bad he hoped he didn't have an accident on the short ride to the house.

He pulled up in front of the house. He'd asked June, the realtor, to leave the door unlocked for him, and he got out on his side and walked around. Holly was actually sitting in her seat, not waiting for him but staring at the house. When he opened the door, she startled. 'What's this?' she said, getting out.

'It's a house,' he said, grinning.

'Well, I can see that! I mean, why are we here?'

'I'm thinking about buying it,' he said.

She turned and quickly hugged him. 'Oh, Dalton, that's wonderful. You need your own place!'

She ran up the sidewalk to the front porch. Pointing at the same spot on the porch that he'd thought about earlier, she said, 'Oh, God, you need a porch swing right there! And paint it some really cool color, like puce!'

He opened the door and she rushed in, running circles around the rooms. 'Oh my God!' she said about seeing the extra room with the French doors. 'This is incredible! And look at this dining room!'

'Wait till you see the kitchen,' he said, and led her in there.

'Oh my God!' She fell to her knees. 'This is the kitchen of the gods!' Rushing back to her feet she grabbed Dalton by the shoulders. 'Please, please let me cook in here! Please!'

'About that—' he started.

'Oh my God! There's room for anything in here—'

'Holly!'

She stopped for a moment and turned around. By the time she did, Dalton was down on one knee and holding out a box. He opened the lid and she saw the most fabulous ring ever. 'Holly Humphries,' Dalton said, 'will you marry me?'

Holly looked from the ring to Dalton to back at the ring. Slowly she closed the lid and pulled on Dalton's arm for him to stand up.

'Way too soon, sweetie,' she said, pulling his face down to kiss him. 'We don't know each other well enough yet.'

'I know you're all I wanna—' Dalton started.

'You know,' she said, smiling, stroking his face with her hand, 'we haven't even had sex yet.'

Dalton put his head down as he turned purple. And he said, 'Ah.' And that was about it.

Holly leaned down to look up at his lowered face. 'Sweetie, are you a virgin?'

'You mean have I done it with someone else?'

'Right,' she said.

'Well, then, yes,' he said.

'Don't you think we should find out if we're compatible there first?'

'But if I've never done it, how can I be any good?' he asked, looking at Holly as she straightened up.

'Well, you might not be at first,' she said. She smiled as she pulled him down to the kitchen floor, 'but I think I can be a real good teacher.' Once she got him down, she leaned over and began to kiss him. Straightening for a second, she said, 'And, ah, don't take that ring back. You never know what's going to happen!'

Milt – Day Seven

I went and picked up the boys from the children's pavilion where Mike and Lucy had stashed them. Jean was saving us seats at the main theater, where there was an end-of-cruise extravaganza going on. Mike and Lucy were sitting right outside the pavilion, their faces to the glass in front of it, watching the kids play.

'You're off the hook for mine,' I said. 'Thanks for watching them. Guess what I had for dinner?'

Mike said, 'What?'

'Squab.'

'What's that?' he asked.

'Baby pigeon,' I told him.

Mike made the same face I'd made earlier. 'Gross,' he said.

Lucy laughed.

I nodded my head in agreement. 'That's what I thought when I found out what I'd ordered, but truth be told, it was mighty fine eating.'

'Yes, I had it once,' Lucy said. 'Little bit richer than chicken.'

'I'll never know,' Mike said. 'Next thing y'all be telling me you ate a mouse or something.'

I laughed and went in to get the boys. But if I wanted to tell the whole truth, I think that little bird was sneaking up on me. I was getting a bad case of indigestion.

'Come on guys, we're gonna meet your mom at the big theatre. They're doing a song and dance thing for the whole family.'

'Whoopee,' my son said with less enthusiasm than I thought was merited.

We made our way through the food court, down the corridor to the pool area, which was uncharacteristically empty, and were halfway through it when it hit me.

An elephant was dancing on my chest, and my left arm felt like it was on fire. I sat/fell on the nearest lounge chair.

'John, get your mother! My phone!'

'Daddy!' Johnny Mac yelled.

That was the last sound I heard.

Johnny Mac – Day Seven

Johnny Mac grabbed his dad as he fell backwards on the lounge chair. 'Daddy, daddy!' he screamed, shaking his father.

Early moved Johnny Mac out of the way and went through the sheriff's pockets until he found his cell phone. 'What number for your mom?' Johnny Mac just stood there, in shock. Early punched him. 'What number for your mom?'

Johnny Mac took the phone, found his mom's name and hit it. She came on after only one ring. 'Hey, honey, what's taking so long?'

'Daddy – daddy—' Johnny Mac tried to get out.

Early grabbed the phone. 'I think he's having a heart attack! Just like my grandpa. He's passed out but he's still breathing!'

'I'm on my way. I'll call the medical team,' Johnny Mac's mom said and hung up.

The two boys just stood there, staring down at the sheriff.

Meanwhile, Back In Prophesy County

Emmett got to the Longbranch Inn before Beth Atkins, so he ordered an appetizer of chili-cheese fries and some sweet tea. He was sitting by a window overlooking the street and saw one of those new Volkswagens, bright yellow, pull up and park. Beth Atkins got out and came in, wearing men's blue jeans, a short-sleeved checked shirt and the same shoes. If she wasn't a lesbian, someone needed to teach her how to dress, Emmett thought.

He stood up and stretched out his hand when she got to the table. 'Miss Atkins, good to see you again.'

She shook his hand and sat down. Loretta was on her like white on rice. 'Getja something, honey?'

'Diet Coke?' Beth said.

'You got it,' Loretta said and moved away.

'What was it we needed to talk about?' Emmett asked her.

'It's this whole idea of Reba Sinclair being Darby Hunt's girl-friend.' No 'dad' or 'father' or even 'that son-of-a-bitch.' Just 'Darby Hunt,' like he was someone she read about in the papers.

Emmett started to say something, but Loretta was back with Beth Atkins' Diet Coke, so he just smiled and waited while Beth thanked her for the soda. Once Loretta had gone, Emmett said, 'OK. What about it?'

Beth was silent for a moment, then sighed real big. 'OK, I hope this is confidential?'

'Unless it bears on the case, then yeah,' Emmett said.

'I don't really care at this point. I don't want my family persecuted by that old woman for something I know none of them did.' Again with the sigh. 'Look, I'm gay.'

Emmett nodded his head. Jeez, he thought, I have gaydar! He was quite proud of himself.

'My family doesn't know, or if they do, they're not talking about it. Anyway, two summers ago I met Reba Sinclair at a women's bar in Dallas. We went out once, but she was very persistent and very aggressive. I told her I didn't want to see her again. I came back here, where I've lived my whole life, except for four years at OU in Norman, and she called me so incessantly I had to have my number changed. Six months later there she is at that new Christian school! And she starts calling me again, harassing me.'

'Why didn't you tell us about it? Or the police?' Emmett asked. She tilted her head and gave him the stink-eye. 'OK,' he said. 'I get it. But what kind of harassing?'

'I came home from work one night and she was in my bath! Asked me to join her! I told her to get the . . . you know what out of my house. "Only if you dry me off," she said, and giggled, for Christ's sake.' Beth shook her head. 'It's been awful. She's waited outside my school twice after work. No one at school knows I'm gay, and I'd rather it stayed that way.'

'How did she find out about your— About Darby Hunt being your birth father?'

'I have no idea! But I know that she knew because she mentioned it once. I was pumping gas and she pulled in and got out of her car and came over to me. I'd already paid cash and was right in the middle of pumping, so I couldn't run away. And she says something to the effect that she knew what happened with my parents, and that because she was a woman she'd never treat me that way. She'd treat me like a princess.'

'Exactly the thing an abuser would say,' Emmett said.

Beth shuddered. 'Don't I know it. I remember the way my father talked to my mother when she got out of the hospital after he'd beaten her. I was only four when he killed her, but I remember. It was sickening. All sweetness and light. "Do anything for you, baby. You're the love of my life, I can't live without you." Crap like that. But the day my mother finally left him, she said to me, "Lizzie," – that's what she called me – "Lizzie, be careful of men, you can't trust them." And then here's a woman saying just the kind of things Darby Hunt said. And believe me, Deputy, it wasn't just that – I was not the least bit attracted to the witch.'

'It seems like I need to have another talk with Miss Sinclair,' Emmett said.

'Do you think she killed Darby?' Beth asked.

'I dunno, but I'd sure like to check out her skill on a hunting rifle.'

Emmett got back in his squad car, thinking about how to get into Reba Sinclair's house without a warrant, because he had damn little to go on to *get* a warrant. 'Hey, Judge, we got this woman who says she's the dead guy's girlfriend, except turns out she's a lesbian who's been hitting on the dead guy's daughter, and we think maybe she killed the guy as a way to win favor with the daughter.' And then the judge laughs. 'Har-de-har-har.'

Emmett thought maybe he should just go home and sleep on it. Not likely that she was going to kill anybody else tonight. Then his cell phone rang. He saw that it was the shop calling, and not on the radio.

'Holly? What's up?'

'Emmett, it's me, Anthony. Here's the thing. Mrs Hunt mentioned that Darby said his girlfriend almost made it to the Olympics one year, so I Googled her, and she did almost make it. Emmett, she was up for the biathlon team for the winter games in 2002, in Salt Lake City.'

'Biathlon? Shit! That's the skiing and shooting one, right?'

'Right. Cross-country skiing and rifle shooting!' Anthony said.

'Damn skippy!' Emmett all but shouted.

Milt – Day Seven

I woke up in a sterile, white room. When I turned my head to the right, I saw my wife.

'Hey,' I said.

She'd been resting her head on her arm, propped on the back of a straight back chair. She startled, then looked at me and smiled. 'Hey, yourself,' she said, leaning forward to kiss me.

'What happened?' I asked.

'You had a mild heart attack,' Jean said.

'Did I die?'

'No, you're very much alive,' she said, caressing my arm.

'No, I mean for a minute or something. I want to scan my brain for any afterlife experiences.'

Jean laughed. 'No, baby, you didn't die, not even for a minute.'

'Where am I?' I asked.

'In the ship's infirmary. Their doctor checked you out, gave you some meds, and you'll be fine until we hit Galveston.'

'Where are the boys?' I asked.

'Lucy and Mike took them. They came out of the food court area right after Early called me.'

'Early called you?'

Jean nodded her head. 'Yes. John's crestfallen that he panicked and didn't save your life. Early is quite proud that *he* did.'

'Yeah? No kidding? Go Early,' I said. 'What time is it?'

Jean looked at her watch. 'Twelve-thirty,' she said.

'Baby, go on back to the cabin and get some sleep,' I told her.

'Absolutely not,' she said.

'What? You're gonna sleep in that straight-back chair? You know you need to get your brace off and rest your legs. If you don't, you won't be walking tomorrow, no-way, no-how.'

'I'll be fine—' she started, but I interrupted.

'Uh uh,' I said. 'Go!' I pointed at the door, a scowl on my face. 'Now!' Then I motioned to her with an index finger. 'But come here first and give us a kiss!'

She laughed and leaned over, giving me a kiss that, had my heart been all that weak, woulda killed me. 'Um,' I said, 'this bed is bigger than it looks.' I wiggled my eyebrows at her.

'OK,' she said, laughing. 'I think you're on the mend. But call me if you need anything, OK?'

'Will do,' I said and watched her walk out the door. She hadn't been gone more than ten minutes when I realized I needed to pee like a racehorse. I was in a fairly small room, with two regulation hospital beds, a gurney and assorted medical supplies. The only door was the one Jean had taken to get out. So, unless I wanted to pee where I was lying, I was going to have to go find a bathroom.

I tried sitting up and found that I could do it fairly well. I put my feet over the side and that felt OK. So I tried standing up. I was a little dizzy at first, but I waited and that went away. I walked to the door. So far so good. I saw a sign just down the hall and recognized it as the bathroom, on the other side of which was Heinrich's security area. I felt good, knowing exactly where on the boat I was, and who I could go to if I needed help. I had no idea where the doctor was or what he or she, for that matter, even looked like.

I opened the bathroom door, made it to the toilet and let loose. It took a while. I must have been holding it in for quite some time. Once I'd finished and flushed, I opened the door just enough to hear voices. Recognizing them, I stayed where I was and listened.

'I told you not to come down here!' Heinrich was saying.

And then Crystal Weaver said, 'But that cop had a heart attack, right? So we're OK. Nobody's going to find out anything!'

I heard kissing noises. 'Lizbet, listen to me,' he said. Shit, I thought, her name's not even Crystal. Phony name, phony hair. And I *knew* the boobs were phony. 'We're too close now to blow this. The old geezer can't get off the ship tomorrow. You need to do the pillow tonight! You should be in there with him right now!'

'I know, baby, I know, but I wanted to see you! You saved me from Josh, and I still have a lot of thanking to do.' I heard more kissing noises. Jesus, Heinrich, I thought. I never had a clue. And I'm a real good investigator. But they hadn't said a word about Lance. The 'old geezer' had to be Vern, and the pillow, the 'do the pillow.' Was she supposed to suffocate Vern in his sleep? And who would question the death of or do an autopsy on an overweight fifty-something man on his honeymoon with a hot number like Crystal? Or should I say Lizbet. Shit, I remembered seeing my phone on the hospital tray table in my room. I couldn't even call someone to save Vern.

How did Heinrich save Crystal from Josh? What did she mean by that? Had Heinrich killed Josh? If so, why? How had he 'saved' Crystal? What was Josh doing to Crystal that required saving?

'Go,' Heinrich said. 'Call me when it's over, then try to sleep.'

'In the same bed?' she said, alarm in her voice.

'Yes. You must wake up in the morning to find your husband dead. That's been the plan all along, Lizbet. Ever since he took out that insurance policy.'

Lizbet giggled. 'God, what a sweetie! A million dollars!'

'Yes,' Heinrich said, his voice getting testy. 'Now you must go! Do it!'

'All right, all right!' she said, her voice fading. 'I just don't want to sleep with a corpse, you know?'

I heard the elevator door close, and Heinrich's voice say, 'Stupid bitch,' as his voice faded, too. After another minute, I looked out and the corridor was empty, so I moved as quickly as my broken body would allow back to the infirmary to my phone. I called Mike Tulia's cell phone.

'Hey, Milt,' his sleepy voice said. 'How you doing, man?'

'Listen to me closely, Mike. Crystal is on her way to her cabin to kill Vern. She's going to smother him with a pillow—'

'Jeez, man, call Heinrich—'

'Heinrich's her partner,' I said.

'Holy crap!'

'Exactly,' I said. 'Mike, you gotta do it. You've got to go to Vern's cabin and save his fat ass.'

'Ah, shit, man,' Mike whined.

'Hey, it's a rotten job,' I said, 'but somebody's gotta do it.'

'Well, fuck,' he said. 'OK, I'm going, I'm going.'

He hung up and I sank back on the bed. When I did my eyes went to the door of the infirmary, where Heinrich, chief of security for the Star Line ship, was standing.

THIRTEEN

Meanwhile, Back In Prophesy County

It took less than an hour to find a judge willing to sign a search warrant. Emmett got Nita and Anthony to go with him and they headed to Reba Sinclair's house. Unfortunately, once there it was hard not to notice Beth Atkins' new yellow VW parked in the driveway. They came in two cars – Emmett in his, Nita and Anthony in another. Emmett radioed Anthony, who was driving, to go around the corner where his car couldn't be seen from Sinclair's front window.

'Don't need a hostage situation here. I'm going to go up to the door like it's nothing serious—'

Before he could finish talking, he heard the sound of a rifle shot and the glass on the passenger-side window blew out. Emmett then felt a sharp sting on the back of his neck as the driver's-side window blew out. He wasn't sure if a bullet had grazed his neck or if the blood seeping down his back was from glass cuts from the broken windows. At that point he really didn't care – he just fell to his side. Lying across the front seat, he called out to Anthony, 'Shots fired! Shots fired! I'm hit, but it's not much. Call Charlie Smith for back-up and get your butts back here!'

They were in city territory. He'd forgotten to call Charlie and let him know he was serving a search warrant on Sinclair. He was gonna get his ass chewed out for this – if everything turned out OK.

He turned on the loudspeaker and spoke into the handset. 'Miz Sinclair! You need to stop shooting at us. You need to throw out your gun and come out with your hands up—'

What Emmett considered to be a reasonable request was met by a barrage of bullets. He started to count them then figured why bother? She was in her own home – she probably had boxes of ammo. He would if he was a world-class-almost Olympic shot. His car was hit with all six shots, one even coming through the front door passenger side, very close to his head. He twisted around until he could open the driver's-side door then slid his body out to the street. He had his gun in his hand but was afraid to shoot for fear of hitting Beth Atkins.

Anthony pulled up sideways to Emmett's car, virtually blocking the street. He and Nita bailed out, guns drawn.

'What do you wanna do, Emmett?' Anthony asked.

'She's got a hostage. We can't go shooting her house. We'd probably kill Beth Atkins.'

Nita handed Emmett the bullhorn from the car they'd been in. 'Hard to get to the loudspeaker,' she said.

Emmett turned the bullhorn on. 'Reba, the city police are on their way. This place is going to be surrounded in a very few minutes. Is Beth OK? Just let me know if she's OK.'

The front door opened and Beth Atkins stood there, her arms raised, Reba Sinclair standing behind her.

'Deputy!' Beth Atkins called out. 'She said for y'all to back off! She wants to leave in her car and she said she'll drop me off somewhere and call you and tell you where.'

'No way, Reba. You're not taking Beth anywhere! Just give it up before the police get here and it really gets bad. Right now all we've got you on is keeping Beth in your house against her will, which is just a minor infraction,' Emmett lied.

'Bullshit!' Reba yelled from the doorway. And Emmett had to wonder how in the world this woman got the job as principal at a Christian school! 'This would be considered kidnapping! I was pre-law at SMU! And you think I killed Darby Hunt, so that's even worse! Just get out of my way or I'll kill this bitch!'

At that moment police squad cars with sirens blazing came tearing down the street, which distracted Reba Sinclair. Beth Atkins tore away from her, falling to the ground. Reba looked after her with a shocked expression and Nita stood up and fired, hitting Reba in her gun arm. She dropped her weapon, her left hand grabbing her bleeding arm.

'Didn't wanna kill her, Emmett,' Nita said.

Emmett stood up and slapped Nita on the back. 'You done good,' he said, and jogged up to the front door.

Reba was crying, looking down at Beth, and Emmett soon realized she wasn't crying from pain but from perceived betrayal. 'Why? Why did you do that? You told me to do this!'

I helped Beth to a standing position. 'I told her to take me out here to tell you her demands, Emmett,' Beth said.

'No!' Reba shouted. 'She told me to shoot her father! And if y'all figured it out, we'd run away together! That's what you said!'

'I told you she was nuts, Emmett,' Beth said, again using Emmett's name instead of her usual use of 'Deputy.'

Emmett looked at Anthony, who had come up behind him. 'Anthony, why don't you cuff Miz Atkins here, just in case, while I take Miz Reba to the ER. We'll meet you back at the station. Just put Beth here in the interrogation room.'

'What the hell are you doing?' Beth demanded. 'I had nothing to do with this! She killed him!' She whirled on Anthony as he tried to cuff her. 'Stop that!' she said, but he grabbed her arms behind her back and cuffed her.

Emmett put some gauze on Reba Sinclair's gunshot arm, taped it up good, then handcuffed her good arm to a metal ring on the back seat of his squad car. On the drive to the ER, and while in the ER, Reba Sinclair told a different story than the one he'd heard from Beth Atkins.

It started off the same: they'd met at a women's bar in Dallas, gone on a date, then Beth had gone back to Longbranch with no plans of seeing Reba again. But Reba had other ideas. She had fallen in love with Beth rather quickly, so sent her résumé out to schools all around the Prophesy County area, and had finally been picked for the Christian school principal's job, mainly because she was willing to take the really, really bad salary they offered. She'd called Beth many times to let her know she was in town and wanted to see her, but Beth always put her off – that is, until about a year and a half ago.

That's when, according to Reba, she found out about what had happened with Beth's parents. Beth called her out of the blue, and asked her out to dinner at the new vegetarian restaurant. This was followed by an intimate evening at Beth's home. It was after sex that Beth began to cry, and told her about what her birth father had done to her mother.

'She told me his sentence would be up in a year and half, said she just couldn't stand the idea that he was going to be free after what he'd done,' Reba told Emmett. 'Do you know what her mother told her right before she died? She said, "Lizzie," – that's what she called her – "Lizzie, you just can't trust a man."' Reba beamed at him. 'But she knew she could trust me.'

Emmett felt a little sick to his stomach. Most of what Reba had told him she could have made up, and the part about Beth's parents was local history. But the Lizzie part? That had to come from Beth herself.

'So what was the plan?' Emmett asked.

'She thought I should start emailing him, go to see him, become his girlfriend. She even had me take that old bat, his mother, up to see him. After the first trip with her, when she didn't shut up the entire way, I brought a thermos of coffee laced with a sleeping pill for her. Did the trick. I could get to the prison without having to listen to her rattle on and on about how awful Beth and her family were.'

'But why did you buy him those expensive gifts?' I asked, thinking of the Harley and the huge flat-screen TV.

'Beth told me to. She said that would give him a false sense of security! Her idea was to kill him when he was in bed with me!'

Reba said, and shuddered. 'I said no way, Jose! I wasn't about to sleep with him. But then she remembered me almost going to the Olympics,' she said, and I could see her in the rear-view mirror smiling timidly, 'and she said I should do the honors. And I knew I could do it clean, no sweat.'

'Did she ask you to shoot her father?' Emmett asked.

'Yes! And I was happy to do it. I love her,' Reba said.

'And after you shot him? Did you tell her?' Emmett asked.

'Oh, yes!' Reba said smiling. 'I went right to her house and told her. She hugged me and said thank you.'

'What did you use?' he asked.

'My favorite! A Marlin 336 XLR, with a five-pound trigger pull. Sweet piece,' she said, smiling. OK, Emmett thought, maybe she is a little crazy.

'I'm gonna need you to repeat all this to the county attorney, Reba. Think you can do that?'

'Sure, if that's what you want,' she said.

Milt – Day Seven

'I was really beginning to like you, Milt,' Heinrich said as he slowly came into the room.

I used the button on the hospital bed to raise myself to a sitting position. I didn't think I wanted him getting to me while I was lying down. 'Look, Heinrich, it's over. Mike's on his way to warn Vern, they're gonna catch Crys— I'm sorry, it's Lizbet, right? Anyway, they're gonna catch her and you know she's going to turn on you.'

'Never,' he said, his entire body oozing confidence on that subject. 'She's my wife; she'd never betray me.'

I laughed. It sounded funny to my own ears. 'Are you shitting me?' I said. 'She was trying to seduce Mike and who knows who else? Oh, and how were you saving her from Josh? I take it you're the one who strangled the boy?'

'It was in my wife's defense!' Heinrich said, his face becoming hard with anger. 'He was raping her!'

I just looked at him for a minute. 'Are you sure about that? That wimpy little fourteen-year-old, who looked anorexic, was assaulting Crys— I'm sorry, I keep doing that! I mean Lizbet? I don't think so. But I gotta know, why did you kill Lance? Was he raping Lizbet, too?'

'I didn't kill Lance!' he shouted as he lunged for me.

It appeared I was to have the same fate as poor Josh. Heinrich had his hands around my neck and was squeezing. The edges of my vision were beginning to blacken. Then the pressure was gone and Heinrich was falling to the floor. Behind him stood my beautiful wife, leaning on one crutch. The other lay on the floor where it had dropped after she'd bashed in Heinrich's skull.

Meanwhile, Back In Prophesy County

After the ER doc got Reba sewn up, Emmett called Midge Murphy, the county attorney, right then and asked her to meet them at the shop, then drove over there. Emmett didn't want Reba realizing she was throwing the love of her life under the bus until after she'd told Midge the whole story.

Unfortunately she figured it out on the drive to the shop and clammed up. But Emmett had a feeling he could get her to open up one more time.

He left Reba with Midge and Anthony in the break room while he went into the interrogation room with Beth. She was still cuffed so Emmett went to her and took the cuffs off.

'Sorry about that,' he said.

She rubbed her wrists and looked at him. 'Why did you do that?' she asked, a hurt look on her face.

'I'm afraid I bought into what Reba Sinclair was saying there for a minute. You know, about you telling her to do it.'

Beth shook her head. 'God! I told you I wanted nothing to do with that woman! Anything she did she did on her own! I haven't even talked to her but a couple of times since she moved here, and both those times were to tell her to leave me alone! I don't want to sound shallow, Emmett, but have you looked at her?' Beth said and laughed.

'Yeah, that does sound shallow,' Emmett said.

'Well, it's not just her looks. Obviously she's crazy! Who else would follow me from a one-night stand all the way from another state? I mean, move here? That was nuts enough, but to kill Darby Hunt?' Beth threw up her arms. 'That's just crazy, Emmett.'

'Yeah, that's crazy all right.'

Emmett got up and left the room, making sure the door was locked behind him, and went into the break room. Midge and Reba were sitting at the table, Reba crying, while Midge held her tape recorder in front of her and Reba tearfully told her everything she'd told Emmett earlier.

Looked like Beth Atkins was going to go down for soliciting the murder of her father.

Johnny Mac – Day Eight

Sometime in the early morning hours of their last day at sea, Johnny Mac's dad had another heart attack. This time a helicopter from Galveston flew out to Life-Flight him to Houston for emergency surgery. Johnny Mac and Early packed their stuff quickly and tried to pack some of Johnny Mac's mom's stuff, but Mrs Tulia told them not to worry about it, that she'd take care of it, and hurried them up to the top deck where the helicopter was going to land. It was the wee hours of the morning and they could see the lights of Galveston in the far distance. The ship would be docking in an hour or so, but the ship's doctor said there wasn't time for that. Mr Tulia and Janna were already up there.

Janna ran to Johnny Mac and hugged him. There were tears in her eyes. 'He's gonna be fine!' she said.

Johnny Mac could only nod. He knew if he said anything he'd start crying.

'As soon as we dock, Daddy said we'd drive straight to the hospital! So I'll see you there, OK?'

Again Johnny Mac nodded. It was windy on the top deck, but got windier when the helicopter reached them and started to descend. Two crewmen, the doctor and Johnny Mac's mom came out of the door with the gurney that carried his dad. There were tubes running in and out of him, a mask on his face and a blanket covering his body. Johnny Mac barely suppressed a sob. Janna reached for his hand and squeezed it.

Mr Tulia put a hand on each of the boys' shoulders and moved them towards the helicopter, bending forward as he did so. Instinctively Johnny Mac and Early did the same, although they were way too short for it to matter. Once all were aboard, the helicopter took off, but Johnny Mac was too worried about his dad to be either scared or awestruck regarding his first trip in a chopper.

Five hours later the boys were curled up on a couch in the cardiac waiting room of Methodist Hospital in Houston, Texas, covered with blankets and sound asleep. Johnny Mac was roused when he heard his mother's crutches bang against a metal table. She was up and a guy in scrubs and a weird hat was walking toward her. The doctor, he figured. Johnny Mac jumped up and joined his mom.

'Mrs Kovak?' the doctor said.

'Yes?' his mom said.

'Doctor Denton,' he said, extending his hand. His mom shook it quickly.

'How is he?' she asked.

'He made it through with flying colors,' the doctor said, smiling. 'We had to do a quadruple bypass on him, and he's going to have to change his wicked ways, but he should be good to go for at least another twenty/thirty years.'

And that's when Johnny Mac saw his mom cry for the very first time in his life.

Milt – Aftermath

I woke up with a crowd around me. Jean and Johnny Mac and Early, Mike and Lucy and their daughter, and Esther Monte and her daughter.

'Hey, gang,' I said. 'We having a party?'

'Man, what *won't* you do for attention?' Mike said.

'Hey, baby,' my wife said, bending down to kiss me.

'Get her a chair, Mike,' I said.

'I've been trying, but she won't sit down!' Mike said.

'Jeez, I'll sit, I'll sit!' Jean said, and accepted the chair Mike brought to my bedside.

Mike lifted Johnny Mac up to sit on my bed. He leaned down and hugged me. 'Don't do that again, OK?' he said in my ear.

'Promise,' I said back.

'OK, so what happened on-board? Mike, did you get to Vern in time?'

'Man, you can't stop a cop, can you? Yeah, I got to the fat bastard before she even got there, told him what you told me. So I hid in his room, let her come in and get the pillow and stick it over his face, then he grabbed her arm and I switched on the lights, and voila, we had her. And by the way, he took Ryan home and told me he was going to stay there, if Lois would let him.'

'She will,' Lucy said.

'And Heinrich? Darlin',' I said to my wife, 'did you kill him?'

'No, of course not!' Jean said. 'He just had a bit of concussion.'

'So they've been arrested, I take it?' I asked.

'Oh, yeah,' Mike said. 'And Crystal – did you know that's not even her name? It's really Lizbet Heinrich! She's Heinrich's wife!'

'Yeah, I knew that,' I said.

'Oh. Well, anyway, she's singing like a bird! Blaming it all on Heinrich, but the kids found proof that she was having sex with Josh—'

'God, Mike!' Lucy said.

'Honey! They're the ones who found the proof, for God's sake! They knew what it meant!' Then, with a worried frown, he turned to his daughter, 'Didn't you?'

'Of course, Daddy,' Janna said, and she and Lyssa giggled.

Lucy shook her head in despair.

'Anyway,' Mike continued, 'she was doing Josh and he was stealing for her, and old Heinrich didn't know a thing about it! But the kids, here,' he put his arm around his daughter and drew her close, 'with all their misbehaving, were able to prove it. Honey?'

Janna smiled sweetly at her father. I was gonna have to warn my boy about girls like this – you could get in real deep with those baby blues of hers. And she said, 'Well,' stretching out the 'well' and encompassing her little gang of brats with a look, 'we were talking one day, and decided maybe we needed to see inside Josh's cabin—'

'That was sealed,' I said. 'With crime scene tape! I put it up myself.' It hadn't actually been crime scene tape as they didn't have any aboard, but did have 'under construction' tape and I'd used that.

Janna's smile faded and she looked at her father. 'You said he wouldn't yell at me,' she said accusingly.

'Milt, don't yell,' Mike and my wife said almost in unison.

'Sorry,' I said to Janna. 'Continue. Please.'

'OK,' she said, giving me a guarded look. Then she smiled and said, 'So, anyway, the boys were stuck in their cabin,' she gave me a withering look, 'but we came up with this idea to double check Josh's cabin. We knew the security crew had already done that, but really, Sheriff Kovak?'

'Yes, Janna?' I said.

She frowned and said, 'I don't think they were very good.'

'Why's that?' I asked.

Again with the laser smile. 'Because Lyssa and I found this box—'

'How did you get in the room? It was locked.'

'Dad, is that really relevant at this time?' my son said.

I gave him a look, but Janna plowed on. 'In the box we found a key card to that room where we'd seen Mrs Weaver and that man – Chief Heinrich, it turns out! – and one of those cheapo cell phones? But this one was used a lot for texts and one thing I know how to do is to find a text history!'

I noticed her parents exchange worried looks. 'And most of the texts were between Josh and Mrs Weaver! And they were gross!'

'We gave both those things over to the Galveston police,' Mike said. 'Last I heard, the police had done some digging, and it looks like Heinrich and Cry— I mean, Lizbet, have done this on other ships, with other cruise lines. She marries these old geezers and demands a honeymoon on a cruise ship, which Heinrich can accommodate. She targeted Vern at a bar, then Heinrich got them on the boat. Who knows if any of her marriages are for real – even the one to old Heinrich? He didn't know she'd been screwing young teenagers to get them to roll drunks for cash for quite a while, it seems!'

'So who actually killed Josh and why?' I demanded.

'Heinrich,' my wife said. 'According to him, he walked in on his wife in bed with the kid, and when she saw Heinrich standing there she yelled rape and Heinrich grabbed poor Josh around the neck—' Jean stopped and looked at the kids. 'Well, anyway,' she said. 'Josh died.'

I squeezed her hand and sighed. Josh's crazy behaviour suddenly made a whole lot more sense. I could only imagine how Mike must be feeling.

'But what did any of that have to do with Lance Turner?' I asked.

'Nothing,' Mike said. He grinned at Esther. 'Your turn!' he said.

Esther sat down on the edge of my bed. 'Well, the steward came to me and asked me to gather up Lance's stuff since he showed no next-of-kin on his paperwork. So I did. And I found a videotape. I'd brought a small player with me so Lyssa could watch a tape before bedtime, which she likes to do to fall asleep, and I played it.'

She turned to the kids. 'I wonder if there's a soda fountain on this floor?'

'By the elevators!' Johnny Mac said.

Esther reached in her purse and brought out several one-dollar bills. 'Take orders and it will probably take all four of you to bring them back, right?' she said, the 'right' aimed at the adults. So they all ordered soft drinks, except me because I wasn't allowed.

When the kids were gone, Esther said, 'The tape showed two men – one was Mr Connelly and the other I discovered was his son, Rose's late husband, Baker Junior. Anyway, Junior was saying, "I know what you did, Dad, and I think it's disgusting!" Or words to that effect. And Mr Connelly was denying it vehemently. It turns out that Junior saw his father hitting on Rose at a dinner party the night before and Junior was threatening to tell his mother if his dad didn't step down from his position at the firm and retire.'

'OK,' I said. 'What's the big deal? Was Lance blackmailing Connelly Senior over this? Hardly seems worth it to Connelly.'

'It must have been pretty much worth it. I showed the video to Rose and she saw the date of the recording, and said the next day was when her husband had his fatal car accident. His brake lines were cut.'

'Jesus!' I said. 'Connelly Senior killed his own son?'

'And brought Rose and her kids into his home!' Esther said.

'Has he been messing with her?' I asked.

'Rose said when she first moved in with them he tried, so she moved into a room with her boys and he stopped. She said she was very careful not to ever be alone with him.'

'I gotta get up!' I said, pulling on the needle sticking out of my arm, through which crap went into my veins. 'We can't have this guy running loose—'

'He's not, Milt!' Esther said, pushing one of my shoulders down on the bed while my wife pushed the other. 'Rose and I went to the Galveston police with the tape while they were on-board ship, and they questioned him extensively. And that's when I remembered he had opportunity.'

'Pardon?' I asked.

'Remember us all wondering how in the hell somebody got cyanide into Lance's wine? Well, you know the Connellys didn't join us that night, but Senior did drop by the table, remember?

Lance went to the bathroom, and Connelly Senior came up to me and leaned down and whispered in my ear that he thought I could do better than Lance and that he felt that Lance was not a good person. He was between me and Lance's wine at the time so I didn't see him drop anything in and with all the trauma of Lance's dying, I totally forgot about it. But he admitted it. With all the evidence piling up – the tape and me remembering him at the table and the death of his son – he just up and confessed. Seems he worked with the CIA during his thirty years in the Air Force and had been issued the cyanide tablet that you hear about? Well, according to him it's true, except it was a capsule. He's been keeping it in a small vile on his key chain ever since.'

'So he's been arrested?' I asked.

'Yes, and by the way, Milt, you might have mentioned that Lance was actually a sleazeball whose name wasn't even Lance! I think I might have been able to get over him a little quicker!' Esther said accusingly.

'Something else to put at Heinrich's feet,' I told her. 'It was his call. But how did Lance get that tape?'

'According to the old man, Lance worked for him in the mail room and, being an opportunist, I suppose, managed to put a nanny-cam sort of thing in Mr Connelly's office. He saw the very heated discussion between father and son – the door, I presume, was closed, but the walls, according to Rose, are glass. So anyway, the next day Baker Junior has his fatal accident, and Lance gets interested in the conversation the two had had the day before, and gets his nanny-cam back.' She shrugged. 'A lot of this is conjecture. Rose and I trying to fill in the blanks. Most of it, however, came from the old man's statement.'

'So why was Lance, or whoever, on the ship in the first place?' I asked. 'And why the hell did he have the tape with him? And he's been blackmailing Connelly for three years? Rose said her husband died three years ago! That's a lot of blackmail!'

'The old man said Lance followed him a lot. He didn't work at Mr Connelly's company anymore,' Esther said, 'but he always seemed to know where he was. He showed up at parties, at the old man's golf course, at the car wash. And the price had been going up and up every month, according to Mr Connelly. He said, and I quote, "He was bleeding me to death!" And then Lance just showed up aboard ship. He found the old man and threatened him with the tape. Oh, and he said Lance only latched on to me so he could stay close to him. The asshole,' Esther said.

'Who, Lance or the old man?' I asked.

'Both,' she replied.

'You said that Rose's husband's brake line had been cut. Didn't the investigators notice this when he died?'

'No, they probably didn't check since it was "an accident,"' Esther said. 'But the old man confessed that he cut his son's brake line.'

I take it the old man didn't know about Lance's past, or the fact that he wasn't actually Lance, before he hired him?'

'No, and he didn't know until the Galveston police told him. He was shocked,' Esther said.

'How's Rose's mother-in-law holding up?'

'According to Rose, she's still shell-shocked. But Rose said all the money in the family is hers, an inheritance from her father, so if she becomes convinced that Senior killed her only son, he's going to have a hard time hiring an attorney.'

'So, Milt,' Mike said. 'You only solved the one murder – with the help of some small friends. You gotta give the other one up to Esther and Rose.'

'With honors,' I said.

EPILOGUE

Milt – *Two Months Later*

I'm doing much better. I've lost forty pounds, had to buy new pants, and am not allowed to eat anything at the Longbranch Inn except a new dish now on the menu called 'The Milt.' It's a grilled chicken breast, liberally basted with picante sauce, and comes with a corn and black bean relish and a green salad. And Loretta is totally in on it – she won't bring me anything *but* the Milt. One day, just for kicks, I ordered French fries with cream gravy – and got a green salad. Chicken-fried steak? The Milt. It's a conspiracy. I wouldn't really eat any of the bad stuff now anyway, but it makes Jean and Loretta feel like they're contributing to my well-being and that they're in control. You gotta give the women a little something every now and then. Personally, and don't tell Jean this, I kinda like the way I look in my new duds. Very studly.

Emmett's nick in the neck from Reba Sinclair shooting at him turned out more serious then he thought – he didn't get it looked at right away and he got sepsis – something that's not good. He was on antibiotics for a whole month and still has to go see the doctor a lot. What with my heart and his neck, we were both out of commission for a while, which meant Jasmine, who was next in line after Dalton in seniority (Dalton said he didn't want it, which was good, 'cause I wasn't gonna give it to him) was in charge for about six weeks. It was not a good six weeks for slackers who liked to jaywalk, kids who wore their pants down showing off their Calvin Klein's, or mothers who turned the wrong way in the pick-up lines at the schools. She also managed to arrest two burglars and a car-jacker. I'm thinking about turning in my badge and letting her run the show. Or maybe not.

Emmett and I went by the shop one afternoon, just to see what was going on, and saw a female there we didn't recognize, although she was sitting in Holly Humphries' chair.

'Hey, guys!' she said with glee and waved, and sure enough it was Holly. But her hair was dark brown all over, all the shiny things were gone from her face, her make-up was normal, and she was wearing a regular dress almost to her knees, with panty hose and kitten heels. She twirled for us.

'What happened to our Holly?' I asked her.

'Oh, don't worry, she's still here. It's just that I'm going to Dalton's house for dinner to meet his mom for the first time. You know, first impressions.'

I nodded. 'Makes perfect sense,' I said.

Shortly after that meet with Dalton's mama, the two announced their engagement and Holly started showing off an engagement ring that wasn't exactly normal. I was flabbergasted when Holly told me Dalton had picked it out on his own. The wedding will be in the fall, after Dalton's mama and his aunt get back from their pilgrimage to Israel, and he's asked me to be his best man. I've accepted. I'm also walking Holly down the aisle, so it will be a hectic day for me, but I think I can man-up for it.

Summer's upon us and Johnny Mac's been bugging his mom and me to go to sleep-away camp. This particular camp is in Texas, in the Dallas area, a Methodist church camp, where Mike and Lucy Tulia are sending Janna for two weeks. Jean heard from Esther Monte that Lyssa's been bugging her about the same camp, and we got a call from Early's mom that he's been asking about the same thing. So it looks like we might do it. All of us drive there – Esther would probably fly in from Atlanta – go out to dinner, take in a show or something. It'll be fun seeing the old gang again. Tell you the truth, except for a couple of murders, that cruise wasn't all that bad.